PARTIAL TRUTHS

PARTIAL TRUTHS

***

SHAHED GHANIMATI

SHAHEDWRITES.COM
@SHAHED_WRITES

Paperback ISBN# 979-8-9912287-0-1

Ebook ISBN# 979-8-9912287-1-8

Printed by Ingram Spark

Cover Photograph: Javier Márquez

Designed by: Monique Comacchio

Library of Congress #2025901896

Dedication

To Gabe, for being the man Camila was hoping for. I will always like like you.

And for anyone who spends countless hours in their 20's pondering, perseverating, and worrying if things will work out: they do. Be kind to yourself, laugh a lot, and appreciate your tight skin.

Prologue

If only she had waited to call. Then she wouldn't have been yelling at him while merging onto the 405 in the middle of rush hour traffic. Maybe if she hadn't started sobbing, she would have seen the brake lights flashing ahead of her. Maybe she could have prevented the accident that slowed the already snail-paced traffic to a screeching halt.

Perhaps if she still had her car, and it hadn't been tragically towed away, she wouldn't have walked home alone that night.

But she did.

And if Ben had only driven past her, not noticing how broken she looked, like her world had just crumbled into a million little pieces, maybe then he wouldn't have offered her a ride.

But it all did happen.

And he did care.

And she got into his car.

And then everything shifted.

PART 1

September 2002

1

"Shit, shit, shit!"

She attacked the couch, tossing throw pillows off in a panic. Her eyes landed on her bag, limp on the floor. A puddle of crochet fabric full of daily essentials from gum to lotion to emergency tampons, and hopefully her keys.

"Fuck!"

"What's going on, darling?" Tyler asked as he stood in the bathroom doorway, batting his lashes. Her roommate dramatically fanned out the long sleeves of his new kimono robe, which fell gracefully off his lanky frame.

"Ooh, that's nice!" she said, popping up from the floor amid her frantic search.

He sauntered into the room, satin fabric billowing behind him. "What's with the ladylike language?"

"I'm late for my Spanish class, and I can't find my fucking keys!"

He folded his arms at his chest, drumming his fingers along the luxurious fabric.

"Why are you taking that class? You're almost done with school, like, forever and you're adding a class now?"

"We've been over this. I need to improve my Spanish if I'm ever going to make it to the CDC office in Mexico City. It's only two nights per week."

"Cami, you know they speak English in Mexico City? Especially at the U.S. CDC office?"

"Tyler, please just help me," she pleaded as she flipped waves of long hair over her shoulder, looking under the couch again.

He floated around the room, lifting piles of papers and unfolded laundry, and held up a huge brass keychain, jingling her keys along with a dozen of her different evil eye charms.

"Oh, thank you, thank you, thank you." She jumped up to grab the keys from his hand and placed a scarlet-colored peck on his cheek. "Thank you! I'll see you later."

She left the apartment and ran down the street, her bag heavy on her shoulder, jostling noisily. By some miracle, last night after her restaurant shift, she had found a parking spot near her building. Now, she got into the car, put it in gear, and peeled out onto Wilshire Boulevard, heading for North Campus. Her gas tank was less than a quarter full, and she made a mental note to gas up before her next evening shift. Westwood wasn't particularly dangerous, but she didn't like pumping her own gas after the closing shift. It hadn't been easy balancing classes, her research, and waitressing, but that was the only way to minimize her student debt. Her fellowship had helped immensely, but it didn't account for her obsession with thrift store shopping and her serious coffee addiction. She and Tyler had kept their rent-controlled apartment in Brentwood since becoming roommates and moving in during their junior year. They planned on living there for as long as possible. There was no way they could rent an apartment for $600 a piece anywhere else within a five-mile radius of UCLA. Sure, the air conditioner crapped out often, and they longed for a communal pool while they baked during the summer. But they adored their Mediterranean-inspired, one-bedroom apartment with its small patio and highly coveted parking spot.

She skillfully navigated the streets and made it to sorority row like an expert, having survived LA traffic for seven years now. She prayed she'd find a parking spot, hoping it wouldn't be an issue before her first class. Since moving to LA, she had become rather devout. Praying for parking spots. Praying for statistically significant research results. Praying for good waitressing tips sans the ass-grab.

One parking spot secured, and she was breathless when she reached Rolfe Hall. Plunging a hand into her black hole of a bag, she was desperate to find something. A clip, a hair tie, or even a scrunchy would do to amass her hair on top of her head.

Her hair was a blessing and a curse. Thick, long, chestnut waves that gave the impression she had just taken an impromptu dip in the ocean. Streaks of gold woven between tendrils that were enviable but also hot. Very hot and sweaty, like her own personal sauna. The night air cooled her skin but not enough. She wrapped her hair up with the random rubber band she found in her bag and smirked, thinking of all the times Tyler joked that the contents of her bag could sustain them for months if ever they were stranded on a desert island.

Other students loitered near the classroom door, and she assumed they were enrolled in the same advanced language course as she was. She slowly paced the walkway, still hot and sticky, and fanned herself with her hand. Perspiration pooled between her breasts, dampening the lace bra peeking from beneath her top. She blew a breath downward, trying to cool her skin, and felt someone staring.

It happened often. The staring. It started when she was thirteen. They were shopping at the mercado when her mother first noticed it. One of the checkout boys was placing a gallon of milk on top of their carton of eggs because he had been too busy eyeing Camila, bent over tying her shoelaces. Her mother promptly wrapped her sweater around Camila's rear and scolded the boy, "Pinche cochino!"

"Mija," her mother told Camila on their way home, "You are old enough now. Men will start to notice you in a way that is not always honorable."

"Yuck, Mom!"

"There is no yuck. It's their nature. They are going to want to own you like algo precioso, something precious. You can use this to your advantage, but be careful. Some of them will think this is an invitation. You must always protect tu corazón as well as your body."

Since childhood, Camila's mother and grandmother had raised her with more than just the notion of gender equality. She was encouraged to see her role as a woman in society as an advantage, something she could use to make a difference. Her responsibility, as a woman born in a developed nation with unlimited access to education and healthcare, was to succeed for all those who were not afforded the same opportunities. Men were a part of society, but not the center of society. They were supposed to be partners by choice and not necessity. It was this constant theme of female empower-ment that led her to graduate school and the belief that men were inherently dishonest and had to be cautiously managed, with two ex-ceptions: her father and Tyler.

"Azzizam," her Iranian grandmother, Mamani, who always referred to Camila as dearest, would tell her, "Even on their best day they will never be smarter than you. They may be stronger, but we are more cunning."

This was almost always followed up with the qualification, "Except for your Baba, he was an angel among men, God bless him."

Even after twenty years, her paternal grandmother's eyes would glis-ten with tears when talking about her son. He was exempt from deri-sions of the male gender. His photo could still be found in every room.

* * *

Ben had arrived with plenty of time as usual. He had slowly walked along the pathway, lined with spruce trees, snaking between the Language Arts buildings, and located his classroom. He was always on time. More accurately, he was always prepared, as he had been in college and high school and all the previous years of education through which he excelled. Teachers would remark on his maturity and organization skills since elementary school. His patience and kindness towards others, and of course his intelligence. His fourth-grade teacher even named her son after Ben in hopes that the name would transplant the same desirable traits she had seen in Ben onto her newborn son. Ben wasn't loud or obnoxious in the popularity that followed him but gained the respect of his peers through his athletic prowess, academic excellence, and ability to be universally friendly. Ben's ultimate goal was always to create minimal worry for his fam-ily while simultaneously generating as much pride as possible. His choices had consistently reflected what would be best for the whole, not solely himself.

He sat on the edge of the cold, cement planter and waited for class to start. For the past year, during these rare quiet moments, he had begun to question his decisions. Until now, Ben's life was a testament to making reasonable and logical choices. But now, with only a handful of months before his professional life was supposed to begin, he had lost the ability to distinguish between what he used to perceive as clearly "right" or "wrong." He rested his face in his palms and gently rubbed circles over his eyelids with his fingertips. Why had he postponed moving to Boston? He had grappled with this question for months. Why spend an extra year in LA? Why take extra unnecessary classes? Was he trying to avoid the impending responsibilities of adult life, or was he finally pushing back against a lifetime of delayed gratification? What he knew was that he longed for control. For the past three years, he had started to feel like he was watching his life speed away toward someone else's dream. His family questioned his decision to postpone his life further, but Ben was tired of being compliant. For years it had brought with it a sense of satisfaction, but now he couldn't remember the last time he felt true joy. His mother sensed his discontent, but when she asked if he was in fact happy, he would reply, "Of course, Mom, there is nothing to be unhappy about."

But that wasn't exactly the same as being happy. He didn't have a joyful life. Instead, he had the promise of a happy ending, but not for another year, and it was his fault for letting it go on so long. His choices had never before led him astray. He longed to feel buoyant, and going to Boston now would have been another anvil holding him down.

He opened his eyes to see the blurred silhouette of a woman come into focus in front of him. As she paced the walkway, his eyes slowly grew accustomed to the light, and her blurred features sharpened into a clear picture, but in the process, he had inadvertently been staring. It was embarrassing to be caught, but Ben had never experienced such a visceral reaction. It was as if a Lilith Fair poster had come to life. Her long patchwork skirt swayed with her steps, her white peasant top teetered off one shoulder to flawless skin. None of the women in his classes wore clothes like this. None of them ever wore their hair down. They were all trying to hide their femininity to achieve gender neutrality, but this woman was like the love child of Stevie Nicks and Shakira and flaunted it.

Camila turned, feeling a pair of eyes track her movements but not in the mood to engage. No one could quite pinpoint the origin of her appeal. She initially found it irritating until she learned to turn it into a game.

They'd ask, "So where are you from?"

And knowing full well it was the details of her genetic lineage in question, she'd say, "San Diego."

Latinos thought she was Latina, Persians thought she was Persian, and everyone else put her in a nondescript "ethnic" category.

She waited in the hallway with the rest of the students and glanced over again to where the staring had originated, expecting the usual request for her phone number but noticed he was looking away. Weird. Normally, she would have been approached by now. Perhaps there would be a brave attempt at witty banter or feigned recognition from a shared class. For the past year and a half, she had been able to politely decline those requests for her number, citing her boyfriend as the reason for her refusal. But this guy had the audacity to stare and then not follow through. He hadn't moved from his spot, seated along the planter across from their classroom. He rested his elbows on his knees, back hunched over like his backpack was weighing him down and occasionally glanced up to see if the door to their class had opened yet. His light brown hair fell in his eyes, and as he brushed it away, she noticed the golden dusting of hair on his strong forearms. She turned away before their eyes met.

Moments later, the students from the previous class emptied noisily, and she noticed how tall he was as he headed toward the door. He held it open with his broad shoulders as the last few students exited, remaining there until the class filled up again.

Camila made her way through the door, avoiding eye contact with him and muttering a quick thank you. She took a seat, hung her bag on the back of her chair, and started jotting down her to-do list for the week. She was planning to defend her thesis in a few short months, and organization would be key if she was going to meet her deadline. The longing for independence gnawed at her after decades of educational supervision, but still, she was digging her heels in to slow her debut into the "real" world. Tyler was already much busier this year, his clerkships having started in June, and Camila wasn't thrilled about countless nights alone. If she was honest, this was in part the impetus for enrolling in the evening Spanish class. There was only so much "No Pudge" brownie batter a girl could indulge in on her own. She needed a distraction and to improve her Spanish. After meeting Tyler at the Clinton/Gore '96 rally held on campus, they had become instantly inseparable and were further convinced of their celestially predestined friendship when they applied and received acceptances to graduate school together.

She was doodling on the corner of her planner when she heard a body sliding into the chair behind her. She felt the shift in the air but resisted the urge to turn around. Thankfully, the professor arrived, quickly delving into the class expectations, timeline, and the projects required for the quarter.

Ben stared at the bundle of hair before him, precariously held together by an overly strained rubber band. A few loose tendrils cascading down partially obscured the tattoo at the nape of her neck. He couldn't decipher the meaning but stared at the foreign script as the rest of the class faded away.

"Ahora, por favor, preséntese a la persona a su derecha," instructed Señora Escobedo.

Camila turned to the woman to her right, introducing herself in Spanish as her peripheral vision confirmed that it was the owner of the well-developed shoulders and seemingly heavy backpack who had taken the seat behind her. The deep tenor of his voice distracted her as her partner introduced herself. "I'm sorry. What was your name again?" she asked the woman.

At the first break, Camila grabbed her bag and walked out into the darkness that now blanketed the campus. She knew better than to stray too far on her own and kept to the walkway as she reached for her lighter. She felt the flicker of the flame as she brought it to the cigarette between her lips, the tip glowing as she inhaled. She gazed up at the moon and exhaled. Her fingers straddled the cigarette as she walked aimlessly along the path, and she felt his eyes on her again.

None of the women Ben knew smoked. It was 2002, and the risks of tobacco were no longer theoretical but well-studied and accepted. He leaned against the wall, hands shoved in his jeans pockets, watching her, mesmerized. She took a couple more drags, flicking the ash with a quick movement, and extinguished the fragment of cigarette in the planter and placed the remnant back in the pack. He couldn't take his eyes off her.

She stopped directly in front of him on the way back into class, looking straight up at him.

"It's not polite to stare."

He was caught off guard. Those eyes. If her hair and curves hadn't been enough of a lure, her eyes were the final straw. Two concentric rings of color, honey-brown around a pitch-black center and jade around the periphery. His voice caught in his throat.

"Smoking is not good for you," he finally said.

"Well, *Doctor,* I know it's a shit habit," she said sharply. "Thank you very much." She saw in his chocolate-brown eyes a mixture of confusion and concern before she broke away and walked back into class.

* * *

"How was class?"

"Fine," she said, plopping down on their futon-extra-bed-only-major-living-room-furniture couch. She dropped backward, keeping her feet on the ground since Tyler had converted it into a full bed this evening.

He gave a strand of her hair a gentle tug. "Just fine?"

"Yeah, class was fine, but some asshole tried to lecture me about smoking."

He laughed. "Uh, lame. It's not like cigarettes can kill you, right?"

She threw a pillow at his head, and he batted it away.

"I'm quitting soon anyway," she said.

"Oh yeah, how is Lorenzo going to like that? I thought he loved smoking after you guys fuck."

"Excuse me? We don't *fuck.*"

"Well, it isn't making love, so what would you call it? That man wouldn't know love if it bit him on his perfectly tanned ass."

"Tyler!"

"What? Don't act surprised. He treats you like shit, and you know it. I'm so excited he moved. Now I don't have to fake smile at that pompous douche."

"Tyler, he's still my boyfriend!"

"Hopefully, not for much longer. Your family would be so pissed if they knew how he treated you. Has he even called you recently?"

"He's busy."

"Yeah, busy trying to screw every woman in a 10-mile radius just to prove a point. I've never met someone who could be so homophobic and closeted at the same time."

Camila pushed herself up from the futon. "Okay, you sprinkled a bit too much sass into your Cheerios tonight. I'm going to bed."

"Goodnight, and I love you."

"Love you too," she said, smiling down at him and placing a kiss on his puckered lips.

* * *

With a new key hook now installed in their apartment, she arrived with ample time for the next class. A creature of habit and superstition, she took the same seat and glanced down at her phone. Shit. She had a missed call from Lorenzo. He'd be angry. He had made it abundantly clear he didn't believe in long-distance relationships and had no interest in waiting by his phone, especially with the time difference. He hadn't always been this rigid. When they had met, he was spontaneous and so cultured. His lack of predictability was alluring, but slowly his carefree manner became exhausting and noncommittal. But still, she had convinced him to reconsider when he suggested they break up before his move. She promised him she would be available whenever he had time to call. Tonight, he would be angry for sure.

The same gawker walked into class wearing jeans and sneakers, a predictably casual ensemble that would normally make Camila cringe but somehow worked on him. He must have been an athlete at some point. His body could not have belonged to a mortal. His thighs seemed hard as stone under his jeans. The muscular contour of his chest visible through his thin shirt. His backpack looked almost comical struggling to span the breadth of his broad back. Her eyes met his, and she quickly turned to face the front of the room. Great, she thought. Maybe tonight he would want to warn her about the dangers of the Diet Coke she was drinking. She felt him settle in behind her, his presence all-consuming. She crossed her legs and ran a hand down her shin, admiring the handiwork of her latest aesthetician. Though her mother had congratulated her multiple times for having avoided the genetic curse of abundant body hair, Camila followed her depilatory practices with diligence and was proud the only hair on her body was on her head.

If Camila would have tempered her pride and turned to face Ben, it would have been obvious he was entirely preoccupied watching her fingers trail down her leg and couldn't have cared less about her Diet Coke. He was only redirected to the front of class when Señora Escobedo greeted them, "Buenas noches a todos."

* * *

She hurried to the middle of the quad where the reception was best. It was one of those evenings when the moon was so bright the entire campus was blanketed with a silver glow. There were never any stars in the sky. LA was so bright that even at night, the city looked like it was merely a backdrop to the noise and congestion.

Fuck! She looked at her watch. Lorenzo would be asleep soon. The line rang and rang. She was preparing to leave a message when he picked up.

He sounded sleepy and irritated.

"Hola, mi amor," she said. "I'm sorry I missed your call earlier. I was rushing to class."

"It's fine," he said, yawning.

She asked him how his day was, and he said again, "Fine."

He was punishing her for missing his call.

"What did you have for dinner?" She asked, hoping to jump-start their conversation.

Ben watched her pacing. He was well hidden from view beneath the arched walkway that led from their class to the library and could look at her without reservation. He could see her in the middle of the quad as if she were a lone performer on a stage. The moonlight shined brightly on her face, giving her an ethereal glow. She was focused on whoever was on the other end of the line. He gazed at her legs, skin the color of caramel, soft-looking, golden. She flipped her long, dark hair from side to side as she walked, and it was obvious she was agitated.

"Camila, I'm tired," Lorenzo told her. "I don't have time to talk about my dinner, which was four hours ago." His accent was more pronounced when he was testy.

"I'm sorry I couldn't answer when you called earlier."

"Sure, fine, we'll talk later."

"Okay, amor, good night," she said to a sleepy grunt and then a click.

She stood there looking at the phone in her palm, and with her other hand pinched the bridge of her nose and squeezed her eyes shut, slipping the phone in her back pocket.

The gathering of students signaled the end of their break. Ben assumed his usual position at the door and held it open as others funneled in. She was the last to enter.

She looked up at him. "You're staring again."

He swallowed hard.

"Sorry," he said, wondering why he was apologizing but distracted by a glimmer of gold nestled between her breasts.

A small evil eye charm rested in her cleavage. He had seen the blue and white ellipsoid shape before. On the first day of class, he noticed several of them dangling off the stack of bracelets that adorned her wrist, jangling as she slid her hand across her planner jotting down notes.

* * *

The following week was more of the same. She actively ignoring him, and he unable to look away. But his eyes didn't hold the same shameless animalistic desire as other men. He didn't undress her with the carnal look that she had grown accustomed to. He stared at her with confusion and wonder, as if she was an equation he had to solve.

Her call to Lorenzo on Tuesday night had left her frustrated. They had been struggling. She was regularly missing his evening calls, and he was becoming progressively moodier and more bored with their conversations. She now regretted signing up for the Spanish class. It added to her already overflowing plate. She was juggling so much and now trying to keep ahold of Lorenzo. It was taking its toll. By the following Thursday, they had only exchanged a few hostile emails with the understanding they would talk on Friday night. Anxious, she couldn't wait for class to end and for night to turn into day. Friday. On Friday they could talk and get back on track.

Given the added stress, it wasn't the best time to quit smoking, but it was never going to be the perfect time. As she paced the walkway, she popped pieces of gum into her mouth like they were Skittles. She saw the gawker again, leaning against the wall, watching her unabashedly. It was becoming irritating. Or was she just irritated with everyone and everything? She didn't wait for him to open the door. She marched right over to him. "Can I help you with something?" she said. This was becoming ridiculous.

He looked up in surprise. "No, why?"

"You are constantly staring at me." She held up her three coral-tipped fingers. "I've told you three times now."

He knew he had been staring at her, but for good reason. He didn't see her pull out her pack of cigarettes like usual during break, and she had been somewhat more fidgety during class, picking at the chipped edge of her desk. He rubbed the back of his neck. "You're not smoking tonight."

"Well, not that it's any of your business, but I'm trying to quit."

He gave her a slight smile. "Good. I'm glad you're quitting."

He was less infuriating when he smiled. Maybe she should be nicer and not take out her anger on this well-meaning stranger. She gave him a small smile back.

"Well, thanks for the support," she said, extending her hand. "I'm Camila."

"I'm Ben," he replied, taking her hand in his.

* * *

Camila untied her apron and cashed out her tips. Her feet throbbed, but she was grateful for the extra shift. This waitressing job was a lifesaver. The tips covered the gas her "vintage" Honda Civic needed to get between home, campus, and her trips to San Diego. Despite the six-figure mileage, the '94 hand-me-down had clocked, she kept it as good as new, or as new as she had received it. The occasional oil change was manageable with an extra shift now and then, and thankfully, no major repairs had been needed.

She raced home to shower off the smell of pizza dough and melted cheese, eager to get on the road. She hadn't seen her family for a full month and missed home.

"Mom, I'm just throwing some stuff in a bag, and then I'm hitting the road," she said into the phone as she ran around the house in her bra and jeans, trying to stay cool.

The other days of the week had conspired to make this feel like the longest week ever, but it was finally Friday.

She threw her bag into the passenger seat of her car, turned on the fan, and dialed Lorenzo's number before shifting into gear. It was 10 in the evening in Boston, and he was expecting her call.

Great. Wilshire was a mess. Everyone seemed to be escaping the city. She was an expert in steering, shifting gears, and holding her phone between her ear and chin. She waited patiently until he answered.

"Hola, mi amor," she said when he answered. She was happy to finally hear his voice free of irritation, though it may have been the calming effect of the cigarette she could hear him smoking. She heard the familiar sound of him snapping his lighter closed with one hand and envisioned him holding the cigarette precariously between his beautiful, full lips. She heard him inhale and blow out the smoke into the receiver. She used to love watching him smoke in bed after they had sex, congratulating herself for being able to satisfy him so completely. She hated the smell on her sheets and the way the smoke would sting her eyes, but she vowed to be more accommodating than his last girlfriend, who had rudely asked Lorenzo to smoke outside. Camila aspired to be a better girlfriend than the mysterious woman who had let him slip between her fingers. He never spoke of his ex except for when he was letting Camila know how she wasn't measuring up. She knew her family and Tyler didn't love Lorenzo, but she saw the potential in her future with him. He was going to be a tenured professor and support her work while she established herself in her own career. They would have children once he changed his mind about having a family, and everyone would finally see that he wasn't selfish. As she reminded herself of his virtues, her thoughts were interrupted by a shuffling in the background.

"Are you free to talk, Lorenzo?"

"Uh, yeah," he said, sounding distracted.

She pushed any suspicion about his attentiveness to the back of her mind, focusing instead on rekindling their usual banter, and heard a muffled whispering. She chose to ignore it.

"How are your lectures going?" she asked, merging on the 405. It was a literal parking lot. It would have been faster to walk to San Diego at this point.

She heard what she figured was his phone falling to the ground. Then an unfamiliar voice. A shiver ran through her.

"Professor Salas is a bit indisposed right now," a female voice said through giggles.

Camila felt her hands go clammy. She steadied her voice and, as calmly as possible, said, "Please put Professor Salas on the phone."

She heard Lorenzo's voice in the background. He sounded angry as if he was scolding someone.

"You know, Camila, this is not a good time." His accent was more pronounced, a sign of his impatience.

Now she was angry. "But we had a date to talk tonight."

"See, that's the problem, Camila. This isn't a date. We don't have a relationship. All we have is a series of appointments and boring phone calls. Nothing is spontaneous."

The traffic had picked up and moved faster than pedestrians now.

"Lorenzo, I am going to be graduating. . ." She stopped midway through her sentence, hearing laughter in the background. "Lorenzo, who's there with you?"

"Why? What difference does it make? I am not going to be celibate until you decide to visit."

"Are you fucking cheating on me?"

"Stop overreacting."

The tears started falling, her body reacting to what her heart already knew.

"It's been less than two months. You can't fucking keep it in your pants for two months?"

"Camila, you are acting like a child. You're out of control. I don't have time for this."

She went silent long enough to hear the giddy voice in the background say, "Professor, come back to bed."

Rage coursed through her. She could not believe he was breaking up with her and all while some slutty co-ed was in the background. She was furious and mortified.

"You fucking asshole," she said through sobs. "Hijo de puta! You don't deserve me. I hate you! Don't ever call me again!" She snapped her phone closed, throwing it in her purse.

All that time she had given him. All the things she did for him against her better judgment. Two years! Tyler had been right. Her family had been right. How could she have allowed herself to be treated this way? After everything her family taught her about choosing a partner who would respect and support her desire to make a difference in the world. Maybe she had thought having an international boyfriend was the first step in having an international life. She should have been smarter instead of falling for his charismatic foreign appeal, which just camouflaged his arrogance and machismo.

But none of these realizations helped stem the flow of tears. Her eyes stung, and she rubbed them with the back of her hand, smearing her mascara across her face as her car inexplicably picked up speed.

But her foot was off the accelerator, wasn't it? And everyone else was slowing down?

Why was the car ahead of her getting closer if she was pressing on the brake?

* * *

"Hey, hey! Wake up! Lady, wake up!"

Camila slowly blinked her eyes open. There was a dusty haze swirling in her car, and she heard a thudding. A metallic taste filled her mouth. Why did her chest hurt?

"Lady, get out of the car!" Someone was yelling through the window.

Why was the car in front of her so close?

Why did her legs hurt?

She slowly turned her head, looking out her window, and saw the concerned look of a strange man. A very well-dressed but strange man. She rolled down her window. "What happened?"

"Lady, you've been in a car accident. The police are coming, but you have to get out of the car. You're in the middle of the freeway!"

She rubbed her temple. Then her fingers made their way to her mouth. When she looked at them, she saw blood. Bright red, fresh blood. Her blood. Her eyes darted side to side as her breath became rapid and shallow.

"Oh my God," she mumbled. "Oh my God, oh my God." Her hands started shaking. She was shivering as if she'd been doused with a bucket of ice water.

Inhale. Exhale. Inhale. Exhale.

The stranger managed to put his hand through the window, unlocked her door, and helped her out.

"Honey, do you have any family near?" an officer asked her, once the messy pile of metal that used to be her car was towed away.

What was she going to do without her car? That had been her mother's car. She didn't have money to buy a new one. How was she going to get to work?

As the panic started to settle in again, the officer put a gentle hand on her shoulder.

"Can I call anyone for you?"

She saw her bag amongst the litter and brush on the side of the road and pointed to it. The officer gathered whatever she needed was there.

Miraculously, her phone hadn't fallen out during the accident, and she dialed Tyler's number, handing the phone to the officer. She had no confidence in her ability to explain where she was or what had happened.

She stared at the other cars that had weathered the accident much better. A gorgeous Porsche. A shiny new BMW. Cars with owners who probably had good insurance and the ability to buy another car in an afternoon. Her car looked like an accordion before it had been miserably towed away. Her "PEACE" and "Amnesty International" stickers on the rear window mocking her as they faded into the distance. She was dreaming about the day she could afford a life that didn't necessitate buying everything secondhand when she heard a familiar voice.

"Cami, baby, are you okay?"

She slowly turned her head to see Tyler's worried face. Tears started rolling down her face uncontrollably.

"Oh, Cami, it'll be okay. We'll figure it out."

She couldn't reply. Her words sounded more like babbling.

The police officer came over to them and said to Tyler, "Sir, I would consider taking her to the emergency room. She's having a panic attack, and she may have lost consciousness in the car before we arrived. She refused to go with the ambulance."

"Okay, thank you. Let's go, Cami," and Tyler placed an arm around her, hoisting her to her feet and helping her walk the few steps to his car.

"Why didn't you let them take you to get checked out?" he asked, knowing the answer already.

"I didn't want them to call my mom in case I passed out."

At the hospital, they walked through the emergency room's sliding double doors, and Tyler answered the receptionist's questions. They were escorted to the triage area, where Camila changed into the hospital gown and proceeded to wait for an hour before the doctor arrived. Tyler didn't leave her side.

"I'm Dr. Parker. Can you tell me what happened, Ms. Malik?"

"I, I, I was driving to San Diego, and then I had a car accident."

"Where were you exactly?"

"Going south on the 405, I was near Santa Monica."

"Oh, so you were the reason I was late to my shift," he said, crossing his arms and smiling down at her.

She was still frazzled and didn't pick up on the joke, but Tyler giggled, making sure the unexpectedly handsome doctor didn't give up on them. Tyler knew her type, and she would be very disappointed to learn she botched the possibility of flirting with Dr. Parker once she snapped out of her current panicked state.

Dr. Parker turned to Tyler, "Were you with her?"

"Oh, me? No, I wasn't with her."

"Do you have any pain, Camila?" Dr. Parker asked.

"I, I have chest pain," she said softly, extending her hand to her left clavicle that had a nasty injury, likely from her seat belt.

"Do you have a headache?"

"No, not really, but my lip hurts too."

Tyler looked down at her and noticed that since he had picked her up off the side of the road, the right side of her lip had ballooned.

"It looks like you may have a laceration of your lip and an abrasion of your left clavicle," the doctor said. He proceeded to listen to Camila's heart and lungs. Gently poking and prodding her stomach and checking her reflexes before completing a rather detailed visual examination where she had to stare into his dreamy eyes and then follow his fingers.

"Okay, I'm going to order a CT scan, and I'll review the results with my attending," he said, pulling the curtain closed behind him.

Tyler sat next to her on the gurney. "Cami, girl, you okay?"

"I think so."

"Okay, if you're so okay, on a scale of one to ten, how hot is Dr. Parker?"

"Um, four?"

"Okay, you must have hit your head. Parker is a solid eight. I'm glad they're going to scan your head!"

She smiled up at Tyler and leaned her head on his shoulder.

After another two hours, the CT scan was complete, and she was back in her partitioned part of the ER.

The curtain pulled back, and Dr. Parker appeared with his attending, Dr. Gordon.

"Hello there, Camila," Dr. Gordon said kindly, "It seems like you had quite the night."

For some reason that statement made her want to cry. It was almost paternal, even though he couldn't have been more than forty years old. Her eyes welled again.

"Your CT scan is normal, but I hear that you have some chest pain. Can you show me where?"

Camila answered using her right hand to motion diagonally from her left shoulder to her sternum.

"I see," Dr. Gordon said. "Are they real?"

Camila was confused. Why didn't she understand the question? Did she have a concussion despite the CT results? Were what real?

He asked her again, motioning to her breasts with his pen. "Are those real?"

Well, now all three men were staring at her chest. Camila finally understood his meaning and looked down to her breasts.

"Um, yes, they're not fake. I mean, they're real," she said.

Tyler was biting on his lower lip, trying to hold back his laughter, realizing Dr. Gordon was trying to exclude an implant rupture and not coming on to her.

"It looks like you got jostled pretty well out there," Dr. Gordon told her. "I want you to take it easy for the next week. No work, no school. Just try to relax at home."

"Okay," she said quietly.

"You two live together?" He asked Tyler.

"Yes, sir."

"Okay, make sure she doesn't overexert herself, and if she starts to behave strangely," he said, "please bring her back."

It took all of Tyler not to reply with a smart-ass comment to that last bit as Dr. Gordon stepped out.

Dr. Parker stayed behind, applying a bandage to her clavicle and examining her lip delicately with his gloved fingers.

"Okay, I'll let the nurse know you can leave. Be careful driving home," he said, giving Camila a wink and a brilliant smile.

Camila zoned out the window as Tyler drove. The pain was physical and emotional.

No car.

No job.

No school.

No boyfriend.

She breathed out a defeated sigh and closed her eyes.

2

"I knew he was no good," Mamani said, parading around their apartment burning esfand to ward off the bad omens she believed were the direct cause of Camila's accident. "That Lorenzo, khar!"

To Mamani, calling someone a donkey was the greatest insult. Though it had never been clear to Camila or her mother, Elena, why such a hard-working mammal should get such a bad rap.

"Your grandmother is right," Elena said, "He was arrogant, Mija." She was in the kitchen, trying her best not to sweat into a massive pot of pozole. Menopause was a bitch.

Camila lay on the couch, nursing a headache, listening to her mother and grandmother. Three days had passed since the accident, and she still didn't feel like herself. Elena and Mamani immediately drove up once Tyler had convinced Camila to call them. They rushed over, stopping at Jordan Market only to buy the esfand that Mamani was now burning to fumigate the house of the evil eye that had precipitated the breakup and car crash.

"He was always talking down to me," Mamani said, raising the esfand to emphasize her point. "Like I didn't understand English. I've been in this country longer than he has been alive!" Though this was technically true, no one had the heart to tell her this was more a consequence of her diminutive stature than his innate arrogance.

Camila must have dozed off. Her eyes adjusted to what little light now filtered through the patio window. Slowly she turned to face the small kitchen table. The apartment was dark except for the dim Turkish lamp that shone down on the three people she loved most. The smell of pozole and warm sangak bread hit her nostrils, and for the first time since Friday, she was hungry. Sitting up slowly, she allowed her brain to adjust to the change in position before attempting to stand. Her whole body was sore. Two large, indigo bruises on her shins were exquisitely painful to touch. She made it halfway before Tyler looked up, "Hey, sleepy, how are you feeling?"

"Oh, Mija, come sit down," Elena said as she rose to bring a fresh bowl of pozole for Camila.

"Camila joon," her grandmother said, "You must eat, or else you will not heal."

She couldn't argue with decades of old-world medicine and mysticism, no matter how unscientific.

Tyler gave her a sweet smile from across the table, used to the hostile but well-meaning takeover when Camila's family deemed it necessary. He was their adopted son and could follow some of the spoken Spanish-Farsi mix. They may have seemed like an odd trio—her American roommate, her Mexican mother, and her Persian grandmother—but for Camila they were everything.

* * *

When she didn't come to class the following Tuesday, Ben thought it was a random absence. But on Thursday, when Señora Escobedo reassigned her partner to a different group for the foreseeable future, an odd sensation settled in his gut. Where was she?

He had no way to contact her. No phone number, no mutual friends, not even a last name. He now regretted not asking for her phone number.

The following week he sat at his desk flipping through the pages of his lecture notes absentmindedly and wondered if she had dropped out of class. Not that it should matter, he told himself. Still. How could one person who had spoken no more than twenty words to him permeate his head? It had only happened to him once before.

He was lost in memories of the past when he sensed someone entering the class. She walked in slowly, shouldering her large bag, her hair in a high ponytail, her lips bare and swollen. He wondered what happened.

Señora Escobedo stood abruptly from behind her desk, seeing Camila, and embraced her when she approached. Their conversation was private, but Señora's compassion and concern were evident. Camila offered a small grin, but Ben could see that her lip was bruised, preventing her usual smile. She wore a loose-fitted top over linen pants that hung from her hips. He noticed bruising around her collarbone. But it wasn't until she came closer that he saw the awful state of her left shoulder and chest. She acknowledged him with a nod and took her usual seat in front of him. He saw a bruise on the top of her hand as she placed her book on her desk.

During their break, she slipped out of the class before he could say hello. He pretended to want a soda and even went as far as the vending machine but couldn't find her.

She had escaped to cry in the bathroom, feeling lonely since Elena and Mamani had left, her emotions still raw from the accident and breakup. Her mother and grandmother had stocked her refrigerator with enough food for a small village, and since Tyler was busy with his clinical rotations, Camila was left alone for hours. Normally, she would busy herself with her thesis or work, but her headaches were still exhausting, and waiting on tables seemed an impossibility. And besides, she was sad, very sad. Alone, she felt the void that had once been filled with hopes of a future with Lorenzo. Now she just had an empty space in her chest. She cried and then cried some more. Though her body had started to heal, her heart was still shattered.

At the end of lecture, as the other students stood to leave, Camila sat back in her seat. She reached up, taking down her hair. As it fell around her shoulders, the air filled with the fragrance of cinnamon and roses. He froze, putting his books in his backpack, and inhaled her scent. He debated whether he should initiate a conversation to ask what happened. But would that have been too bold? What if she didn't want to share? But it's reasonable to inquire after someone after a long absence, right? He oscillated between respecting her privacy and showing his concern as the window of opportunity was narrowing. Finally, giving up on the possibility of starting a conversation, he headed towards the door, glancing back to see Señora Escobedo take the seat next to her.

Outside, he walked slowly toward the south side of campus where he had parked. He enjoyed the campus at night. There was a magic in the silence. He stopped at Kerckhoff for a cup of coffee and spent the time wondering what had happened to her. An accident of some kind, and the bruise on her hand looked like an IV site. Why was it so hard for him to talk to her? She was just a classmate. He didn't understand the tension between them.

At the parking structure, he got into his car and exited, pulling out onto Strathmore to cut through the apartments heading for Brentwood and home.

As soon as she was outside, the cold hit her. She wrapped her sweater around her arms, but the fabric snagged on her healing skin, and she let it fall off her shoulder, choosing to tolerate the cold rather than risk ripping off a fresh scab. After class, she had detailed the traumatic events of the past two weeks for Señora Escobedo, who listened with empathy, and though it had helped to hear her supportive words, it had brought it all to the surface again. The disappointment, the betrayal, the emotional and physical pain. Tears slid down her cheeks now, and she tried to focus on her walk home. The streets weren't empty, but she knew better than to walk around Westwood after dark, distracted. She picked up her pace but startled at the slightest sound. Cars sped by along the freeway on the opposite side of the cemetery, and from where she was, she could see the bright lights on Wilshire. The street to her right looked terrifyingly dark, but she didn't have a choice. Tyler was on call, and a taxi would be no less frightening as a single woman. As she debated her unpleasant options, a car pulled up to the light. She tried to avoid drawing attention to herself. There was, after all, a path near campus affectionately called the "rape trail," and she didn't want to contribute to that horrid urban legend.

She heard the automatic window roll down and turned away.

"Hey!" A deep male voice shouted from the window.

Shit.

Just look ahead, she told herself. When the light changed, she'd sprint to the fire station, where there was more light and a dozen brave and hopefully handsome men waiting to rescue women in danger. She felt her heart rate gallop, and her hands grow clammy.

"Hey, Camila." The voice was coming from the same car window.

Wait, how did the murderer/rapist know her name? And why was he driving a Volvo?

She cautiously peered into the car window from a safe distance but couldn't see inside. The car made a sharp illegal right turn and pulled up along the curb. The driver-side door opened, and he came out leaning against his car with a smile that melted the ice that had grown around her heart.

"Can I give you a ride?" he said.

"Oh, Ben, hi," she said.

She should have declined but was exhausted from worrying about a potential assault and still too sore to give any attacker a good chase.

"I live in Brentwood. Is that out of your way?"

He smiled. "No, I live there too."

He came around to open her door. She sat down, buckled her seat belt, wiped her face clean of tears, and inhaled deeply. His car was clean. It smelled like Tide.

They didn't speak for a few blocks until they stopped at the light on Sunset.

She was surprised to recognize the song as she heard the faint sound of Bob Marley's voice from his stereo. What did this seemingly privileged white guy driving a European car know about discrimination? But maybe she should withhold her judgment, given she was depending on the privilege of his car at this very moment. She hummed along and noticed a faint smile form on his lips.

He reached over to turn up the sound as he heard the acknowledgment of his music selection.

"Do you have time for a coffee?" she asked, breaking the silence and glancing toward him. She wanted to offer something in return for his generosity, and she wasn't ready to be alone. "There is a coffee shop in Brentwood called Coral Tree," she said. "Does that work?"

"Sure," he said. "I know it."

He could tell she had been crying. Why was she so sad? He caught her eye for a moment. A moment was all he could take between the newness of their friendship, if it could even be called that, and the undeniable attraction of being 20-something and in close quarters with the opposite gender.

More silence.

They parked, and again he came around to her side to open the door. Lorenzo had rarely opened doors for her. He was chivalrous only when it was to his advantage.

They walked up the few steps to the coffee shop's entrance, and Ben held open the door.

"Hi, what can I get you two?" Asked an exquisitely beautiful barista with an array of ear and nasal piercings.

"I'd like a Mexican mocha, please." Camila said and looked up at Ben beneath her long black lashes, "What would you like?"

"Oh, I'll have a cappuccino. But I'll get this," he said, wallet in hand, not seeming to notice the gorgeous woman taking their orders.

"No, please," Camila said. "It's my treat. You did rescue me." She placed a hand over his, gently pushing his wallet back. His skin felt warm beneath her cold fingertips.

"I just gave you a ride, but thanks," he said, looking down at her.

She paid for their drinks and turned to him, "Why don't you grab us a table? I'll wait for the drinks."

He sat in the corner away from the other late-night caffeine consumers, watching her as she meandered through the few shelves of spices, chocolates, and coffee accessories. She picked up a bottle of cardamom pods and sniffed under the cap, replacing it on the shelf with a quick twitch of her nose. She was like nothing he had ever seen before. Each time he saw her, she surprised him. The colors, the adornment, the fragrance. Everything was loud and unapologetically unique.

She walked over carefully, carrying two cups brimming with hot, steamy liquid. He rose and pulled her chair out before taking his own on the other side of the table again.

"Thank you for saving me from being murdered," she said.

He laughed. "You're welcome."

God, she was pretty. Like, very pretty. Like he shouldn't be thinking this given how distraught she looked when he found her.

"So, you've been here before?" she asked.

"Yeah, a few times."

Must be nice, she thought. Coming to Coral Tree was a calculated decision for her. Spending four bucks on a drink was a luxury reserved for special occasions.

"And you live nearby?" she asked, holding her cup beneath her lips.

"Yeah, just a few blocks down, closer to Bundy."

Okay, this guy must have a sweet life. Like most things in LA, housing was all about location. The closer to the beach, the more expensive the real estate. The fact that her place was on the west side of the 405 and still under $2,000 per month was nothing short of a miracle, and here was this guy, neighbors with the Brentwood Country Club.

She licked chocolate foam from the corner of her mouth as he watched her intently. "So, I suppose you're wondering what happened to me," she said.

"I can't imagine. Besides, I'd never assume anything about you. Although, I think you presume to know all about me. I may surprise you."

She smiled at him like she had been caught. He wasn't wrong. She made a sport out of sizing people up before getting to know them. It saved time, and she was usually right. Camila had decided Ben was a preppy California boy who had been raised with two parents who could afford to buy him a European car, enjoy regular vacations, and bless him with genetic superiority manifested by his above-average height.

"Okay, then what are you thinking?" She asked, playing along.

"I was wondering what your last name is."

"Why?"

"I didn't know how to find you," he said. "When you missed class."

She smiled, "There are easier ways to find me than through the campus directory."

He looked at her inquisitively.

"You could've asked for my phone number," she said.

He shifted in his seat but said nothing.

What was with this guy? She was practically throwing her digits at him, and he seemed less than interested. And she was known to be more than just moderately interesting to most men.

"My last name is Malik. Camila Malik."

He smiled. "Nice to meet you. Again."

She smiled back a bit too wide and winced, her fingers flying up to the healing cut on her lip.

"Are you okay?"

"Yeah, it's just my lip isn't completely healed. I was in a car accident two weeks ago."

"I'm sorry, that's horrible," he said as the cause of her absence became apparent. "Are you feeling better?"

"Kinda. But still not 100%." She slid her sweater down. "That's what this is about," she said, motioning to her clavicle and shoulder. He glanced at her skin but didn't see damage, only soft, smooth skin, the color of late summer.

"That looks painful."

"It is, but I imagine it could have been worse given what my car looked like when they towed it."

"That's why you were walking tonight?"

"Bingo."

"Did you walk to campus?"

"Yeah, walking to campus isn't the issue. I always have work to do on my thesis, so I just get in early, grab an office, and work."

"Thesis?"

She took a sip, warm, chocolate liquid coating her throat, enjoying the hints of cinnamon that lingered on her lips.

"I'm in the doctoral program at the School of Public Health," she said.

"Cool, what department?"

"Epidemiology."

He wondered how they had not met before now.

"When do you finish?" he asked.

"Well, first, you should never ask a graduate student that question. You can never really be finished, but I'm planning on defending in the spring."

"Oh, sorry, but that's great. What's your focus?"

"I have a couple projects right now. But I'm working on a paper for my advisor at the moment. So, it's really her research."

As she dove into the details of the paper, it occurred to her that this stranger had taken more interest in her academic life than Lorenzo ever had.

He stirred his coffee, watching the tiny bubbles swirl, and took a sip. As she continued talking, he sat back, crossing his arms, his shirt stretching around his biceps and shoulders. He couldn't look away, the way her eyes shone, the way her hands flew around for emphasis as she explained her project. He envied her passion and enthusiasm. He was searching to find his purpose again. It wasn't a question of performance. He could always perform, but he lacked motivation. He was taking this year to find inspiration, and currently, she captivated him, even though she shouldn't have.

"I want to work for the CDC but abroad, improving access to health care for high-risk populations," she said. "I've never considered this my home. I feel like I belong everywhere and nowhere at the same time."

"Won't you miss your family?" He didn't know anything about her. Why he assumed she even had a family was beyond comprehension.

"I know they'll visit me," she said. "There's more for me to do in this life than be a mother or wife. I just can't. I won't, really. I need to do more." She smiled at him.

His eyes were the same color as chocolate pooling in the bottom of her cup. His looked darker now than the honeyed color she noticed when they had first met a few weeks ago.

"Well, I should get home, or my roommate will be worried," she lied. Tyler was at the hospital, but she wanted to leave. She was exhausted, and being with him expended more energy in a way she couldn't explain.

"Let me drop you off," he said.

"Oh, my building is just across the parking lot," she said as they left the café.

"Camila, I am not sure I'm going to let you cross a dark parking lot at night after I went through all the trouble of rescuing you," he joked.

She smiled. "Okay, well, if you stand right here, you can watch me cross safely into my apartment building."

"Deal."

She quickly looked both ways and crossed San Vicente as he watched her carefully. Making her way between the parked cars, she reached the gate to her building and turned to wave, and he raised his hand in reply. It had been a long time since she'd been treated kindly by a man without the expectations of physical intimacy. It had been even longer since she'd felt the tickle of affection and flutter of anticipation that lingered as she opened the door.

3

"Shall we?" Ben asked as she leaned over, placing her notebook in her bag. He saw the same charm dangling from her neck. The same little eye looking back at him with a blank, cautious stare.

"Coffee?"

"Sure."

A few weeks had passed, and they were in a routine. She assumed her usual position in the passenger seat of his car and noted that the seat hadn't been moved since last week. She made herself comfortable, tucking her feet beneath her and throwing her bag in the footwell. She heard the layers of violin, guitar, and the rasp of a familiar voice from the stereo, "I love these guys! I can't wait to see them live one day."

"They're great live. I went last May at the Staples Center."

"So cool. This is one of my favorites," she said as she reached over to turn up the music.

"They played this one that night, but my favorite is 'Don't Drink the Water.'"

"That's kinda heavy. Most guys I know like 'Crash Into Me' for obvious reasons," she said with an eye roll.

He laughed. "Well, I guess I'm deeper than most guys."

"No, you're not. I just haven't completely figured you out yet."

They assumed their usual table at Coral Tree and waited for the barista to make their drinks.

"How was your weekend?"

"Fine, just studied a bit," he replied.

"What are you studying, by the way? I realize I don't even know if you're an undergrad or a grad student," she said.

"Does it matter?"

She shrugged, not sure if it did. "Well, I mean, kinda."

"Why? If I'm a lowly undergrad, you won't hang out with me?"

"I am not that highbrow, thank you very much, but if I'm older than you, you should know."

"Why? What difference does that make?"

"Dude, can you just answer the question!"

He laughed, "Don't worry. I'm a perfectly grown-up twenty-seven. I'm at the business school."

Before she could ask what exactly he planned on doing with his MBA, her name was called.

"I'll be right back," she said as she hurried to the counter, her dress swishing with every step, as he wondered what mysteries lay beneath the layers of floral print.

She gave him a flirtatious wink as she headed back, ferrying their drinks, the light glinting against her large gold hoop earrings. They dangled to the tops of her shoulders. He smiled back at her. Everything about her was bold.

She sat across from him, placing a cookie between them.

"I think we earned a treat," she said, a broad smile forming on her red-stained lips.

He smiled at her and looked down.

"What?" She asked, sensing there was something he wanted to say.

He looked straight into her eyes, intent on learning more about the mysterious woman seated before him.

"I wanted to ask you something, but I'm not sure if it'll come across as rude," he said.

"Listen, that's one thing you don't have to worry about. You can ask me anything." She nibbled on the cookie. "I don't have anything to hide."

Their conversations had remained light with a cordial but cautious tone. Neither wanted to sabotage the fledgling friendship that was just taking root, and yet they both wanted to dig deeper. They mutually skirted around the periphery of more controversial topics, waiting for the other to take the leap.

He shifted uncomfortably in his seat. "So, how does someone named Camila Elena Malik not speak Spanish?"

Strange. She loved hearing her name roll off his tongue. She wondered what that tongue would feel like running along her skin. That was odd. She usually had more self-restraint. He was a classmate, a friend at most. He was also a bit tame for her taste. A little too wholesome.

"Oh, I see," she said, laughing. "A little stereotyping, are we?"

"I didn't mean to offend," he said, reaching across the table for her arm and stopping midway when she laughed.

"I'm just kidding, Ben. Ask me anything."

He smiled at her sheepishly and rubbed the back of his neck.

"Okay, so my parents met at Berkeley," she said. "At the International House."

"Where were they from?"

"My mom is from Mexico City. She was studying education. My dad was from Iran. He was in the engineering program."

She could see him following her story intently, responding and reacting at the right moments. His eyes didn't trail off to other tables or customers. He was singularly focused on her.

"I love thinking about all the choices that were unknowingly made and the random paths that were taken to bring them together. Across oceans and continents. To the moment they saw each other and knew they were meant to be."

"So, you believe in fate?"

"Of course! Everything happens for a reason, Ben. Even us sitting here is not by accident. There is an energy in this world. What you put in is what you get."

He had to admit, he was intrigued himself, thinking of all the reasons he was now sitting across from this fascinating woman. His eyes roamed over her face, taking in her eyes, mouth, skin. "So, what happened when they met?"

She had heard the story told and retold so many times from her mother's perspective and then from Mamani's. Each time, Camila had tried to imagine what it would feel like to stand in front of her own soulmate one day, for the first time.

"Well, it was all very romantic. Fast, but romantic, apparently." She leaned on the table as she detailed the events of a lifetime ago. Her love for retelling the story was only surpassed by how much she had loved hearing it as a child.

"My mom was reaching for a book at the library, and he appeared at her side, grabbing it for her. She and I are about the same height, but he was much taller." She laughed.

"Clearly those genes didn't get passed down to me." She paused to sip her drink. "You know you're quite attentive."

He smiled. "I like a good story. Keep going, please."

"They were inseparable from that point on. Three months later they moved in together, and, a year later, I was born. But then the revolution in Iran started. My mom says Dad felt as if he were split in two. There wasn't a right choice or a wrong choice. Just an impossible choice. He had this life here. A wife and child, but all his friends and family were back in Tehran, part of a movement that was supposed to help change the trajectory of his country."

She finished her coffee and noticed how intently he watched her. She placed the cup down and tucked a loose tendril of hair behind her ear.

"So, after about three years, he couldn't stand being on the sidelines of the revolution with all the news coming from back home. He wanted to go back to Iran and help even if it meant leaving us for a while. My mom knew exactly what it felt like to be away from everything you know and see things change back home. Things that you wanted to be a part of. Their relationship wasn't about coercion or guilt. She would never have asked him to stay."

He looked surprised. "So, he left?"

"Yeah, I was a little over three years old."

"Did he come back?"

"No, he was killed in a car accident a few weeks after he arrived."

He looked as though she had caught him off guard. "I'm so sorry," he said. "Do you remember him?"

"I remember shadows of him, like his silhouette." She smiled. "I remember feeling loved."

"Your mom sounds like a very strong woman to let him go in the first place."

"Yeah, she's pretty amazing. She's always saying, '*Sometimes when you love someone so much, you have to let them go.*'"

He was captivated by her candor. He wondered how his life would have been different if his mother had followed the same mantra.

"But wait, how does this explain why you don't speak Spanish?"

"Oh," she said with a small chuckle, "when my dad died, his mother left Iran and moved in with us. My father was her only child, and she had already lost her husband. I was all she had left, and she hadn't even met me. My grandmother told me she kept pictures of me all over her house. She had never even met my mother, but they just clicked and made a new little family for me. She didn't speak Spanish, and my mother didn't speak Farsi. All they had in common was me and the English language. So, I grew up speaking English."

"I get it."

"They also didn't want me to stand out anymore."

He looked confused. "Anymore?"

"I don't exactly look like Shirley Temple, now do I?" She laughed. "I was always shorter than the other girls in my class. Always darker. Always the one with crazy hair that could never be tamed."

He couldn't imagine a time when she didn't stand out, but only in all the best ways.

"So, puberty fixed the height issue," she said. "I guess now I'm considered average, but it brought attention I didn't want into my life in a different way." She rested her elbows on the table, and her bangles tumbled down her arm. "I realized quickly that even though I still felt like a little girl, that was not the reaction from the outside world," Camila said. "It was jarring at first. I mean, I was at a wedding once with my mom, and a grown man asked me to dance. I was 14!"

"What did you do?" Ben asked.

"I totally freaked out. That's what I did."

Ben laughed and sat back into his chair. "Seriously, did you dance with him?"

"No! I ran and hid in the bathroom until my mom came to find me," Camila said, hiding her face in her hands. "The poor guy was probably only twenty-eight or twenty-nine years old, but to me, he might as well have been 50! I just felt so uncomfortable. I knew he wanted something from me, not exactly sure what, but I didn't want any part of it," Camila said.

Ben placed his cup down, leaning back into his chair and folding his arms across his chest, making his biceps look particularly large. "In his defense, I bet you looked older than 14," Ben said.

"I did. That was the problem. I had the mind of a 14-year-old and the body of a grown woman," Camila explained. She sat upright and pulled her hair up onto a pile on top of her head. Her earrings picked up the light as she continued to explain.

"I know it may sound crazy, but I still remember the feel of his hand as he put it on the small of my back. I mean, listen, I wasn't violated in any way, but all I wanted to do was scream. I couldn't understand why he didn't know I was a kid, and I felt somehow it was my fault. Like I was going to get into trouble because he wanted to dance with me."

Ben had a sharp twinge of guilt realizing that he too had been ogling her for the good part of the evening. "Well, that's the thing about men: we're pretty basic. Even the most powerful men, perhaps especially those in power, can falter when presented with a beautiful woman."

"I don't think you would do that," Camila said with conviction, ignoring the implication that he considered her beautiful.

Ben smiled away the compliment. "I'm not saying I'm above it, but I haven't been put to the test yet. But I'm only human, Camila."

Camila found his honesty refreshing. He didn't hide his intentions behind a gentleman's façade. But she had lived enough of life as a woman in LA to know she should still be leery of what may lay beneath the surface. Only time would reveal if this friendship would continue or evolve into something more or dissolve altogether. She was attracted to him but not enough to get hurt.

"Are you comfortable in your skin now?" Ben asked.

"I know I'll always be like a novelty to some guys. Something they can have and then regale their friends with stories about how they nailed this exotic chick. I've never been enough for any one culture to accept me. I'm too much for one and too little for the other." She swirled her hands in the air. "I belong in the ether. Eventually, I realized my differences were my assets, and now that I know how to wield my powers, I feel less like a victim," she said. "If someone can't handle my appearance, it's their issue and not mine."

"You sound like a magician."

Camila laughed out loud. "But it is kinda like magic, isn't it? My appearance alone can open some doors with no effort and close others instantly."

Ben understood what she meant. For a man who prided himself on having above-average willpower, he was finding it difficult not to stare with the way her nipples brushed against her top. He found himself expending more energy than usual to maintain eye contact.

"Well, that is definitely something I will never experience," Ben said.

"Are you kidding me? Of course you experience it. I bet you experience it every day without realizing it," Camila said. "Let me explain," she said, seeing his face contort into confusion.

"Please do, Camila."

She stared at him before she said, "Well, first, I'm sure you've never not belonged. I'm sure you have always been the golden child of your family. I'm sure you were always picked first for teams; you never had to worry about a prom date, and strangers still come up to ask you how tall you are, assuming you must have been some kind of extraordinary collegiate athlete."

That was only partly true. Life had been easy for him. At least for the past fifteen years. But he wasn't going to share those details yet. Or ever.

He shrugged. "I guess." She was so straightforward, he thought. Cutting through all the bullshit most people usually skirt around. He had never met anyone like her.

"So, am I right, Ben?" She asked, smiling broadly with confidence.

"Okay, only part of that is true," he said. "They usually don't ask how tall I am. They try to guess."

They both started to laugh at her stealth-like accuracy.

She looked at her watch. "Oh God, it's so late! You probably have stuff to do, and I'm on the early shift tomorrow. I should go."

"Early shift?"

"Oh, I'm a waitress at CPK," she said as they packed up to leave.

"So, you have a job besides your graduate work?"

"Well, the bills aren't going to pay for themselves, Ben," she said with a wink.

* * *

"Hey, I can pick you up tonight," Tyler told her the following week. He had been on night rotation, and she had been left to her own devices, or rather Ben's, since their biweekly outings had become dependable.

"It's okay. I have it covered."

"Really?" he said, chopping carrots in the kitchen. "How exactly?"

"Well, if you must know…"

He paused his chopping. "Of course, I must," he said, popping a piece of carrot in his mouth.

"There's this guy in my class, and we usually grab coffee after."

"What!? Cami! How many weeks have you been withholding this delicious little nugget?"

She laughed deviously. "He's just a nice guy. He doesn't give me the creeps. He hasn't even tried to kiss me, and I had to practically beg him to take my phone number."

Tyler gave her a confused but worried look. "Are you sure he wouldn't be more interested in me?"

"Ha, I'm pretty sure he's straight, but I guess you have a point."

* * *

Ben ordered an Earl Grey tea. "No cappuccino tonight?" she asked. He smiled, "I thought I'd mix it up."

He never changed anything. What was going on?

"Just when I thought I had you two figured out," said the now-familiar barista. "Most people order the same drink each time. But tea? That's a first."

"We're trying to keep you on your toes, Bella," Camila said. "Hey, I like the red," she continued, motioning to Bella's fire-engine red hair, a change from her usual purple.

They inhabited their corner table as they had for weeks now. He had noticed that her phone didn't consume her anymore. No more checking it during breaks. The change started when their friendship had. She seemed less agitated, less anxious.

He leaned in. "Can I ask you a question?"

"Sure, Ben, anything," Camila said and leaned on the somewhat sticky tabletop with her elbows.

"Why were you crying that first night I picked you up?" He had patiently waited, hoping the subject would have naturally come up by now.

"Well, right before my accident I was on the phone with my boy-friend, and he broke up with me."

"Oh, I'm sorry."

"Don't be. He was an asshole," she said, waving her hand as if she were shooing away a fly. An asshole fly.

He gestured to the necklace she always wore. "Did he give you that?"

"Oh, this?" She lifted the necklace off her breasts, where it hung, dangling the evil eye charm over her fingers.

He nodded, trying to look only at her eyes.

"No, he didn't buy me much. I bought this for myself. It was my first major purchase, and then I kept adding to the collection. I have eyes everywhere."

"I've noticed."

"They keep me safe," she explained. "It's the symbol of the evil eye, you know, though it didn't keep that asshole away from me." She shrugged. "So, who knows?"

"How long were you guys together?"

"About a year and a half. I kept trying to convince myself I loved him. You know, to make it all fit. But I was pushing the river."

"Pushing the river?"

"You know, when the world is showing you what direction you

need to take but you insist on going the opposite way."

"I see." He smiled. "Fate."

"Exactly!"

"So, it was fate that you got into a car accident?"

She sensed the gentle sarcasm in his tone. "No. Well, yes! It was Lorenzo's fault because I was yelling at him and started crying and couldn't see, so I crashed into the car in front of me. And, if I hadn't totaled my car then we wouldn't be sitting here together now, would we?" She smiled coyly. "It's all destined. It could have been worse. It was all the good karma I had built up, all the prayers from my mother and grandmother that kept me safe." She said with conviction.

He smiled. "Not the airbags?"

"You think you're funny, huh? But one day you'll see, Mr. Non-believer. Life will change for you, and it'll be the direct result of all the good or bad you've put out there."

But life had already veered off course for him, and bad had turned into good, but he doubted it was due to anything he did. Ben had been raised in the church of religious ambivalence and the golden rule.

"Lorenzo? That was his name?"

"Yeah, he was a grad student in the Biochemistry department, but he moved to Boston when he got a tenure-track position. I called him that night, and some girl was in the background."

"Ouch!"

"Yup, that's one thing I can't handle. Being the other woman."

He swallowed hard.

"It's okay." She laughed to herself. "He was a bit much at times."

"Like what?"

"Nothing," Camila said.

"Camila, what? You said I could ask anything, so tell me." He was intrigued now.

"Okay, but remember you asked for it," she said. "Well, he liked to talk during sex. Like dirty talk." A shiver of disgust ran up her spine.

His mouth fell open but was still interested in hearing more.

"It always made me cringe, but I didn't want to seem prudish. But it wasn't even about that. It's just not my thing."

Ben shifted in his seat, feeling uncomfortable.

"Listen, I felt the same way as you look right now. It would instantly take me out of the mood. I think the world can be divided into groups of women who enjoy that kind of talk and those who don't. I am yet to find someone who belongs to the former."

He ran his hand through his hair, trying to get the image of Camila having sex out of his head.

She pushed her chair back from the table. "Okay, I should go, but next time it's going to be all about Ben. You know so much about me, and I know very little about you."

* * *

He noticed that time was now punctuated not by hours of the day but by days between seeing Camila. Maybe it was attraction, maybe it was loneliness, but the momentum of the week would peak as he anticipated Tuesday's class, and after Thursday, he would have to spend the next four days tempering his excitement for their next class. Tonight, they were comfortably seated at their usual table, nursing their drinks.

"Okay, so now I get to ask you anything I want, right?" Camila said. "That was the agreement last time."

"Yes, anything you want," he said, setting his cup down in preparation.

"Okay. Where did you grow up?"

"Connecticut."

"Do you have any brothers or sisters?"

"I have two sisters. One older and one younger."

"What do your parents do?"

"My dad is an ER doctor at Yale," he said.

She pointed to the scar on his upper lip. "Did he fix your lip?"

"Yeah, kinda," he said, looking uneasy.

"Gosh, you are overwhelmingly descriptive. You can feel free to elaborate, you know. This isn't a deposition, Ben. I'm not going to hold your answers against you."

"Okay, okay, I'll be more specific," Ben said with a laugh.

"Okay, good. So, let's try again. Your mom, what does she do?"

"She teaches kindergarten. I mean, she teaches kindergarten, which is a classroom full of small people who need frequent bathroom breaks and often cry," he corrected himself with a bit of sarcasm.

"Very funny. Now are you going to take this seriously or what?" Camila said.

"I'll be serious. I promise," he said and placed his hand on his heart. "She does teach kindergarten. She's been teaching in the same school for the past 25 years. It's in a cute little cottage with its own vegetable garden and chicken coop in the back. She says it's good for the children to be around animals. She could have retired a few years ago, but she just loves it."

"So did you used to go help her when you were little?"

He shifted in his seat. "She would bring us there sometimes. We loved being with the animals and playing in the grass. It was peaceful."

She smiled. "Wow, this sounds all very idyllic."

He imagined it did sound heavenly, the way he described it at least. He had never considered himself a natural liar, but he seemed to be born to it, the way he was lying with ease.

"Where did you go to undergrad?"

"Yale," he said.

"Okay, fancy pants." She got a smile from him at that. "Okay, just a few more questions. When will you be done with your MBA?"

"At the end of the year."

"Isn't an MBA a two-year program?"

"It usually is, but I'm in an accelerated program."

"What's the rush?" she said.

Before he could evade the question, they were distracted by a sudden, loud crash. Bella dropped a tray of cups and saucers.

Camila stood, startled by the noise, and called over to Bella. "Do you need help?"

"No, honey, I'm okay. Just a hazard of the job," she said, kneeling to pick up the pieces as one of the back house staff came to lend her a hand.

Camila sat back down. Ben was grateful she was no longer standing directly in front of him. She had worn skin-tight jeans tonight, accentuating her hourglass figure and making her look even more curvaceous. As if that were humanly possible.

He really did try hard not to stare. But she was wearing a tube top that hugged her tightly, and her shawl did little to hide anything. Her necklace dangled on her chest, and she played with the charm at the end of it while she talked, drawing his eyes to her like a cat to a string.

He usually held himself to a higher standard and could easily avoid whatever tempting bit of flesh a woman would display before him, but with Camila it was impossible. Even if she was wearing a burlap sack, he would've found it hard to look away.

"So, I wonder where Señora Escobedo wants the class to go for the Spanish immersion experience next weekend?" He needed to change the subject.

"I figure it'll be fun wherever we go. It's like a scavenger hunt."

"So, we have to make sure we speak Spanish the entire time, or we don't get credit?"

She broke off a piece of the brownie they were sharing. "Exactly," she said.

"I can pick you up."

She smiled. "Sure, that would be great."

It was near the end of October, and the evenings were cooler. She tightened the emerald-colored shawl around her shoulders. The color made her eyes pop, reminding him of the green of a stained-glass window.

They finished their drinks and made their way to the door where he would normally watch her cross the parking lot and enter her building.

"Oh, here is my number," she said, handing him a scrap of paper. "I'll see you Thursday."

He told her goodbye and watched her disappear behind the gate. He looked down at the paper he held in his palm and sighed. A knot forming in his gut. This was wrong. He needed to stop this before it became too difficult.

4

October 2002

Camila had the rare luxury of extra time the following week and casually made her way to Powell Library to spend a few minutes sitting on the steps before Spanish class. Watching the sun set over the dorms along the west side of campus was a simple pleasure she enjoyed best in solitude. She had walked miles across this campus during the years she had been both an undergraduate and graduate student. Now that graduation was looming, she was starting to feel the pang of nostalgia set in.

Camila was ready for a life that could make a difference. With enough experience in the field and patience working her way through the necessary bureaucracy of government institutions, she could eventually land herself a position that could have her traveling the globe as a CDC country director. Improving her language skills was a step in the right direction. She pulled out the stack of research articles she had been reviewing and set the pile in her lap. It was going to take hours to prepare the presentation that was supposed to secure the funds for her postdoctoral project. She looked up as a shadow fell over her, blocking out the warm rays of sun that were gradually shifting from burnt orange to deep crimson.

"Where did you come from?" Camila asked and smiled up at Ben towering over her.

"I was heading up from the business library. What are you doing here?"

"Watching the sunset before class starts. Want to join me?"

He didn't remember the last time he had made space in his schedule to just enjoy a sunset. Ben sat to Camila's right and watched the sun make brush strokes of color across the sky past her face. He tapped the papers in her lap. "What are these?"

"I have to review these and put together a proposal to fund my post-graduate project," she said.

"Looks daunting."

"It's not so bad. I'm professionally and emotionally invested," Camila said.

"I have an idea," Ben said and stood abruptly. "Let's ditch class tonight. You tell me about your project, and I'll take us to Diddy Riese. My treat." He extended his arm out to her.

"Sounds great, but I didn't peg you as the tattoo type," she said, running her fingers across the childlike lettering covering his forearm before taking his hand and standing up.

Ben blushed from her touch. "I lost a bet to an eight-year-old and then couldn't get the ink to fade without losing too many layers of skin."

"My project can wait. First, let me ask, does this eight-year-old belong to you?"

"No," Ben laughed. "I try to help out at a shelter a few times per month."

"What kind of shelter?" Camila asked as they walked away from their class together.

"It's for women and children, primarily victims of domestic violence. I started tutoring the kids a few months ago, and last week I bet one of them if she got an A on her math test, she could give me a tattoo."

"Now I understand the hearts and flowers," Camila laughed. "What made you start volunteering?"

"I don't know. I'm trying to be more purposeful in the way I choose to spend my time," he said almost completely truthfully. There were so many things he had given up over the past few years on the journey to his career and well-planned-out future. He didn't play tennis anymore. He made time for a run, but that was more medicinal. What he had recently realized was that as his life was marching along in an orderly fashion, life was actually passing him by. So, when he experienced this crisis of self-realization, he decided to take this year and reconnect with himself. To learn something new, make time for the things that interested him but were usually pushed to the side to make space for what was required of him. This was supposed to be a year away from the pressure of grades and class rank and performing.

They started walking toward Westwood Plaza as the sun set completely and transformed the sky into a deep purple. She noticed how he gently placed his hand at her elbow each time they crossed the street and purposely had her walk along the inside of the sidewalk.

"So, your project?" Ben asked.

She flipped her hair to look at him directly as they walked together. "Well, I'm working on a data set collected from indirect sex workers in Cambodia. It was the basis of my thesis, and if I can get the funding, then I'll be able to go to Phnom Penh for a few weeks with the in-country team."

"What an amazing opportunity, but what's the difference between indirect and direct sex workers?"

"Good question. Direct sex workers work in brothels, where it is easier to implement safe-sex practices like universal condom use, especially when you have government involvement. Indirect sex workers are more challenging. These are women who wouldn't normally consider themselves sex workers but will participate in high-risk sexual behavior for money. They are more difficult to track, and as a result can fall in between the cracks of health care strategies, which leaves them more susceptible to STDs, like HIV."

"That is such a vulnerable population."

"Yes, I mean if I hadn't won the celestial lottery, I could have been born there, and that could have been my life."

"I'm sure your research makes you very thankful for all the opportunities you have here," Ben said.

"Yes, absolutely, but it's not enough to just be grateful. I have to do something to help. These women don't engage in these encounters for recreation. It's a matter of necessity and lack of options. Imagine if feeding your children and preventing them from a life of destitution depended on entertaining strange men. It would be stomach-turning, but any mother would tolerate it for the sake of her children."

"Your work will make such an impact," Ben said, envious of the opportunity to make a lasting difference in the world.

"I hope so. If we are able to give these women more choices, then perhaps they wouldn't feel trapped into a life that is dangerous for them and their families. Anyway, I only have one life to try and make an impact, so I figure do something that is worth it, right?"

Ben felt her fervor was contagious even though he had craved stability his entire life. In his career, in his family. He didn't have a fraction of the fire Camila had. Even his relationships had been well planned out and orchestrated to minimize any unexpected emotional fluctuations. But now amid his private personal crisis, he was finally realizing his strategy had resulted in a life devoid of passion.

They took the last two seats outside the store as the line began to wrap around the corner. Camila had seen the famed storefront every day on her way to and from work, but it had always been either too early or too late to indulge. Ben pulled his chair closer to her to make space on the sidewalk. Their legs touched under the table, the friction causing heat to radiate up his torso.

"Ditching class, homemade tattoos from minors, and now ice cream? What has gotten into you tonight?" Camila asked. "Thank you, by the way," Camila said, tapping her ice cream cookie sandwich against his like a toast.

"You're welcome," he said with a mouth full of ice cream. "I don't know. I wanted to talk to you more than go to class."

"Well, I'm pretty compelling with all my sex worker talk. By the way, did you know how much self-control it took for me not to yell 'Rocky Road' in there?" Camila said.

"But you got Chocolate?"

"Oh my God, you don't get it?"

"Get what?"

"*The Goonies*? Please, tell me you've seen it."

"I haven't actually," Ben confessed.

"WHAT!" Camila yelled and turned the heads of a few nearby customers.

Ben looked around to gauge the response of those near them to Camila's outburst, but much to his surprise, no one cared. He was continuously aware of how his behavior may impact others. Never be too loud, too demanding, or too bold.

"Well, now I see your two flaws. Eating toothpaste-flavored ice cream and a fundamental deficiency in the basics of American cinema."

"I'm not sure *The Goonies* won any Oscars, and mint chip is a perfectly reasonable choice," Ben said, licking his ice cream with exaggerated enjoyment.

"It would have been cheaper to lick a tube of Crest."

"That's big talk for someone who was just treated to ice cream," Ben said.

"If it means I can mock your taste, I will happily pay for myself next time, messy," Camila said as she dragged her finger along his palm to clean up a trickle of melted ice cream that was making its way toward his wrist. She licked her finger and made a face.

"Oh, come on, it's not that bad," Ben said.

"Mmm, just like Colgate," Camila laughed.

He really enjoyed her laughter. It was full, open, and sincere.

"Okay, fine, what's your favorite movie?" she asked.

"Easy, *The Untouchables*," Ben said.

"The movie about the righteous, handsome, truthful police officer who sacrifices everything to do what is right?"

"That's the one," Ben said.

"Wrong," Camila said, dismissing him.

"What? You can't say wrong. There is no one correct answer."

"Of course there is. *Working Girl*."

"That movie with the big hair and shoulder pads?" Ben said in disbelief.

"You mean that classic movie about the struggles of an underprivileged woman clawing her way up the corporate ladder despite what the world throws at her, who fights for what she wants even when she is told she can't have it? Then yes. You clearly didn't watch it properly."

Ben was stifling his laughter by the end of Camila's sermon, "What is the proper way to watch a movie?" Ben asked.

"With me," Camila said.

"I'll make a note of that," he said.

"Most things are better with my input," Camila said.

"I can only imagine."

"Of course. For example, you haven't noticed the small puddle of melted green ice cream on the front of your shirt because I have made this experience all the more thrilling for you."

Ben looked down to see a pool of ice cream seeping into his shirt, then looked back up at Camila. "I may actually believe you," he said and started to dab at his clothes.

Camila popped up and quickly returned with a pile of napkins and a cup of water. An expert in getting pizza sauce out of her clothes, she dipped the wad of paper into the cup and proceeded to pull his shirt away from his chest and slide her hand under the stain to wipe at it like he was a clumsy toddler.

Ben looked around uncomfortably, scanning the crowd for familiar faces after realizing he was being groomed in public. He gently pushed her hand out from under his shirt.

"Thanks."

"I think I made it worse," Camila said and bit her lower lip.

"No, I think the wet halo around the green stain makes it less obvious for sure," he said, mocking her.

"Asshole," she said and batted his hand away.

"Now can I drive you home?"

"I'm not sure I want you to anymore," Camila said with an air of superiority and stood as Ben pulled out her chair. "I may be better off walking in the dark. You look like a mess," she said and lightly pushed against him, her hand feeling the firm wall of muscle beneath his shirt. A rosy hue spread across her cheeks.

"Let's go before I make you walk home," Ben said.

"You wouldn't do that. You are too noble to risk my safety," she said.

"Is that so?"

"Absolutely, you're chivalrous, and I'm a delight, and you know it."

Ben sagged his shoulders as he shook his head laughing.

"Fine, Camila. I give up. You're delightful, and your skills at stain removal are unparalleled."

Camila looped her arm in his as they crossed back over Le Conte Avenue and back onto campus. Being this close to him, she was able to appreciate the subtle scent that enveloped her senses when the wind gusted past him. She wasn't sure if it was deodorant or cologne, but whatever the source of the clean, crisp fragrance, she wanted to drink it up. They remained intertwined as they slowly strolled to his car. She enjoyed the feeling of her hand resting on his sturdy arm and realized that she just enjoyed being with him. He felt solid next to her not only physically but also in virtue.

"I bet you've never done a bad thing in your life," Camila said.

"I've never understood the fascination with being bad. Why not live a life free of complications?"

"Because that is not life, Ben." Camila slowed her pace to a stop, not wanting the conversation to end by arriving at their destination prematurely. She couldn't recall the last time she cared so much about what someone else thought or felt they actually cared about what she had to say in return. She turned to face him, the quiet of a deserted campus surrounding them. She knew he couldn't be entirely honorable because of the glint of desire she saw a few times before they would break eye contact, but she didn't want to test his convictions. Not yet.

"Life is messy, Ben. Figuring out the mess is what defines us. An easy life is like food with no salt. You'll be full, but you won't be satisfied. A man who likes mint chip can't possibly want a bland existence," Camila said with a smile.

He looked down at her, speechless. In one afternoon, she had cut to the essence of what he had wrestled with for the past year. He didn't know women like Camila existed. She welcomed chaos while he had spent the majority of his time bubble-wrapping his life from any potential turmoil. As Ben drove away from Camila's apartment that night, for the first time he felt a buoyancy he had never known.

5

The light of the moon cast a silver tint around them, adding to the palpable thrill she had begun to feel whenever they were together. Her feelings for him had morphed from mildly irritated to friendly fascination to full-blown infatuation. She thought of him more often than she wanted to admit to Tyler. It wasn't just physical attraction; that was undeniable. But she had also started to develop feelings of attachment. She would rehash their conversations and wonder what they would discuss next. There was still so much about him that was a mystery. She yearned for hours of time for their conversations to naturally meander into more personal territory. She hoped that this weekend would lend itself to further discovery, emotionally and physically.

"Okay, on Saturday night just call me when you're outside and I'll come out," Camila said to Ben as they departed the cafe the following Thursday.

"I wonder what we're supposed to wear. It's a restaurant and a club, right?" she asked.

"Yeah, that's what Señora said."

She could tell by the expression on his face he was apprehensive. In reality, he was dreading the possibility that dancing may be in his near future.

"Okay, well, I'll see you Saturday then." She turned to walk across the street and stopped. She wasn't used to things moving this slowly. At this pace, the polar ice caps would be gone before he even asked her out on a *real* date. So, without knowing exactly why, she stood on tiptoes, kissing him on the cheek, and then ran across the street. She turned to wave at him as she entered her building.

Breathless, she leaned against her apartment door as soon as she closed it behind her and found Tyler sitting on the floor, his Tarot cards splayed before him.

"What's up, buttercup?" He looked preoccupied with the future before him.

"Nothing," she said.

"That's not a nothing, nothing." Tyler was well-versed in Camila's many moods.

"I just kissed him!" She covered her mouth with her hand.

His face lit up. "Mysterious Spanish Class guy?"

She smiled. "Uh-huh."

"How was it?"

"Well, it was only a peck on the cheek, but I think I like him. He's so cute and thoughtful and smart. He's just so slow with, you know, making a move."

"Maybe he's being a gentleman?"

"In LA?"

They both erupted into laughter.

* * *

"Okay, what do you think?" she asked, a few days later, as she twirled into the living room.

Tyler looked up from his notes, surrounded by piles of books, one pencil behind his ear, another held between his teeth. His neurology clerkship final was approaching, and after a six-week rotation slugging it out in the neuro-intensive care unit, he needed to pass this test.

His mouth dropped open, seeing her, and the pencil fell.

"Holy shit, you look like a Latin Jessica Rabbit!"

She spun around again for emphasis. Her red dress clung to her curves in all the right ways. The cap sleeves accentuated her delicate shoulders, and the frilled hem at mid-thigh highlighted her toned legs. Her hair was swept to one side with a large red rose tucked in at the nape of her neck.

"I got it at a consignment shop," she said. "The tips have been good lately," she said.

"Well, if he doesn't make a move tonight, then he's clearly gay, and you can send him my way."

Ben knew something was shifting in his friendship with Camila, and worry consumed him. The desire he felt to be with her at times was illogical. He'd find himself thinking about her over breakfast or during one of the long runs he was now making time for a few days per week. Planning to spend hours together tonight was both exciting and terrifying. This year was supposed to be dedicated to rediscovering himself and making time for new interests, but that didn't include new women. He was waiting outside of his car as she walked out, and his heart stopped for a split second.

"Nice flower," he said as he held the door open for her.

She slid into the passenger seat. "Thanks," she said.

She was buckling her seatbelt when he entered his side of the car, and he couldn't help noticing her crossing her legs. For a brief moment, he wondered what they would feel like beneath his fingers. They looked smooth and soft and tan with the flirty hem of her dress brushing her thigh. God, he needed to focus on the road.

He was unusually quiet tonight, she thought. Maybe he was nervous because he was going to finally make a move. She uncrossed and crossed her legs, and she caught him tightening his grip on the steering wheel. They drove for an hour, not saying much, the radio playing in the background, before getting to Anaheim and parking in a lively part of town. He helped her out of the car, and they walked up to the restaurant together, where a muscle-bound bouncer eyed her up and down. As if he were going to devour her. And in front of Ben.

She flashed the bouncer a smile as they walked past, and she caught him glaring at Ben as if to say, *Why the fuck is she with you, gringo?!*

The place was huge, two stories, with tables winding all along the top balcony and surrounding the dance floor. Music filled the space with a vibrant and infectious rhythm. They joined their classmates at a table with Señora Escobedo and had to yell to talk over the live band. Per their teacher's instructions, they ordered their meals in Spanish and were on their way to receiving full credit for their outing when someone got the bright idea to go out onto the dance floor. Camila jumped up as if she had been waiting all night for an invitation to dance.

"Come on, Ben, won't you?" Camila asked.

He shook his head. "No, thank you. I know my strengths and weaknesses."

"Okay, but you'll be missing out." She smiled as one of their classmates grasped her hand and pulled her to the dance floor.

For the next half hour, Ben sat alone at the table watching Camila salsa dancing nonstop. She moved with grace, spinning, hips swaying, her hair flying behind her. She seemed to enjoy being dipped and twirled by each partner who approached her. They knew the moves, how to turn her, how to guide her, and she knew how to be led.

Señora Escobedo moved to sit in the empty chair next to him. "Ella es muy bonita, no?" she said to Ben, watching Camila on the dance floor. "You should go dance with her."

Señora Escobedo wasn't blind. He knew she had seen them together in class and during break. He also knew Camila had told her she'd broken up with her boyfriend a few months ago, the reason for her car crash.

"Yo no bailo, Señora," he said, smiling.

Nudging him, she said, "Well, even if you don't dance, this may be a great opportunity to learn."

The music slowed, and Camila stood on the dance floor catching her breath, lifting her hair to fan her neck. A few eager dance partners approached, but she declined, gracefully. One seemed hopeful and a bit too determined, and Ben saw her backing away as a man grabbed a hold of her wrist and Camila struggling to break free.

"Excuse me, Señora," Ben said and made his way to the dance floor in a few large steps.

"Dance with me?" he asked Camila as he towered over the perpetrator, giving him an intimidating stare.

She smiled up at Ben.

"Yes," she said, pulling her arm free of the other man's grip.

Ben slipped his arm around her and held her close, her right palm against his left.

"You rescued me again," she said, looking up at him with a smile.

"Well, now you need to rescue me," he said, his arm around her waist causing his stomach to flutter. "I'm a bit out of my element here."

"You're doing fine. Just let yourself move to the music. There aren't any steps, just feel the music."

Her eyes flickered up toward his face, and again she noticed the faint scar that extended from his lip. "So, how did you get that?"

"Oh, an accident a long time ago."

She could sense his reluctance to explain further and was satisfied with the answer. She leaned her head against him and heard his heartbeat, their hands intertwined on his chest. She felt the hard muscles of his arms around her and loved the feeling of her hand in his. She was ready to admit it now. She liked him. He was kind and good and handsome. She was tired of having to fight for a relationship. Everything was so easy with Ben. The only issue was the incomprehensibly long time it had taken for him to ask her out. And, technically, he still hadn't. They were together at a school-related activity, like children on a field trip. This was not a date.

He felt her body against his, her warmth. He inhaled the floral scent of her hair. The faint smell of roses. It reminded him of the rose water he washed his hands in before eating at a Moroccan restaurant once. Dear God. This was not what he wanted. This was wrong. He shouldn't be holding her. He shouldn't be swaying with her to music clearly intended for lovers. Still, he slid his arm a bit further around her, coaxing her closer.

She loved every second in his arms, swaying with him.

When the music stopped, she looked up at him. "Thank you for saving me," she said, and he let her slip out of his grasp. Their hands lingered together.

"There were others who would have rescued you," he said.

"But I don't know them. I don't want their hands on me."

He let go of her, making his way back to their table as a fast-paced song started again.

"Oh no, you're not going anywhere," she said slyly gripping his hand. "I love Celia Cruz!"

"Oh, Camila I don't know how to dance." He was pleading now.

She loved his honesty. How he didn't pretend to be an expert when he wasn't and make a fool of himself. He was confident enough to be vulnerable about his abilities. She loved that he trusted her to lead him.

"It's okay. I'll teach you. It's not hard."

Two hours later, they made their way back to the table to find it deserted. His sleeves rolled up, his collar undone, his skin glistening. He rested his hands on his hips as he caught his breath, and his shoulders looked broader. She could see the muscles under his shirt contracting and relaxing with each breath. She wanted to walk over to him and unbutton his shirt, run her hands down his sweat-soaked chest, push him up against the wall, and ...

"Now *you're* staring," he said with a smile.

She was totally caught.

She grinned. "Don't flatter yourself."

He nodded toward the door. "Shall we?"

"Sure."

In the car, she leaned her head back on the seat and let out an exhale. She took off her heels. Her feet ached after hours of dancing, and she tucked them beneath her.

"Tired?" he asked, and she nodded, turning her head toward him.

Kiss me. Kiss me. Kiss me. She hoped telepathy would work, but he was much more interested in talking on the way home. A nervous sort of talkativeness.

"How did you learn to dance like that?" he asked.

"Like what?"

"You know, like *that.*"

She laughed. "Well, I grew up in an all-female household, and between the salsa music and Persian music, we had a dance party nearly every night."

He liked the thought of her and her mother and grandmother dancing around their living room. Her joy was somehow infectious, and he found himself less burdened when she was near. The image of her as a child made him smile. He didn't have as many happy memories growing up. Well, at least not until later.

They turned on her street just as it started to rain. Okay, this was going to be it, she thought. He had rescued her on the dance floor and then twirled and spun her around for the past two hours. They had been slowly getting acquainted with each other over the past two months like some Austen-style courtship. It had to happen tonight. Sometime between driving from the restaurant and walking through her door, he would kiss her. She could feel it. The rain was coming down enough to cool the balmy mid-October weather. The windows were fogging, and the headlights of oncoming cars blurred through the windshield.

"I think I have an umbrella in the trunk," he said when they pulled up in front of her building. "Stay there, and I'll be right around."

She sat there shuffling her feet in excitement. She didn't remember the last time she had anticipated a kiss so much and quickly fluffed her hair and applied balm to her lips, looking in the vanity mirror. The door opened, and he extended his hand, gently pulling her out of the car and under his umbrella. He walked her up the few stairs to her door, his hand soft on her low back while holding the umbrella to protect her from the rain.

She turned at her door and said, "Well, this is me."

He stood there, the rain pattering, the light of the patio faint in the dark doorway. She could feel the butterflies in her stomach and the tingles in her toes as she waited for him to lean into her. Her high heels helped traverse the vertical distance between their lips.

What was taking him so long? Did her breath smell? Was he nervous? He didn't seem the type of man to be nervous about anything. Did she have something in her teeth? Was she too sweaty from all the dancing? Didn't he feel what she'd been feeling over the past few weeks? He needed to put her out of her misery, or she was going to burst.

She glanced at his lips, then his eyes, and saw him looking at her. Why wasn't he saying or, more importantly, doing anything?

She suddenly heard the loud creak of her front door swinging open, and there stood Tyler carrying a bag of trash and wearing his robe and little else.

His expression said he realized he had stumbled upon something private. "Oh!"

"Hey Tyler, what are you doing here?" Camila said, through gritted teeth, her tone really implying, *I'm going to fucking kill you, Tyler. Your timing is fucking impeccable.*

His eyes widened. His eyebrows lifted. "I'm taking out the trash. What are you doing here?"

"This is my home too, if you haven't forgotten," she said, thick with sarcasm.

"Hey Tyler," Ben said softly over her shoulder.

She spun around, her hair swinging, and saw in Ben's face shock and shame.

"Hiya, Ben," Tyler said. "How are you?"

"I'm fine, thanks."

Camila was confused. "Wait, how do you two know each other?"

"Tiffany was my clerkship mentor last year," Tyler said. As if that explained anything.

"Who is Tiffany?" she asked. Confusion and irritation painted all over her face.

"Ben's girlfriend," he said. "I guess congratulations are in order. I heard you guys are engaged now."

Camila felt as if her heart was free-falling to her knees. Like she was drowning in a tsunami of unwelcome information.

"Thanks," was all Ben said.

"Well, I should go throw this out," Tyler said, lifting the bag of trash. "See you around, Ben."

"Bye, Tyler," he said, looking at his feet.

Camila couldn't believe what she had heard. It was like swimming in the ocean and having wave after wave crash on you.

Tiffany. Crash

Girlfriend. Crash

Fiancée. CRASH

She felt stupid and disappointed. More stupid than anything else. And it was his fault. He never said anything about having a girlfriend, let alone making her his fiancée, for two months. *Two FUCKING months!*

He had held Camila and moved with her on the dance floor. Their bodies had pressed up against each other. And he, well, he made her feel like he was interested.

She looked up at him now, and his eyes met hers. She wasn't going to cry, but she didn't want to be around him just in case.

"I'm going inside. Thanks for the ride," she said flatly as she turned to walk through the door Tyler had left wide open.

"Camila," he said.

"I'll see you later." She said over her shoulder with finality and turned to close the door behind her.

Ben closed his umbrella and headed back out to his car. It wasn't raining anymore, but it felt like everything was still coming down around him. He never expected the night to end like this. If he had been honest with himself, he knew what they had between them wasn't platonic. He had felt it when he drove her home that first night and each night afterward when they would share stories of their previous lives over a cup of coffee. Why hadn't he mentioned Tiffany earlier? He knew why. He may have been embarrassed to admit it to himself, but the truth was he liked Camila more than he expected, and it had shocked him. It had scared him. But he loved Tiffany. He was proud to be with her and proud of her. They had been together for three years now. He hadn't lied about Tiffany. He truly loved her. But she was gone. Across the country, in a different time zone, working a hundred hours per week, with barely enough energy to stay awake through their attempt at a nightly phone call. They knew this year would be tough, but that's why they were getting married in four months. By March they would be husband and wife, and it wouldn't matter how much distance was between them. They would be legally wed. He just had to last for four more months.

It had never been a problem before. They could have spent days and weeks apart. He would never have even fathomed glancing at another woman.

And in one night he had danced with another woman and held her in his arms, swayed with her, and smelled her hair.

He was a good man. He was not his father. He would not hurt the women in his life.

Tyler opened their bedroom door carefully, making sure the coast was clear. But, unfortunately for him, Camila was still awake, seated on her bed preparing for his interrogation.

"Hey, Cami," he said cautiously.

"Spill it," she said. "Now."

"Spill what?"

"All of it, Tyler!" She sounded hysterical.

"Okay, well for the record, you never told me the name of the mystery man you've been hanging out with each week after your class. No way I would ever guess it was Ben Cole Martin."

"Is that his full name?"

"Yes, and it's a perfect name, just like him."

"What's that supposed to mean?" She was irritated.

"Just that. He's perfect, Cami. He doesn't make mistakes. Not in class, not in life. He was class president his second year, and he's Alpha Omega Alpha. He was even voted to be part of the Gold Humanism Honor Society."

She sighed, frustrated. "Okay, in English please."

"Cami, he is the golden boy of our entire school. He is morally scrupulous, smart, and socially functional, a rare combo in med school. To top it off, he is part of the power couple that is Ben and Tiffany."

That name again, like a dagger in her gut.

"What is she like? Is she nice?"

"Well, as nice as a robot can be. For as much as they are both crazy smart, he is the only endearing one. She has about as much charisma as our dining table. Don't get me wrong. She's not mean. She's just not warm and fuzzy. She was a great mentor to me, but she is singularly focused on being the best. If you get in the way, she just steps over you like a carcass in the middle of the road."

"Do they live together?" She was wincing on the inside.

"No, she's an ER resident in Boston."

Camila was silent.

Tyler joined her on the bed, nudged closer to her, and put his arm around her shoulders. He sensed her disappointment. "Were you trying to corrupt our perfect little Dr. Martin?" he said.

"No, honestly, I wasn't. I didn't know. He never mentioned a thing about another girl. But now it makes sense. Why I had to literally beg him to take my phone number."

"Hmm, I wonder," Tyler asked out loud.

"I didn't even know he was in medical school! I feel like such an idiot!" She said, dropping her head into her hands.

"Yeah, I think he's taking a year to get his master's, but in what, I don't know."

"He's getting his MBA," she said. "He told me he's at Anderson."

"Well, there you have it."

"And I wasn't trying to corrupt him. You know I would never do that if I knew he was dating someone else. That kind of karma is terrifying. But he danced with me tonight, Tyler. Like, really danced with me. I felt him hold me. He didn't leave an awkward space between us. He held me." She looked up at him, her eyes filling.

"Oh, my darling," he said, letting her rest her head on his shoulder, "I am sure you're not the first one to be lulled into submission by his effortless charm and fucking amazing arms and his tight ass."

She chuckled. Tyler always had a way of making her laugh when she needed it the most. And he was right. Ben's ass was fucking incredible.

* * *

For the first time since the quarter started, she wasn't looking forward to Spanish class. When Tuesday rolled around, she didn't want to see him. She was embarrassed. Not that she had a reason to be embarrassed. No one knew she had hoped he would kiss her a few nights ago. But it had been written all over her face. The plan was to show up right as class started, allowing no time to talk.

She walked immediately to her seat, not turning around. He tapped her on the shoulder with his pen.

"Hi, Camila," he said, like nothing had happened. Like he hadn't kept his *fiancée* a complete secret from her.

She couldn't ignore him, but she barely turned her head, making a minuscule amount of eye contact, and squeaking out a faint,

"Hey," before swinging back around and trying to focus on anything else. During break, she immediately ran outside and proceeded to call her mom. She rattled off the mundane events of the day, filling the entire fifteen-minute break before walking back to her desk right as class resumed.

He knew she felt snubbed or ashamed, though he was the one who should feel ashamed. And he was ashamed. He had been caught in an inadvertent lie. He didn't mean to lie; it was an error of omission. He was planning on explaining everything on the way home to her apartment, but before he could catch up with her after class, he noticed Tyler waiting for her and watched as they hurriedly walked away.

Thursday came quickly, and again she avoided him like the plague. The time hadn't helped her forget the feeling of being made a fool. She begged Tyler to pick her up again.

"Cami, this is ridiculous. You can still be friends with him," Tyler said, trying to ease her embarrassment while sneaking away with her after her class let out.

She looked over her shoulder. "I can't now. I'm still mortified," she said.

"You shouldn't be. You didn't do anything wrong. No one did, at least not yet."

Her eyebrows shot up. "Tyler Bradley, don't you dare imply that anything will *ever* happen between me and Ben!"

"Okay, okay, don't get your panties in a bunch." He smiled down at her as they linked arms.

All her evasiveness hadn't helped. Ben sat behind her dutifully each night and would greet her, trying to think of reasons to engage in conversation. But for the first time in his adult life, his mind went blank. All he could do was stare at the back of her neck and watch the thin gold chain she wore glimmer in the fluorescent lights of the classroom on Tuesday night. Or he'd count the freckles on her back that were unobscured by the halter top she wore Thursday. He could smell the lotion she used as it wafted off her skin. All he wanted to do was let his fingers travel the short distance between his desk and her back so he could run his hands over her caramel-colored skin.

What was going on with him? He was shocked with himself. He was so grateful that Tiffany was flying in this weekend for Halloween. He needed a weekend dedicated to his relationship to finally act like himself.

6

"You've been moping for too long, young lady," Tyler said on Saturday morning.

Camila was sitting in her pajamas. It was past noon, and dishes were still piled in the sink from rage baking the night before. "I'm not moping. I've been working on my thesis, and I picked up some extra shifts." It had been days, but the sting of Ben's confession was still raw.

He gave her a knowing look. "Okay, you're moping while you're keeping yourself busy."

She hated (and loved) that he knew her so well. She had been moping. She was still embarrassed and terrified at how close she had come to committing karmic suicide. She had done some regrettable things in her past, but cheating with a married, or near-married, man was inexcusable. That kind of energy was life-changing.

She plopped down on the futon and held her head. "Okay, so I'm still humiliated."

"Listen, come out with me today. There's a party at a house in Malibu. My peds intern lives there with her parents. She's having a pool party. Come along."

She thought about it, weighing her lack of options. She could tell he knew she had no other pressing engagements, and she was just spinning her wheels.

"Let's go," he said. "It's insanely hot out, and there'll be a bunch of my friends there, and you look smoking in a swimsuit. The best way to get Ben Cole Martin out of your head is to have other men drool over you."

He wasn't wrong, she thought, picking at her week-old nail polish. She tussled her hair and pulled her legs up to her chest. She was irritated and embarrassed that anyone could make her feel like such a fool, intentional or not.

"You don't have to say his full name each time, you know."

"Of course, I do!" he said. "A name like that begs for the full regalia his parents intended."

"Okay, fine, I'll come, but you can NOT leave me alone. I won't know anyone."

"Promise."

A few hours later, she had done a respectable amount of work on her thesis, and Tyler had re-reviewed his Pediatrics Blueprints for his impending exam.

"Cami," he yelled at the bathroom door. "We got to go, girl." She had been occupied with a thorough and almost surgical approach to hair removal. "There's a fine line between fashionably late and missing the entire party," he said.

She swung the door open and leaned against the frame, highlighting the curve of her hip.

"Holy shit! Damn, I guess you're not moping anymore."

"Thanks." She pranced over to him. "Let me just grab my sarong."

They drove west on Sunset toward the coast and gawked at the mansions lining the streets only a few miles from their own humble one-bedroom abode.

He pulled his counterfeit Ray-Bans down to get a better look at the corner property while the light was red. "God, could you imagine living here?"

She laughed. "We do live here, Tyler."

"One day, I'll own one of these, and you'll come visit me," he said, waving his hand out the window. "You'll lay by my pool in that exact bikini with your Jackie-O sunglasses and hat. And I'll be fabulous in my all-Versace poolside attire, and we can stare at my pool boy together!"

"Sounds perfect."

A few miles of twisting canyon roads later, they arrived at an estate that overlooked the Pacific. It was breathtaking. They parked and walked the gravel-lined path to the door. A sign directed guests to the stunning pool around the back. Camila usually felt out of place around Tyler's classmates upon first meeting them. They seemed to come from privilege and had an unattainable amount of self-confidence. Camila didn't lack in self-esteem, but hers had been earned through countless trials, and she had been able to fight the odds stacked against her as a minority female. The few times she had encountered Tyler's friends, it was apparent they came from a different type of privilege. Where Camila was privileged to have come from a loving home with a roof over her head and food on the table, they were born into expecting nothing less than the best. As if they were entitled to it. They owned class rings, rowed crew, and graduated from "one-name schools," as Camila told Tyler.

"I didn't even know Smith was a college," she said to him after her first such encounter.

She scanned the crowd and realized that Tyler was right. They were quite late. Food had already been served, drinks had been enjoyed, and a few guests were leaving as they had arrived.

A tall brunette in a magenta Lilly Pulitzer cover-up greeted them.

"Hey Tyler, you finally made it. I was ready to give you a crap assignment next week if you flaked on me."

"Me? Never, darling," he said, placing two air kisses on her beautifully bronzed cheeks.

"Cassandra, this is my fabulous roommate and best friend, Camila."

"Thank you for having me," Camila told her.

"My pleasure. Any friend of Tyler's." She smiled. "Make yourselves at home. Have fun!" she said as she yelled a greeting at another guest across the pool.

"Tyler, this place is ridiculous," Camila whispered.

"I know. Her dad is in the industry. I think he's a producer or something. Not sure why she chose medicine, but I respect her more for it after seeing this place."

She surveyed the expansive landscape. "Yeah, I get that."

"Okay, let's throw our stuff on a chair and get a drink."

Tyler secured a tequila shot from a passing tray before making it to the bar on the far side of the grounds.

Camila opened her bottle of Evian. "I can't believe she got an actual bartender."

He laughed. "I guess it's expected, right? I mean, she couldn't drag kegs up here." He grabbed her by the hand. "Hey, let's go chat with some of my other classmates," he said, pulling her along.

Camila was beginning to feel comfortable standing amongst Tyler's friends when she saw his face drop. After years of friendship, she knew from the slightest change in his expression, something was on the horizon.

She crossed the few feet between them and whispered discreetly, "Are you okay?"

"Um, yeah, I'm okay, but, um, you may not be," he said under his breath. "Don't freak out, okay?"

"Why? Is my boob hanging out?" She glanced down, making sure she was still tucked into her triangle top.

"No, no, you look fucking fabulous, but someone you know is here."

She knew better than to swing around. She kept her eyes trained on Tyler. "But I don't know any of your school friends," she said. Then noticed him gesturing with a tilt of his head to someone behind her.

She turned in slow motion and saw amid the crowd a familiar head of tussled brown hair. Ben. An equally attractive woman accompanied him.

Camila spun around to face Tyler and hoped her face accurately portrayed the mix of anger and fear that swirled inside her.

"I swear to God I didn't know he would be here, and especially not with her," he said before she could even formulate the question.

She groaned, fidgeting in place. "God, Tyler."

He squeezed her hand. "It's fine, Cami."

She moved next to him and sipped her water inconspicuously. "It's not fine, Tyler," she said.

As Ben and his fiancée came into view, she absorbed all that was Tiffany.

"Tyler, she's so put together. God, I must have been delusional to think he'd be interested in me."

He pulled her in front of him. "Hey, hey, listen to me. You are beautiful, Cami, and I'm not just saying that because I have impeccable taste in friends. You are a wondrous, intelligent, and sexy woman.

Who cares if he's here? We are going to have an amazing time." He fixed her with his stare. "Also, you look delectable. I mean, who can wear a tangerine-colored string bikini? And that chain belt makes me want to lick something off your stomach, and I'm gay!"

She cracked a broad grin. "Okay."

"So, tits up! Let's do this," he said just as Ben and Tiffany arrived in their circle of friends.

Her eyes met his, and she saw his lips part as he gazed at her from top to toe. Her nipples tightening as his eyes traveled over her skin. She looked away, and her eyes landed on *her*. She looked pristine. Shoulder-length, jet-black hair, not a flyaway in sight. She was dressed in all white without a solitary smudge, a fashion miracle. She was slender and narrow. No curves. No garish colors. And all of it accented with a large, crystal-clear diamond suspended from her left ring finger.

"Hi Tiffany, what a surprise! Great to see you!" Tyler kissed her on the cheek she offered him. "Hey Ben, nice to see you again," Tyler said, unable to avoid a cheeky tone.

"How are you, Tyler? Staying out of trouble, I hope," Tiffany joked.

Great, she was nice too.

"You know it," he said, and Camila noticed Tiffany looking at her.

She had never wanted to wrap herself in her sarong more. Forget a sarong. She would have preferred a nun's habit. If she could crawl inside and stay there, it would have suited her just fine.

Tiffany introduced herself, extending her hand.

"I'm Tyler's roommate," Camila said. *Not the woman who's been lusting after your fiancé.*

"Oh, you are the fabulous Camila I've been hearing about. What a small world."

You don't know the half of it, Camila thought. "Yes, I guess so," she said.

"Well, I've heard so much about you," Tiffany told her.

Well, I've heard shit about you, she wanted to reply, but instead said, "Oh, I hope all good things."

"Absolutely. But Tyler and Ben both forgot to mention how stunning you are."

Okay, she was not only nice but confident enough to dole out compliments.

"You're too nice," Camila said.

"I would never be able to pull off that color," Tiffany continued, as all three pairs of eyes landed on her.

"Oh, thank you," Camila said. The last thing she needed was everyone staring at her.

"Hey, Tiffany, what are you doing here?" called someone from behind.

Tiffany turned to greet another guest approaching them. "Ah! Jeff, so good to see you!" She pulled him into the group. "Jeff, you know Ben. This is Tyler, my mentee from last year, and his roommate, Camila. Jeff and I graduated together last year."

"Wait, I know you," Jeff said, keeping his eyes laser-focused on Camila.

She gave him a confused look before realization settled on her face. "Oh, yeah, you were the doctor in the emergency room."

"That's right," Tyler said.

"Yup, I'm Dr. Parker," he said, extending his hand toward her.

"You sound like a prick, Jeff," Tiffany said, laughing. "We're at a party. Who introduces themselves as a doctor?"

He blushed. "Sorry, I'm Jeff," he said.

"It's okay," Camila said. "I did meet you as Dr. Parker. Nice to meet you again, Jeff."

"Can I get you a drink, Camila, to apologize for my prickishness?" He asked, extending his hand.

She raised her full bottle. "Maybe after I finish this one," she said.

Once Tyler and Tiffany started reminiscing about their last year together, Camila excused herself. She didn't want to stand there avoiding looking at Ben or, worse, attempt to make civil conversation. She made her way to a table covered with the remains of what must have been a delicious and abundant display of food and picked up a nibble of pineapple. She sucked the juice from the morsel of fruit, hoping its sweetness would replace the sudden bitterness in her mouth. She turned to face the pool as the shouting and cheering escalated. Ben was standing, waist-deep in water with the ball poised overhead. He had a hungry and determined look as he aimed for the goal, but all Camila noticed were the powerful, defined muscles of his chest and the long lines of his arms as he swung the ball backwards to gain momentum. She turned away from the party and looked out over the horizon. It was too difficult to have him so close but also so inaccessible. The sun warmed her as she closed her eyes and tried to suppress the urge to burst into tears.

She felt him before she heard him. He had a way of taking up more space than physically necessary, like he was sucking up the air around her.

"Hi," he said, startling her.

God.

"Hi," she said.

He had stepped out of the pool to the dismay of his classmates, who were still committed to their makeshift game of water polo. "I didn't know you'd be here," he said, shaking his wet hair and inadvertently getting her wet, and she took a step back to avoid getting sprayed.

He hadn't been able to speak since seeing her in her bikini with her wide-brimmed hat and the golden hue the sunlight left on her skin. It was safer if he kept quiet rather than try to control what might pop out of his mouth.

"Tyler brought me," she said.

"Yeah."

Silence.

He watched her suck the chunk of fruit, its juice dripping through her fingers adorned with gold rings that matched her belly chain.

"You're staring again," she said. "And this time your fiancée is here."

"Sorry. You're distracting," he said more honestly than he had planned.

She turned to face the table again, only allowing him a sagittal view of her body. He didn't know her well enough to decipher whether she was hurt or angry, or both.

"We can still be friends," he offered quietly.

"You made me feel stupid. You lied to me, Ben."

"I didn't lie to you," he said with a subtle defensiveness.

"Okay, fine, you told me a partial truth."

"A partial truth?"

"When you leave out bits of the truth," she said. "You're not making anything up, but you are not being completely honest either."

She was right, he thought. He had become excellent at withholding the entire truth over the past year. From his family, from his fiancée, and from himself. He hadn't told Camila the entire truth either. He still didn't know why. Maybe because everyone in his life knew him as Ben the medical student or Ben, Tiffany's boyfriend, and now fiancé. He liked that Camila was interested in only him. Ben. On his own, not qualified by any other attachments, achievements, or future aspirations.

Thankfully, she had been able to avoid him since the fateful evening they danced together, but now that he was in her space, she found herself longing to be near him again. Pool water was still periodically dripping from his hair, landing on his skin. She had never seen him without a shirt. They had never been this naked around each other. His clothing didn't do justice to the muscles underneath. Lean and toned, veins coursing from his hands to his shoulders. He looked like a half-finished sculpture.

"Yeah, you're right. It was a partial truth," he said, and she tore her eyes away from his chest and back to his face.

"I know you didn't think of me as just a friend," she said. "At least to me, you didn't feel like just a friend. But who knows, maybe I made it all up." It was a horrible habit—dismissing herself. She was trying to quit. Her self-deprecation, whether in life or academics, made it seem as if she was hedging her bets.

A few moments of agonizing quiet passed. She divulged too much.

"You didn't make anything up," he said.

His confession surprised and comforted her.

"Can we try to be friends?" he asked, and she heard the caution in his voice.

She was never one to hold a grudge. "I don't know," she said, half-joking. "Do you have any other bits of your life you've omitted? No long-lost children or money laundering schemes?"

"No," he said, grinning shyly.

She smiled back at him. "Okay, then we can try," she said, finishing her piece of pineapple and licking her fingers.

The ball of nerves that had been growing in his gut released at her acceptance of a truce. It was all he had to offer. And he had missed her, their conversations, her effortlessness, and the way she looked at him.

"I see your hand is missing a drink," Jeff said to Camila as he came up to them.

She flirted back. "Yeah, it seems so."

She was pleased to see the irritation on Ben's face.

"Hey, Ben, do you need a drink too?" Jeff asked.

"No, I'm good," he said. "I'm going to find Tiffany."

Jeff slid his arm around Camila's back, landing his hand on her hip. Irritation crawled along Ben's skin.

They took their drinks and found themselves in the pool. Jeff had managed to corner her between the edge and his body. A fuchsia-colored light blanketed the sky.

"You healed up pretty nice," he said, running a finger along her clavicle.

"Yeah? Well, I had a good doctor," she teased back.

It felt nice to be wanted again. To play by the rules, no matter how fucked up they were. She knew how to deal with the Jeffs of the world. Ben was too complicated and off-limits in every way imaginable.

She placed her hands on Jeff's wet chest as he pulled her lower body flush against his. She felt him respond to her, and it was reassuring. She tilted her head back and laughed at whatever he said to her.

Tyler stood with Tiffany and Ben as they watched them from across the pool.

"Seems like your roommate is making friends quickly," Tiffany said.

"She's fantastic, really," Tyler told her.

"She really is so beautiful," Tiffany said. "And those eyes."

"Yup, anyone who's able to get ahold of her should consider themselves very lucky," he said both to no one and one specific person.

"She's rather particular about who she spends time with."

Ben's eyes met Tyler's for a moment before he glanced away.

* * *

"So, you seemed cozy with Dr. Parker," Tyler joked on their way home.

She glanced out the car window, the wind blowing her hair, as Tyler sped down Sunset. "Yeah, he was a good kisser, and I wanted the attention," she said.

"Well, that's very insightful of you. So, I found out what happened."

"With what?"

"Tiffany had been planning to visit Ben this week for a while; it's her vacation week. Why he didn't tell you, I have no idea." He glanced over at her, smirking. "Well, actually, I know exactly why."

"Why?" she said as he turned onto their street.

"Cami, are you serious? You are so different from Tiffany. Poor guy probably didn't know what hit him. He probably never had to deal with those conflicting emotions before. He really is a good person."

"Well, that's saying a lot coming from you, Tyler."

Maybe that was consolation enough. He had been interested but taken. Perhaps they could have a friendship. But only a friendship. Their coffee dates had been carefree. She made him laugh, and he took a genuine interest in her and her work. She was enjoying spending time with him as much as she did with Tyler. But she knew better than to share that with her roommate and best friend.

"Are we still going to West Hollywood for Halloween tomorrow night?" she asked a few minutes later.

"Fuck yes! I have so much blue body paint that you have to help me apply!"

"Fabulous!"

* * *

Halloween in West Hollywood was something to behold. Nothing compared. The street was blocked off for miles. Party-goers stunned and astonished with wild and extravagant costumes. There were booths handing out free samples of everything from condoms to THC-laced candies. KIIS FM always had a booth, and the possibility to win free concert tickets filled the air with palpable excitement. Camila and Tyler had attended every year as a famous duo, a famous, sexy duo—Batman and Catwoman, Zeus and Hera, Superman and Lois Lane. This year was no different.

As she slathered him with blue body paint, she expressed a valid concern, "How are you not going to stain your car?"

"Don't worry about it, Jasmine. You just focus on keeping your chest in that top." He widened his eyes in jest. "They really didn't have a larger size?"

"Stop it! The rest of it fit perfectly, so I just stuffed my chest into the top. It is the best Princess Jasmine costume I have ever seen."

She had matched the sheer blue cut-out pants with a gold belt low on her hips and a black wig with a long braid that draped over her shoulder. She had applied gold tattoos that wrapped around her arms and a small jewel nestled in her navel.

"Okay Genie," she said, "I think this is all the blue I can apply before you get some form of pigment toxicity."

"But look at my pecs in this color. No wonder Genie looked ripped!.I may have you apply this daily."

They piled into his car with a few other friends and headed down Santa Monica Boulevard. Parking was always challenging, but they squeezed into a spot on Doheny through some ingenious parallel parking skills and set out for an epic evening of disinhibition.

"Well, I don't know how we'll get out of this spot, but whatever!" Tyler announced as they started their walk into West Hollywood towards the Abbey.

The costumes were amazing. Nothing was left to the imagination. Snow White and her seven sexy roommates, all clad in matching speedos, an all-male take on The Spice Girls and the classic tributes to Mariah Carey and Madonna. They found another group of friends along the way, and Tyler downed a few Jell-O shots they smuggled in, camouflaged as actual Jell-O in Tupperware. Camila felt great, having earned more than a few compliments on her costume, her body, and her hair. There was something special about getting compliments from men with impeccable taste and no interest in pursuing her romantically. She had almost forgotten the debacle with Ben when she heard someone calling her name.

She swung around, her long, fake braid following behind like a lasso, but her smile crumbled once she saw the source of the voice. Tiffany approached, her hair cut in a perfect bob under her cloche hat, a pencil skirt wrapping her narrow hips. Camila felt nauseous.

"Hi, Tiffany!" She sounded overly excited, compensating for her disappointment.

Tiffany hugged her, and Camila saw Ben. He looked unbelievable in a fedora, a crisp white shirt adorned with suspenders. He wore wingtip shoes. He was freshly shaved, with a new crew cut, and his arms were testing the tensile strength of his shirt.

"Hi, Ben," she said.

He leaned down, holding a fake machine gun in one hand, and with his free arm hugged her.

"Hello," he whispered in her ear, and she caught an intoxicating whiff of cologne. To the outside observer, it looked like a platonic embrace between friends. For Camila, it felt like her heart and stomach had jumped on a rollercoaster that was running off the tracks.

"Hey everybody!" Tyler appeared in all his blue glory, eight Jell-O shots in and feeling no pain.

"You look fabulous!" Tiffany told him.

He slid an arm around Camila and stained her shoulder blue. "Don't we though!"

"Hey, Tyler, where can I get some of those Jell-O shots?" Tiffany asked.

"Come with me, Bonnie. Your wish is my command."

He grabbed her hand, leaving Jasmine and Clyde alone.

"You're blue," Ben said.

"What?"

He thumbed her skin where Tyler had deposited his body paint.

"You look blue," he said and noticed a gentle flutter at the base of her neck. He didn't know why he had hugged her or why he was touching her now, but he was, and he liked it. Her skin was soft and warm beneath his fingers.

"Oh, yeah, our place is covered in blue paint thanks to Tyler," she said, grinning. "You look nice."

He let go of her and snapped his suspenders against his chest. "It was Tiffany's idea. You look great, too."

His eyes roamed her body and lingered at the points of adornment—the gem in her navel, the gold paint on her arms, the dust of glitter across her décolleté. He met her eyes, and she flashed a radiant smile. A flush of heat spread from the top of his head down into his chest and settled in his groin. He shifted side to side, trying to dislodge the warmth growing below his belt.

She shouldn't have enjoyed him looking at her, but she did. Men stared at her all the time. That's what men did for as long as she could remember, uninvited and salacious. But she *wanted* Ben to look at her, her skin seared by his gaze.

This was bad. Really bad, she thought.

This was headed nowhere good, she was certain.

"You cut your hair," she said and reached up to run her hand along his hair, relishing the softness that slid through her fingers.

"Yeah, well, I'm committed to the character," he told her.

"Really? You know what happens to them in the end, right?"

"Well, we'll revise the ending," he said. "Perhaps something less gruesome."

"Sure, but be careful. Some endings can't be rewritten."

Tiffany and Tyler returned arm in arm, she slightly stained blue and he half-smudged to his normal color. Both in need of a chaperone.

Tiffany fell into Ben's arms. "Okay, I think you've had enough," he said as she reached up, placing a sloppy kiss on his mouth. He wrapped his arms around her. Camila thought he looked larger than usual, next to her delicate frame. She looked over at Tyler looking at her. He was sober enough to notice her face deflating.

"Okay, we have to go too," Tyler said. "You know places to see people to do, or whatever that saying is. See you guys!"

"Oh, bye! I'm heading back to Boston tomorrow," Tiffany said, throwing her arms around Camila. "It was so nice to finally meet you!"

"You too," Camila said.

Because it had been. Tiffany was nice, which made falling for Ben that much more horrible. Camila and Ben glanced at each other once more and acknowledged their parting with a mutual smile.

A few hours later, Camila climbed into the driver's side of the car, feet sore, skin dewy. They drove home in silence, and she thought Tyler had fallen asleep.

"Why does seeing Tiffany make you feel so bad about yourself?" he asked.

His intuition shocked her, even though he knew her better than anyone. "I don't feel bad," she lied.

"Cami, look at yourself. You look like Jasmine on her way to a colonoscopy."

She smiled. He always knew what to say. She thought for a few seconds before being able to adequately verbalize what it was that was gnawing at her insides.

"It's because she is everything I'm not."

"Stop it, Camila," he said sweetly.

"Seriously, she's tall, and I'm short. She's slender, and I'm curvy. Her hair is sleek and posh, and, well, just look at mine," she said, pulling off her wig, releasing a wavy mane of hair that tried to escape from her scalp in every which way, making her look like a lioness. "I bet she doesn't even curse."

Tyler's face dropped, and he locked eyes with Camila as they waited for the light to change.

"Fuck," he said, "You really like him."

"Yeah, I'm a fucking mess."

"Camila, he'll never leave her. It's not in his DNA. He's too good. He is genuinely a good person. He's *that* guy."

"I know. But I can't cut him out of my life cold turkey. Not just yet," Camila said.

"Do you think it'll get easier the longer you wait?"

7

November 2002

It was as if an eraser had been taken to the last two months of their friendship. By the next week, their coffee dates resumed. Well, not dates. Camila couldn't date another woman's man, and Ben couldn't lust after a woman who wasn't his fiancée. Or he shouldn't.

Instead, they danced around their mutual attraction.

She desperately tried to relocate him from the "potential" portion of her brain into the "off limits" portion.

"I get a do-over with getting to know you," she told him as they drove away from campus the following Tuesday.

He smiled at her as they pulled up to the traffic light. "Yeah, I guess you do."

"So how long have you guys been together?" she asked once they were seated inside.

"Who? Me and Tiffany?"

"No, you and the Dalai Lama." She rolled her eyes. "Yes, you and Tiffany."

He laughed. "We started dating the end of my first year."

"Wow," she said, shocked at the speed of their courtship.

"Too fast?"

"Who am I to judge? I'm someone you just met." It was an un-called-for provocation, but she was still hurting. A part of her wanted her words to hit him in the middle of his chest.

He cleared his throat and said, "We saw each other daily, so it all moved quickly."

"I see," she said. "Do you guys live together?" She was wincing on the inside.

"Yeah, we moved in together during my second year since she was always at the hospital. Otherwise, we would never see each other."

Fuck, they cohabitated, and he still had kept it a secret. She chose not to highlight the absurdity of the situation. "So, are you moving to Boston then?" she asked.

"I have one more year, but I've lined up a few external rotations for next year."

"Sorry, what's that?" She said, shifting in her seat.

"Instead of staying in LA and rotating through different hospitals here, I'm going to do the same but in Boston." There was deafening silence before he said, "So we can be together until I graduate and move out there."

It was bombshell after bombshell with this guy, she thought. It seemed that he was dedicated to this new transparent version of himself.

She took another sip of her too-hot drink. "When do you graduate?" she asked.

"Next year, but I move back East at the end of Spring quarter."

There it was. Their friendship had an expiration date. They would both be leaving come June.

"So did you go to med school because your dad is a doctor?" she asked. An obvious follow-up question, she thought. But her mind was calculating and spinning with dates. They could be friends. Anyone could keep a friendship safely platonic for a few months, she reasoned. Then in a few years, she could look back and laugh at her youthful romanticism. She was an adult, and so was he.

He looked away, rubbing the back of his neck.

He had spent so many nights in hospital rooms as a boy until they were rescued. He found the sterile walls, fluorescent lights, and smell of antibacterial cleanser comforting. They had always been an indication he was finally safe. But she didn't need to know that.

"Yeah, I did," he said.

When he looked back, she was watching him.

"What?" she said. "What else do you want to say?"

"Why do you think I wanted to say something else?" he smirked. She had an uncanny ability to read him. He wondered how it was possible for her to understand him so well. Her intuition was terrifyingly accurate. Her desire for the entire truth never faltering.

"Well, you do that." She motioned to his hand resting on the back of his neck. "Whenever you have more to say, you do that."

He dropped his hand, smiling. "You know me that well, do you?"

"I'm trying."

"My dad is the best person I know," he told her. "Stephanie says I idolize him."

She tilted her head, looking confused.

"Stephanie is my older sister," he said.

"Oh, how much older?"

"Three years. She's married and lives back East."

"Tell me more about your dad," Camila said, settling back into her chair.

"Well, he's smart but also honest and kind. We never had those weird father-son struggles that movies like to exaggerate. He is the one who encouraged me to take a year off to study something else, even if it meant more long distance for me and Tiffany. He said once med school is over, I'd have to essentially hand over the next six to ten years of my life, so if I want to explore any other options, I should do it now."

"Hence, business school?"

"Hence, business school," Ben said as he sighed and sat back in his chair. "I had considered business school after Yale but chose medicine instead. I think he's worried I lack passion in my life. That I'm just going through the motions."

"Do *you* think you lack passion?"

Ben chuckled, "I have calculated passion in small doses."

Camila ran her hands through her hair in mock frustration. "That is the least passionate thing I've ever heard."

"My dad loves my mom and us with everything he has, and I think he wants that intensity for me too. He wants me to really live life and not let it just happen to me. He's truly who I want to be." He stopped abruptly, realizing what he had done.

"What?"

"I'm sorry, Camila."

She smiled. "Don't be. I asked to hear more." She placed her hand on his, giving a gentle squeeze. "He sounds great."

"Yeah, but that was thoughtless of me." He swallowed hard. "I mean, you had already told me that your dad ..."

"It's okay. I've never known anything different," she said, her hand lingering on his. "I like to imagine my dad would have been the same way if he lived. But that doesn't mean I don't want to hear about yours."

They didn't make eye contact for a while, and when they did, he felt genuine regret for what he considered an insensitivity. Their hands turned and their fingers intertwined. Instinctively, he stroked the back of her hand with his thumb. She didn't draw her hand away.

"I'm okay, Ben. You don't need to feel sorry for me. I think my dad would have been very proud of how passionately I live my life. I want to taste it all, experience all the love, excitement, and joy the world has to offer. Sure, it was lonely at times, and I wished I had a sister or brother when I was little. Someone who would understand me in a way the grown-ups couldn't. Someone to keep my secrets. Someone to share a silent language with. But even though my family is small, when we love, we are fierce in our love."

He didn't know what possessed him to do it, but he leaned forward and brought her hand to his lips.

It wasn't a kiss. It was a brush of skin.

But the feel of his mouth, his warm breath on her skin. She wanted more, much more, and at the same time, she needed him to stop.

"Ben," she whispered, "I'm okay."

He placed her hand gently on the table and dropped back into his chair.

* * *

"What?" Tyler yelled to her from the bathroom.

"HE KISSED ME!"

"I can't hear you over the music," he shouted.

She marched over, turning down their well-used copy of the *Immaculate Collection*, and watched as he bleached his tips with gloved hands.

"Cami, you know this is a time-sensitive process. I don't want orange tips. I need frosted ones, like Justin Timberlake!"

She grabbed his face with her hands, forcing him to look into her eyes. "He. Kissed. Me!"

"What? Who? Not, Ben!"

"Yes."

"Holy FUCK!" He sat on the toilet, crossing his legs. "Tell me exactly what happened."

"Well, we went to Coral Tree like we usually do, and we were talking about our dads, and then he felt bad because he thought he hurt my feelings, since, you know my dad is not around."

"Okay, okay, okay, get to the kissing," he said.

"I AM! Okay, so he took my hand and kissed it."

She leaned against the wall and closed her eyes while stroking the top of the same hand his lips had brushed minutes ago.

"Okay, so not as scandalous as I was hoping, but still, since we're talking about Ben Cole Martin, we can liken his gesture to the normal person's version of a hand job."

"Tyler!"

"What? You know I'm right."

"I know, right?" She was smiling.

"Okay, listen, Cami, I don't mean to be a shitty wingman, and this is all fun, but you have to put this out of your head."

"I know. I was doing *just* that. Until he took my hand tonight."

"You have to get him out of your system. I don't know, maybe rub one out thinking about him, or whatever it is you straight girls do, and get on with your life."

She opened her mouth to object and then clamped it closed. She popped up on her toes and planted a kiss on his cheek before prancing to their room.

"Hey, I'm giving you one hour," he yelled after her. "Then I'm going to need to come in. So, hurry up."

She slammed the door shut.

It didn't take much effort. She closed her eyes and imagined being back at the pool party in Malibu with Ben. But only Ben. Alone in the pool. She lay back on the bed, slipped her hand beneath her jeans, her Rabbit next to her. In her dreamlike haze, he lifted her out of the pool, her feet dangling in the water as she leaned back. His hands along her legs, her waist, then he leaned over her, untying and yanking at the strings of her bikini with his teeth. She imagined his mouth grazing over her hip, between her legs, and she grabbed the Rabbit and climaxed with a loud moan. On the other side of the wall, Tyler yelled, "Good girl! And in record time, I'll call Guinness!"

"Shut up!" She yelled back, laughing as she stared at the ceiling, her body limp and her head in a fog.

* * *

The following Thursday they were back at the Coral Tree Café. As she looked at him over the edge of her cup, Ben felt she was more alluring than usual with the smoky dusting of eyeliner accentuating her almond-shaped eyes. As if it wasn't already difficult to look away, the black pigment made her honey sage-colored eyes look deeper and more suited for the bedroom.

He motioned to his eyes. "How do you do that?"

"What? The eyeliner?"

"Yeah."

"Lots of practice," she said, laughing. "It's actually a very old practice from centuries ago. Men and women used to wear it. It was supposed to symbolize devotion."

"How do you know all that?" he asked.

"I was an art history major in college, and also I like makeup," she said with a mischievous smile. "What? Doesn't your fiancée wear makeup?" She couldn't bring herself to say her name yet.

He shifted uncomfortably in his seat. Was he ready to talk about Tiffany with Camila? He felt a mixture of anxiety and shame. Talking about her would only highlight his lack of transparency. He was still ashamed of the lengths he had taken to hide the whole truth and confused as to why. This year was set aside to rediscover himself, not discover a new partner. He had begun to worry the previous version of himself, who was perfect for Tiffany, was now too different from the current version. Ben was coming to terms with newly realized interests and desires and was searching for something more unrestrained and tempting.

"You don't have to get weird about it," she said. "I've met her now."

"I'm not being weird," he said.

He looked directly at her but felt embarrassed.

"So, is she your best friend then? The person you'd want next to you if the world was ending."

"No," he said, surprising himself with his sudden and candid answer.

Camila looked shocked. "Really?"

"We were never platonic. When we first met, it was immediately physical. We weren't friends to start, but we are friends now."

She really couldn't imagine Ben and Tiffany being physical. She couldn't imagine Tiffany getting tussled in any way. But perhaps they had nice, normal, calm sex, the kind that didn't require thick walls and self-restraint to avoid startling neighbors and roommates. Given an opportunity with Ben, Camila would have dug her nails into her headboard and woken the dead. As forbidden images of her and Ben together coalesced in her mind, she shook her head quickly, trying not to lose herself in the imagined version of them. She tried to refocus on their conversation.

"I don't think I've met the person I'd want next to me if all of this was ending. Have you?" Ben asked honestly.

"I guess I haven't found that person yet either. The person who is not only my friend but also stimulates my mind and satisfies me emotionally and physically. Supports me in being the best version of myself. I know he's out there, but I have to wait for the forces of nature to pull us together."

"You really believe that? That there is one person out there for you?" Ben asked.

"I believe it more than anything. Listen, the world is full of people that I haven't met, and I'm not saying I couldn't live a very happy life with one of them, but I believe in my very core that there is one person I'm *supposed* to be with," Camila said.

"Where did this philosophy come from?" Ben asked, envious of her faith.

Camila smiled and leaned her elbows on the table. "You think I'm nuts, don't you?"

"I wouldn't say that," Ben replied and laughed. "I just don't know if I believe it. I just haven't ever witnessed it or felt it myself."

"You've never felt a tidal wave-like push to be with someone? Like a force so uncontrollable you couldn't avoid it even if you tried?"

"No, I really haven't, but isn't that just lust?" He didn't know whether to be hopeful that he may yet get to experience what she was describing or disappointed that he hadn't felt it yet.

"Oh Ben, it's so much more than lust. It's not just physical. That's part of it, but it's also a connection and friendship and understanding. It's like taking all the best parts of your best friend and elevating it to another level."

"That sounds exhausting," Ben said, intending to provoke her.

"Yes! And how wonderful to be exhausted by passion and love and devotion. If not that, then what is the whole point of all this? I want to die feeling thoroughly spent by all my experiences."

Ben thought about his own relationship. He and Tiffany had a connection. They had understanding, and a friendship had developed, but they never had an energy between them that could be described as overwhelming or unstoppable. They had a steady and constant relationship free of extremes or volatility. What he had craved since he was young. Listening to Camila, he was convinced that any relationship with her would be more tumultuous and fiery than he would want.

"Okay, I am going to convince you, but let's start slowly. Who is your best friend?"

"My sister, but she may lose her title soon," he said with a grin and finished the last of his drink.

"Well, I want to marry my best friend, but Tyler thinks vaginas are gross, so that won't work," she said, shrugging her shoulders.

He laughed out loud. That was rare. It made her heart leap. She laughed too.

"So, we both just have to find the qualities of our best friends in people with romantic potential," Camila said. "I mean, I'll have to, since you already have."

Their awkward silences were infrequent, but when they did occur, they were excruciating, always accompanied by a heavy helping of sexual tension.

She ran her fingers gently over the small rose buds held in the small vase on their table. She picked up the vase and brought it to her nose, closed her eyes, and inhaled. She noticed he was still watching her movements in silence when she opened her eyes, and she broke the spell first.

"But if your fiancée is not your best friend, then your sister knows things that she doesn't?"

"Yeah, I guess," he said, polishing off the last of the muffin they were sharing after she'd declined the last bite.

"I don't know if I'd like that," she said. "I mean if I were her."

"I'm not sure Tiffany cares. But she isn't the one threatening my sister's position," he said, raising one eyebrow.

Was he implying that it could be her? That one day she could be his confidante. Perhaps the attraction she felt was really a miscalculation, and what she truly felt was a connection that wasn't romantic at all. "Oh really? Huh, if I'm in the running to usurp your sister as 'best friend in chief,' then I should warn you I won't keep my opinions to myself."

"I wouldn't expect it," Ben said.

"And we can't have secrets between us. It's not my style. Life is too short for us to lie to each other."

"Of course. I wouldn't want it any other way," he said.

The nights had grown colder, and the tight red sweater she was wearing looked like a second skin. Her hair piled on top of her head, the large gold hoop earrings catching the light.

"You know you never order the same drink twice," he said.

"I want to try it all. It's such a splurge for me. These coffee dates. I mean outings."

He smiled. "Outings?"

"Don't make me blush. You know what I mean."

"I like to see you blush," he said without thinking, uncharacteristically direct and flirtatious.

"Stop it," she whispered, serious.

He reached for her hand.

"Camila, we can still be friends," he said, and she withdrew her hand.

His smile vanished, and she immediately regretted dodging his touch and felt the need to explain.

"You can't touch me like that anymore. I know she exists now. I want to be your friend, but we need boundaries." She was the one who needed boundaries because she had none when they first met, and she got hurt in the process.

"Okay. We'll have boundaries."

"Thanks, it's easier that way," Camila said.

"Easier for who?" he asked.

"For both of us, but especially me. I have amazing willpower, but I can't have you tempting me."

He smiled. "Well, that's one thing I've never been accused of."

"I'm sure you have tempted many women in the past, but maybe you've just been oblivious," she said, licking a few crumbs from her finger.

He was staring again, unnerving her.

"The obliviousness is highly likely," he said. "But I'm not the one doing the tempting right now."

She slowly pulled her hand from her mouth and dropped it into her lap.

Normally, he could control his urges. He prided himself on being able to avoid a low-cut top or tight skirt, but with Camila, everything about her was enticing. Instead of feeling less of a pull, he was being dragged under by desire. The desire to talk to her, to see her more often, to find excuses to touch her.

* * *

The air was dry but cold and felt like a stinging slap. It whirled around them as they walked from Ben's car to the cafe a few weeks later.

"So, what are you doing for Thanksgiving?" she asked.

"I'm flying out to Boston."

To be with Tiffany, she said to herself. It was all in the unsaid words—the truth of what separated them.

"Oh, that's nice," she said, swallowing her feelings. She had been focusing on reframing their friendship. Every morning she'd read her meditation for the day and pray she'd be satisfied with being his friend, *just* his friend. And every night by the time she crawled into bed, she indulged in fantasies about him. All the prayers in the world wouldn't have helped her.

"And you? What are you doing for Thanksgiving?" he asked, sipping his cappuccino once they were situated at their table.

"Oh, my mom, Mamani and me are going up to visit my Aunt Sima in Oakland," she said and sipped her frothy fall-inspired drink as the wind shook the trees outside.

"Your mom's side or dad's?"

"Neither." She laughed. "She's my mom's best friend from Cal. She's the only other person in my life who knew my dad. She's single with no kids, so naturally she has an amazing house in the Oakland hills."

She held up the scone they were sharing. "This needs some orange blossom jam."

His confused look prompted her to explain.

"It's this fabulous jam that my grandmother makes that's like a soft perfume on your tongue. I can eat it by the spoonful."

He was trying not to think of all the things he'd like her tongue to be doing to him instead of that scone. "How long are you going to be up there?"

"Um, Wednesday through Sunday, why?"

"My best friend lives in the city. We played tennis together at Yale."

"Are you trying to set me up on a blind date, Ben?" She was mocking him.

He smirked. "Maybe." He had been thinking about introducing her to one of his friends. For two reasons:

If things went well, he could guarantee she'd be in his circle of friends even after this year.

If she were attached to someone else, someone he knew, then it would snuff out his desire to grab her, push her up against the wall, and take her right there in the coffee shop.

Maybe.

"I think you guys will get along," he told her.

"Okay, then. Give him my number. If he has the balls to call me, then maybe I'll entertain going out with him," she said.

Though it had seemed like a well-thought-out plan, the moment the words left his lips, he regretted them. He didn't want the constant torment of suppressing his growing feelings toward Camila, but the idea of her in someone else's arms was its own torture.

Later that evening, she asked him, "By the way, where are you guys getting married?" She realized she didn't know this key bit of information. "I know it's in March, but where?"

He rubbed the back of his neck. "Oh, Maui," he said.

"What? What else? You're rubbing your neck again."

"Well, would you want to come? Actually, I'd like you to come."

She smiled at him. Maybe this was the first step in building their friendship. The finality of watching him marry Tiffany would definitely put an end to the wondering and the 'what ifs.' She could use the vacation to clear her head and reprioritize her life. "I'd love to."

"You and Tyler, of course."

He was allowing her to bring a plus one, but a plus one who wouldn't want to sleep with her.

What did he care who she brought? He was getting married. She could sleep with the entire island if she wanted to.

He was so fucked.

"Oh! I have miles to use since I canceled my ticket to visit Lorenzo," she said, smiling. "You know, after he fucked his TA."

Ben laughed. "Um, great?"

They were slow to end the night. They loitered around each other, wondering who would make the first move despite the chill in the air.

"Okay, well, have a great Thanksgiving," she said, reaching up to give him a hug, pressing herself against his firm, solid body. His arms wrapped around her, but instead of separating after the normal allotted time for a platonic hug, they lingered. She inhaled his smell, and he let his hands travel up her back before she pulled back enough so her head was directly beneath his face. He leaned down and placed a small kiss on her forehead.

So much for boundaries.

She had to leave.

"Okay, bye, Ben."

"Bye, Camila."

The way he said her name. It was a miracle she made it across the street.

She entered the apartment to find Tyler at the table with his latest boyfriend. This one more serious than the series of handsome, well-groomed men he usually brought home.

"Well, look who decided to join us."

"Be nice, Tyler," Bobby said.

She sat down at the table without an invitation and dropped her head onto her outstretched arms.

"Okay, what is this?" Tyler asked, moving the remnant of what looked like a romantic dinner she had interrupted.

"He kissed me again."

"Again?" Bobby asked, "I thought he was engaged?" Tyler must have kept him up to date.

"He is," Tyler said. "Okay, that's a lot of kissing for two people who are *not* together."

"We were saying bye, and I hugged him," she said, mumbling, her head face down on her arms. "But we lingered, and he kissed me on the forehead."

"Oh, the linger-hug, well, clearly that can happen," Bobby said.

"Um, excuse me, Mr. Fun Bobby, that better not be happening for you!" Tyler exclaimed.

"Never, honey," he said, giving Tyler a kiss on the cheek.

She lifted her head and propped it on her hands.

"Okay, listen, you're going away for Thanksgiving," Tyler said.

"Your family is just the distraction you need."

"Yeah, you're right," she said, hoisting herself up from the table. "But for now, I have a date with my Rabbit."

* * *

"That was delicious, Aunt Sima," Camila said as she helped clear the table.

"You are so welcome, honey. Can you put the kettle on when you're in the kitchen?"

"Sure," Camila said and went into the kitchen.

Her aunt gave her mother a knowing look as they headed toward the porch.

"What's up with her?" Sima asked, taking out her pack of American Spirits. "She seems distracted." She tapped the cigarettes against the package and handed one to Elena.

"Yes, we noticed it too," Elena said.

"Girls," Mamani said, appearing behind them. "We are old enough to know there's only one thing that can do that." She extended her hand for a cigarette of her own.

"But I thought she broke it off with that other guy. What was his name?" Sima asked.

"Khar!" Mamani said.

"Lorenzo," Elena said, taking a long drag on her cigarette. "And yes, they broke it off."

"Shhh," Mamani said. "She's heading back."

"Camila," Sima said as Camila peeked through the glass door. "We're going to the movies tomorrow night. Want to join us?"

"Oh, I have a date. It's so cold out here. Is smoking worth it?"

"It's one of the few joys left in life, honey," Sima said, joking.

Instead of presenting a litany of evidence linking tobacco and cancer, Camila rolled her eyes.

"Wait! Who do you have a date with?" Elena looked shocked. "We just arrived yesterday!"

"Oh, he's a friend of my friend Ben," she said. "I figure it's time to date again."

"Sounds good, Azziz," Mamani said.

"I'll go get the pie," Camila said and walked back to the kitchen.

"Well, if she has a date, then it can't be that guy back home, right?" Sima whispered.

Elena flicked her ash into the saucer acting as an ashtray. "I don't know. She has mentioned this Ben person many times, but then last week she told me he's getting married and that she may go to Maui for the wedding."

Mamani fell silent with her lips moving, and then she quickly blew a breath out as if she were fumigating a room.

"Uh oh, what is it?" Elena asked, knowing that Mamani had just wafted a prayer all over them to protect someone or something.

"I don't know, but something is not right. I worry about how much heartache she can handle."

The next evening Camila prepared for her date with David. Apparently, he did have sufficient balls. Not only had he called, but he had made plans with a designated time and place.

She dried her hair, styling soft waves around her shoulders. She wore a form-fitting dress, knee-high boots and applied a dab of perfume along her neck and wrists. It hadn't occurred to her to ask Ben what David looked like. She assumed he would be a variation on Ben. It was just one date after all. A free meal, according to Tyler. She wasn't nervous about meeting David. She was, however, nervous about driving Sima's stick shift into San Francisco and trying to find parking. But whether it had been Mamani's special prayer or the city emptying out for the holiday weekend, she was able to squeeze her car into a spot a block away from his apartment. He buzzed her in, and as she made her way up the stairs, she heard an unfamiliar voice greet her from above.

"Hi," said David, looking over the railing. His dark skin made his smile all the more radiant. When he was standing in front of her, she noticed he wasn't as tall as Ben but had a jawline that made her salivate. He shook her hand and gently pulled her into him and placed a delicate kiss along her cheek, close enough for his breath to tickle her ear. She stepped back and noticed his arms filled his coat out nicely, and his torso tapered into a slender waist. An expectant thrill made her smile more broadly, a thrill she had long missed.

8

December 2002

A week later, after class, Camila asked Ben how his Thanksgiving was while she sipped her white mocha. They had strolled in the direction of Ben's car and found themselves rushing to seek shelter in Kerckhoff when the rain started. It was unusually quiet, but the quarter was coming to an end, and finals were approaching. Each table was occupied by a student, their nose buried in a textbook or feverishly writing notes.

"Thanksgiving was great. We ate turkey. Oh, and Tiffany says hi. What did you think of Dave?"

They hadn't spoken over the holiday weekend, and she snorted out a laugh at his eagerness.

"I assumed you would have heard from him directly," she said.

"I did, but I want your version."

Now she was intrigued. "Wait, what did he say?"

"He said you were beautiful, fun, and that you guys had a good time but mutually agreed that since you were long distance, nothing would ever come of it."

"That about sums it up."

He was becoming a professional liar, or rather a partial truth teller. The full truth would have divulged David's detailed, hour-long call the day after his date with Camila in which he gave a play-by-play of their evening.

"Okay, so it went well?" Ben had casually asked David on the phone as he closed his notebook.

"Went well?" David told him. "That's one way of putting it. She's so fucking hot. Does Tiffany know you guys are friends?"

Ben was instantly irritated. "Yes, she does," he said, surprised at how sensitive he had become.

"Holy shit! I mean, besides her tits and ass, she's cool too. I had a terrific time, man."

He wasn't sure he wanted any more details. "Great, that's good."

"I mean from the moment she came in, it was an exercise of self-control," David said. "She had on this body-hugging dress and a pair of boots begging to be kept on when we did finally get, you know."

That last bit of information stuck in Ben's throat. He assumed they just had dinner. Why he assumed this was unclear and naive knowing David's reputation.

"Hey, you still there?" David asked.

"Yeah, sorry, I got distracted with something," Ben lied. The lies were rolling off his tongue now.

"So, yeah, we went to dinner and had a great time. She was fun to talk to, and when we weren't talking, I was pretty sure she was eye-fucking me the whole time."

Ben squeezed the bridge of his nose, trying not to focus on the image of Camila fucking anyone.

"So, then we go dancing, and she's fucking perfect. I mean her body up against mine, arms around my neck. She even smelled fucking amazing."

Ben knew exactly how David felt, and envy did not fully capture what he was feeling. Maybe rage, more specifically jealous rage. He should have ended the conversation there, but curiosity ate away at him. If he couldn't experience being with her, then at least he could live vicariously through David.

"Then we go back to my place, and before we even get in the front door, we are tearing each other's clothes off. I mean, we get into my room, and she's in her underwear and boots. Holy fuck, man, I nearly came right then."

"You slept with her on the first date?" Ben hadn't intended to holler into the phone.

"Dude, relax! First, it was all consensual, but we didn't have sex. Almost, but not completely."

"What the hell is *almost sex*?" Ben felt on the verge of a nervous breakdown.

"Dude, you *know*."

Now David was getting coy? "No, I don't think I do," Ben said.

"I think you've been with Tiffany too long," David joked. "Like, we did everything but."

Ben huffed a sigh of frustration. His curiosity had further inflamed his anger.

"But here's the best part. She gets up to leave, and I'm prepared for the awkward, who-is-going-to-call-who conversation, and she says, 'Thanks, David, I had a great time. Maybe we'll see each other again soon,' then leaves! No expectations, no obligations. She had a good time and then left. I had to chase after her just to walk her to her car."

Ben rubbed his temples and squeezed his eyes shut.

"Want to hear the best part?" David said. "There's nothing down there."

"What?"

"You know, *nothing* down there. Like totally bare, clean as a whistle."

And with that grenade thrown, David ended the conversation, "Okay, man, I gotta run. Thanks again. I owe you big time," and hung up the phone.

Now, Ben, sitting with Camila, was intelligent enough to know there were three versions of the story: David's, Camila's, and the truth. He may never know the truth, but David's version had traumatized him enough that he wasn't sure he could have handled the truth. He didn't get much more detail from Camila, though.

"I had a great time," she said. "I am open to seeing any of your other friends if they're all like him."

The hell he was going to introduce her to any of his other friends.

What she didn't tell Ben was that more than once she had imagined David was him. When they were dancing, or when David was hovering above her in bed, or she was moaning with his head between her legs and his arms wrapped around her thighs. She thought of Ben.

But that was her secret.

Well, hers and Tyler's, who got the accurate version of the evening.

"You let him do what?!" Tyler said.

"Hey! This is a judgment-free zone! How many times have I heard about your slutty escapades?"

"Noted. But, for the record. I never used the word 'slutty.' I'm just shocked. You don't even know this David. It's not like you."

"I know. I was surprised how comfortable I was with him too. Maybe because he's an extension of Ben," she said, and felt her mouth dropping open as the words escaped.

"Oh shit. Did you just psychoanalyze yourself?"

"What? No!"

"Uh-huh, are you going to look at me with those pretty eyes of yours and tell me you didn't let this guy go down on you because you mentally transplanted Ben's face onto his?"

"Stop it, Tyler! I'm trying to be good."

He smirked. "Clearly."

* * *

Once Ben's anxiety subsided after hearing the details of Camila's date, things went back to normal between them. Spanish class, coffee, the stares, and the longing poorly hidden from one another.

"Hey, so I am having a little party for my birthday next weekend," she said, a week later as they were leaving Coral Tree. "Do you want to come? Just a few friends from my program, obviously Tyler and my family."

"Yeah, that would be great," he said.

It was a delicate balance, his desire to be near her and his need to quell his attraction. She was outwardly doing a better job of keeping them in the "just friends" zone than he was. In public, she spoke to him and treated him as if he were a eunuch, and he wondered if she ached for him in private.

Ben was conflicted with feelings that felt natural but illicit. He loved Tiffany. He knew he did because he had only ever said the words "I love you" to her and only after reflecting long and hard on whether he could imagine himself with anyone else. His previous relationships had been fleeting, both because he was young and preoccupied with his career. He would have sacrificed any relationship, no matter how committed, to move to LA once he received his acceptance to medical school. Ultimately, that's what prompted the breakup of his previous relationship with Jill, his girlfriend at Yale. She was waiting to dump him once she was accepted to law school too, so it was painless. They had both agreed to bide their time until different graduate schools naturally separated them.

Tiffany was different. There was a seriousness to her that gave their relationship depth from the start. Since they were both on the same path, the sacrifices and expectations were clear and nonnegotiable. So, when Ben decided to take a year to pursue his MBA, it wasn't the most pleasant of conversations. But at the urging of his father, who clearly saw Ben's dampened spirit, he decided to throw a wrench into Tiffany's and his own well-manicured plans.

"This doesn't really work for us, Ben," she had told him after dinner. It was the middle of interview season. She had lined up interviews on both coasts, hoping they would settle near her family in Pasadena or by his family back East.

He knew it wouldn't be easy. His decision to dedicate a year to rediscovering himself would keep them separated for an additional year, which would then trickle into potentially more time apart if either decided to pursue fellowship. Add in the variable of delayed fertility because no female resident in her right mind would skip out on being chief resident her senior year because of a poorly timed pregnancy, and suddenly they'd be well into their late 30s before hearing the pitter patter of genetically blessed little feet. Ben's sudden desire to prolong his studies was going to place her squarely in the advanced maternal age category. All so he could add three little letters to the end of his last name. Or so Tiffany believed, since Ben couldn't tell her the full truth, which was that he wasn't even sure what he wanted anymore and needed a year away from everyone and everything to figure it out. That kind of self-indulgent indecisiveness was not welcome or understood by someone like Tiffany, who had once been described as a "take-no-prisoners gunner with a heart of stone." It was a compliment from her chief resident during her surgery rotation that touched her so deeply she almost produced a tear.

Tiffany wasn't the type to get angry or loud. She'd never lose control, but she was furious. In her dependable, silent, icy, closed-off way.

"You know this relationship was always about choice and not codependence or coercion. You know me better than to expect any compromise on my part," she had said.

"I wouldn't want you to do that," he told her.

"Well, I wouldn't. So, we'll just deal with the extra year apart."

They had successfully managed the time apart, making time for short trips across the country when possible. Between her rigorous intern schedule and Ben's classwork, they could only ever sacrifice two days together between holidays. It had been enough. Enough until he met Camila and realized he wanted more.

* * *

With flowers and a gift in hand, Ben walked into Camila's apartment, and his senses were immediately assaulted with the smell of cumin, cinnamon, and cardamom. Gipsy Kings blared from the stereo. Surveying the room, he didn't recognize anyone except Tyler, and they exchanged greetings with a nod. Tyler was standing by a table covered with a brightly colored serape cloth and fragrant platters overflowing with unfamiliar but delicious-looking food. A majestic woman in her 50s was by his side. But as soon as Ben's eyes finally locked onto Camila across the room, the other guests evaporated.

"You came!" she said, approaching him.

"I did." He smiled down at her, trying not to stare at her cropped peasant top, with its button clinging on for dear life.

They didn't hug, and it felt awkward. He half-thrust the bouquet of flowers at her. "These are for your family," he said.

She held them to her chest and inhaled deeply.

"I'll go put them in some water. Make yourself at home."

"Tyler, mijo," Elena asked Tyler, not taking her eyes off the table as she arranged the food and made space for her famous Mole de Pollo.

"Sí, Señora Elena."

She gestured in Ben's direction with a slight nod of her head. "Quién es ese hombre?"

"Ese es Ben," he said.

Elena knew after so many years together, whenever she was worried about Camila, Tyler was her ally. He was the adopted son, the stable, handsome, well-educated partner they had hoped Camila would find. Unfortunately, with one notable non-negotiable deal breaker on his end.

"Él es muy guapo," she told him.

Tyler leaned in and whispered, "Sí, es muy guapo y muy *engaged*."

"Ah, donde está su prometido?"

"Boston," he told her.

"Oh, Dios mío," she said, quickly kissing the evil eye charm dangling from her neck and then making the sign of the cross.

"Exactly," he said, matching her worried look with his own.

Not two minutes later, while Tyler was fussing over the vase holding the flowers Ben had brought, he noticed Mamani join Elena in the kitchen. She leaned toward Elena, who reflexively bent down to offer her ear to the much shorter Mamani. A few whispers, then Tyler heard an unmistakable "Ben," then "Boston," then Mamani saying, "Khak to saram," which he knew literally translated to dirt be upon my head or the Persian equivalent to Dios mío.

They saw Tyler eavesdropping and motioned him over.

"Tyler joon, this Ben seems too interested in Camila to be engaged," Mamani said. With age came the uncanny ability to sum up a situation after only a few minutes.

The three of them noticed how Camila and Ben had spent every moment together since he walked through the door, like a moth to a flame. They saw the sparkle in her eyes when he looked down at her and how attentive he was, but always with an invisible wall between them. To the inexperienced observer, they appeared to be friends, classmates. But to the trio standing in the kitchen, the energy that swirled around Camila and Ben, the heat between them, was calamitous. They all exhaled a collective sigh of dread.

"Thank you for the flowers," Camila said.

"They were for your family, to be honest," he said.

"Well, thanks." She winked at him. "That's a good way to win points."

"I got you something too," he said under his breath.

"You didn't have to do that," she said, looking up at him, and he couldn't move. It felt as if they were the only two people in the room. Her silhouette soft and ethereal, like a spirit beckoning him closer.

From the kitchen, her mother called, "Mija, come here for a second."

The spell was broken.

"Excuse me, I'll be right back for that gift." She winked at him again.

Finding himself alone, he explored the small apartment that had been kept hidden until now. It had been a mysterious place, piquing his interest every night she'd cross the parking lot and wave good-bye. He saw the timeline of pictures on the walls. Tyler and Camila through the ages: on the beach, hiking in Joshua Tree, beneath a massive sequoia tree, swimming in Lake Arrowhead. He turned to notice the mirrored pillows haphazardly thrown on the couch and the blush-colored light from the standing lamp draped with a floral scarf with a pattern like that of her skirt. The lamp warmed the room with a rosy glow in harsh contrast to the solid white door that guarded the bedroom behind it. A space kept off-limits to him but not to his thoughts. He allowed his mind to wander through the door momentarily, imagining the sanctuary on the other side full of alluring secrets. If they were together, if he allowed himself a moment of indulgence, he would know what her sheets felt like and what side of the bed she preferred. If it was her lotion that left the subtle scent of roses on her skin and what she wore to bed. If they had met before, before when he wasn't sure, but before at some point when they could have had a chance, then he would know. And this part of her wouldn't be a mystery. He saw a desk tucked in the corner that was serving as a makeshift bar for the evening. He picked up a bottle of water and noticed a group of smaller, black-and-white photos in antique frames. He recognized a much younger version of her grandmother, who had the same hazel eyes she did. A beautiful border of mosaics framed the picture of a young couple smiling at the camera. He bent down, peering into the photo looking for answers.

"That is my Amir," Mamani said as she came beside him. Bending over the desk, he was eye level with the delicate older woman.

"Oh, hello. I'm Ben," he said, politely extending his hand.

She offered her small hand in return. "I know."

The difference in their size was comical. But Ben surmised that after years of loss and sadness, something as insignificant as stature didn't trouble her.

"Amir?" he asked with care. "That is Camila's father?" He used the present tense as she had. He hadn't lost anyone in his life, but he imagined if he had, using the past tense would break his heart each time.

"Yes, he was my light, my gift from God."

He could hear the quiver in her voice. He pointed to the picture of the couple. "This is them in college?"

"Yes, I brought this picture from my house in Tehran. Amir had sent it to me, and I used to look at that photo of Elena before we met and wonder what kind of woman had been able to tame my son's wild heart, what kind of love they shared to make him so joyful in the letters he wrote me. He had been so devastated by the changes in our country before he left," she said. She shook her head as if trying to rid herself of the painful memory of his death. "But the world has a way of answering those questions."

She sat down in the chair next to the desk and motioned for him to take the other. She wanted to learn more about this man. Mamani worried that Ben and Camila were both too young to understand the power of their palpable magnetism and the devastation it could cause.

"Do you have love in your life, Ben?" she asked.

Normally, he would've been uncomfortable with such a private inquiry by a stranger, but he saw the pain in her eyes and realized she was not prying for curiosity's sake but for reassurance. To know that someone's love still endured.

"Yes, yes, I do."

"Hmm, that is good. Don't let it slip away. Care for it. This world is one big circle," she said and moved her aging fingers in a circle in demonstration. "Love her, and she will love you back. This universe takes account of the energy you give and gives it back with the same intensity."

He now appreciated how years of living with this mystical woman had turned Camila into a passionate disciple of karma.

He heard Camila approach before she appeared. She looked more exotic than usual with bangles stacked along both wrists and an anklet jingling with each step. She bent down, her hair cascading down, and placed a kiss on her grandmother's cheek.

"My love," Mamani said, her face bright with hope, folding Camila's hand with hers.

"Is my friend bothering you?" she asked her grandmother, smiling at Ben.

"Oh, no, Azziz, he is a very good boy. At my age, you can tell." She rose slowly, patting him on the shoulder, heading to the kitchen again.

She took the seat across from him, left warm by her grandmother.

"Are you having fun?"

"Yeah, thanks for inviting me."

"Don't tell Tyler, but after him, you're like my closest friend," she said shyly.

His chest swelled. He hadn't been sure if he was alone in struggling with the emotions ballooning between them.

"Your secret is safe with me," he said.

"Do you want something stronger to drink besides water?" she said.

"I don't really drink too often."

"Really?" she teased. "Do you have any vices?"

He looked at her without saying a word.

Camila tucked her leg beneath her patchwork skirt and plopped down on the couch with her plate of food. Ben sat on the floor next to her, his stomach full and a clean plate at his side. He recognized her skirt, the same one that had caught his attention the first night of class. From where he was sitting, her calf rested inches from his face, her foot dangling, the anklet jingling with each movement. He felt the urge to run his hand along her shin. Or even better to pull her down to him, legs opened. This was David's fault for giving such a vivid description. He didn't need to know her grooming habits. Instead, he focused on her bright red nail polish that matched the shade she had applied to her lips.

She leaned forward, and her hair fell between them, and she tossed it to the other side, and a tidal wave of fragrance washed over him, the scent of rose water and cinnamon.

"Did you eat enough?" she asked.

"If I eat any more, I'll need to have my stomach pumped."

"Perfect then." She smirked at him. "You'll still have room for tea and cake."

He let his head fall back, and she ruffled his hair in reflex, and he closed his eyes, letting the world once again fade into the background.

He didn't want to leave. He lingered, helping Camila clean up. They found themselves alone, Camila sitting at the table, running her finger through leftover whipped cream and licking it off. It had been a delicious cake. Only crumbs and one lonely piece remained. She broke pieces off into small bites, trying to fool herself into not eating her third slice. She glanced over to Ben arranging her throw pillows back on the couch.

"Hey, no more cleaning," she said. "Come join me."

"I think there shouldn't be much left."

"I hope my mom and grandmother get over the shock of seeing you clean up."

He laughed. "Why do you say that?"

"Except for my dad and Tyler, men are generally dismissed. Lower-order primates who are helpless and useless all at the same time."

"Ouch!"

"Well, present company excluded, of course," she said as he joined her at the table.

"That was an excellent cake," he said, surveying the damage she had done.

"Yeah, it's my favorite, like a huge tiramisu."

He scooped up a fingerful of mascarpone dusted with cocoa and sucked his finger clean. Her mouth watered watching him.

"Can I give you your gift?"

"You really didn't have to," she said, clapping her hands, "But yes, yes, yes!"

He placed the small, wrapped package in front of her. Quickly, she tore through the paper, turning the book over in her hands.

The Alchemist

"Have you read it?" he asked. "I think it's very much in line with your thoughts about fate and destiny."

She let out a small gasp as she covered her mouth, looking up at him.

"Yeah, I've read it. It's my favorite book. Ever."

"Oh, good. I was hoping you hadn't read it. But at least you like it."

"Ben, this is perfect. I lost my copy years ago while backpacking and never replaced it. Thank you so much."

He ran his finger through the last bit of the cream filling.

"Hey!" She said, laughing. "You can't eat the last bit of my birthday cake!" She grabbed his wrist.

"Fine!" He gestured for her to take the last bit from him.

He was surprised when she pulled his hand across the table and took his finger in her mouth. Her eyes locked with his, she sucked the cream from his finger, her tongue quivering against it. As she leaned forward, he fought hard to ignore her cleavage, as her breasts rested on the table before him. He froze, rigid, her tongue lapping his finger, her teeth grazing him just as Tyler walked out of the bedroom.

She looked up and pulled back from Ben, who quickly dropped his hand into his lap.

Tyler stopped midway to the front door, taking in the scene, Ben's finger in Camila's mouth, and quickly looked away.

She knew Tyler was contemplating whether he should speak. He resumed his journey to the door and paused with his hand on the knob. Camila rested her elbows on the table and covered her face with her hands.

"I'll clear this off the table," Ben said, giving him an excuse to hide in the kitchen.

Camila and Tyler stared at each other from across the room. His eyes said it all. *What are you doing?*

She slowly shook her head.

Be careful. Tyler mouthed at her before leaving.

Ben leaned against the kitchen counter, arms crossed across his broad chest.

"I'm sorry," she said.

He was wrestling with the conflict brewing between his head and his heart. It had felt amazing. He wished he could have leaned over the table and met her mouth with his. But he was a rational man, a good man, one that didn't hurt women. The feelings that Camila stirred in him challenged everything he knew about himself.

"I didn't mean to make you uncomfortable," she said, getting up but keeping her distance.

"I'm not uncomfortable." *I'm turned on.*

"I'll see you in class next week?"

"Yeah, I'll see you then."

9

January 2003

They had spent the past four weeks apart. Punctuated with a couple of quick phone calls. Camila had busied herself with her dissertation and being spoiled at home with Elena and Mamani's cooking. Both women had shared a feeling of unease after seeing Camila's interaction with Ben and took it upon themselves to investigate.

"How is Tyler, mija?" Elena asked Camila, gathering the supplies for her famous flan.

"Good, he's with his family for break."

"And how is your *other* friend, Azziz?" asked Mamani, who was sitting at the kitchen table and sipping her tea through the sugar cube she held between her teeth.

"Which friend, Mamani?" She was teasing her grandmother. Even though there had been a good number of friends at her party, she knew exactly who was being asked after.

"The one who couldn't keep his eyes off of you and looked like he wanted to be more than friends."

She grinned at her grandmother, "Mamani, you're going to have to be more specific," she said, winking.

"Ben, mija. Your grandmother is asking about Ben," her mother said, with little humor.

"It's not nice to tease your elders," Mamani said as she pinched Camila's side.

"Oh, Ben," Camila replied, mocking both women with her feigned ignorance.

Camila started to crack eggs into the bowl. "He is fine, and he is *just* my friend." She caught her mother and grandmother exchanging glances. "What?" she said to both.

"Azziz," Mamani said, "in my day, a man only looked at you like that if he had *unfriendly* intentions."

"He's engaged," Camila said. "There are no looks or anything else. There can't be." She gasped, dropping the eggshells onto the counter as she examined the contents of the bowl. Two yellow orbs stared at her from the bottom, two yolks from the same egg. She stepped away as if the bowl held a family of snakes.

Her mother and grandmother slowly approached and looked inside the bowl. Elena involuntarily released a small cry and crossed herself. Mamani whispered a prayer. Camila didn't need to hear the words. It was an omen. This was the universe warning her to tread lightly. That she had already crossed the line with Ben. That she should have never touched him, that she should have stopped meeting him, and at the very least not have sucked whipped cream off his finger.

Elena shook her head. "This is bad. We can't use these eggs for the flan."

"Yes, very bad," Mamani said and dumped the cursed eggs into the trash, and the egg cracking resumed in a separate, untainted bowl.

Ben had his own interrogation at home. Questions from his sisters. Why had he taken a year off for an MBA, and why was he making his life more difficult by taking an unnecessary Spanish class? His sisters never pulled punches.

"Did you get uncomfortable with the tiny bit of free time you had?" Stephanie said, pouring herself a cup of coffee. "You had to go fill it with an unnecessary class."

"Leave him alone," their father said, looking over his journal and knowing the emotional turmoil that had led Ben to make his decision to postpone moving to Boston for a year and from his expected path in life. "This will make him more competitive with the match next year."

"Thanks, Dad," he said, pulling on his running shoes. "I'll be back. I'm going for a run."

"Escaping is more like it," his father muttered under his breath and glanced at Ben, who was appreciative of the support.

An hour later he locked himself in the bathroom under the pretense of showering and took out his phone to punch in Camila's number.

"Hey, it's me," he said.

"Hi, me," she said sweetly. "How are you?"

"How was Christmas morning?"

"Busy. My mom's friends are coming over tonight, so I'm helping with the tamales and dolmehs."

"Sounds delicious."

"I'll try to freeze some to bring back for you. How was your Christmas morning? Did you get anything good from Santa?" she asked.

"I got a new pair of running shoes and some CDs I wanted."

"That's nice. How is Tiffany?"

"She's good. She comes tomorrow."

"That'll be nice. I'm sure she misses you."

"Yeah."

Silence.

"Well, I should probably go," she said. "My mom is getting antsy. Thanks for calling."

"Anytime."

She never called him. She had no business calling an engaged man. They were only friends. But when he called her, it made her euphoric, high, weightless. His voice an audible caress that could never become tangible.

The calls to her were short and always private. He hid in his bathroom, pantry, and on the trail behind the house, seeking as much distance from his family as possible when they spoke. He didn't want to bother explaining who Camila was and why they were friends and how he felt tethered to her in a way he couldn't understand himself.

"Hey, I'm seeing you in class next quarter, right?" she asked a few minutes into their call on New Year's Day. "I assumed you were taking the class, but it occurred to me you may not."

"Yeah, for sure. I'm signed up."

A sigh of relief reached his ear from the other side of the phone. He didn't need to sign up for Spanish Winter quarter either. But he did. He lied about why to himself and everyone else.

"So how were the crowds last night?" he said.

"So cool! I had always wanted to be in Times Square, so I tagged along with Tyler and Bobby. It was freezing, though. I nearly froze my nips off," she said, giggling.

"Where are Tyler and Bobby now?"

"Well, since I was tagging along, I'm on the pull-out sofa, and they're in bed. But I don't care. It was totally worth it to see the ball drop in real life and not on TV for once."

He envied Tyler's closeness to Camila. Ben always felt he was an arm's distance away from knowing her completely. Not only because of the newness of their friendship but also because of the mandatory space they kept between them.

"Did you make a New Year's resolution?"

"No, you know that's not my style. If something needs to change, I just do it. I don't have to wait for a date on the calendar. Did you?" she asked. In reality, when the ball had dropped, she had closed her eyes tightly and prayed to stop pining after unavailable men.

"Nah, I don't believe in that stuff," he said. It was a few hours into the first of the year, and he had already failed at sticking to his resolution: to stop daydreaming about women who were not his fiancée.

"I should have known. Too cosmic, right? Not concrete enough," she said, prodding him.

"Listen," he said, "just 'cause I think we have a little more say in what happens than whether a series of stars align or if the wings of a butterfly flutter doesn't mean I don't believe in setting tangible goals and achieving them."

"So, you mean to tell me that after all this, you don't believe it was fate that brought you and Tiffany together?"

"No, Camila, I don't. I do believe it was our birth year and our academics and goal-oriented personalities."

She laughed. "Wow, said like a true romantic."

"Well, I never claimed to be one."

"You'll see Ben. One day you'll see. Something will come sweeping into your world, and you won't know why, and you won't find a logical explanation, and you'll have to believe in fate eventually."

* * *

The night air was brisk as they walked to his car.

"I missed this," she said, smiling up at him, their bodies occasionally grazing as they walked.

"Me too."

The feeling between them had been a combination of excitement and longing when they first saw each other in class earlier in the evening and was only enhanced by the cold weather that forced them to huddle together.

"Will you be in class during Spring quarter too?" he asked.

"Yeah, you?"

"Yup."

"Do you have time tonight for coffee?" she asked. She sounded hopeful, and he told her he did, suppressing his eagerness, having waited for this exact moment for four weeks.

The car quickly gathered the heat from their bodies, and the windows fogged as they drove off campus. Heading west on Sunset Boulevard was eerily peaceful this time of night. The winding road was deserted except for a few cars pulling into the high-gated entrances of Bel Air.

"So, I was thinking, six months have passed since you decided to take a year for yourself," Camila said as Ben parked the car across from the cafe and turned off the ignition.

"A little more than halfway there," Ben said as they both sat in the car.

She turned toward him. "Any great revelations so far?"

"No revelations, but I think I can see some things more clearly. Other things have gotten a little murky."

"Like?" Camila asked.

"Well, I've missed medicine. I've missed learning with my hands and being pushed to see where my breaking point is."

"You miss being sleep-deprived and berated?"

Ben laughed. "Kinda. Medicine is like a shared trauma. Every day I'm there, every experience pulls me deeper into an exclusive pool of people around the world who have all seen humanity at its best and most tragic. It's an odd little community. We've all seen birth and death. We've all had our hands in someone else's body. We've caused people pain in an attempt to help them, and we've had strangers put their trust in us for no other reason than our profession. It's humbling."

"Ben, that almost sounds spiritual."

"Are you making fun of me?"

"No, I'm being serious. This is the first time you've talked about medicine like it's your calling and not just you picking the path you think everyone wants you on."

"I think I needed this time to take a moment and breathe. To understand what it is I want from life."

"And the other things? The ones that are less clear?" Camila asked.

"I'm figuring them out, but I'm not sure it matters. There is already too much momentum for me to make any sudden movements."

Bella waved at them as they walked through the door and started making Ben's cappuccino before Camila placed her order.

They sat at their usual table with their drinks, and she unwrapped her scarf and let her hair down from the messy bun perched on her head. She shrugged her sweater off one shoulder.

He motioned to the moonstone ring on her finger. "Is that new?"

"Oh, yeah, I got it for Christmas from my mom," she said, spinning it around her finger.

"I hadn't seen it before."

"You are quite observant, aren't you?"

"Well, I like you," he said, staring down into his drink. He was having difficulty grappling with the more intense stew of emotions that had begun percolating over the holidays. Seeing her in person was like a catalyst.

She smiled brilliantly. "Of course you do. I'm fabulous," she said, tossing her hair over her shoulders.

He had tried dismissing his feelings before without success. Now he was planning on trying brutal honesty instead.

"I'm not joking," he said. "I've tried to ignore it. But it got worse over break."

She looked at him with a seriousness to match his own.

"It caught me off guard," he said, rubbing his neck. "I haven't felt about anyone the way I feel about you. Not since Tiffany." He leaned on the table, gripping his cup for strength. "I just wonder if…"

"Ben, don't. You can't wonder."

But she had wondered the same thing endlessly. What if they had met a few months earlier? "I'm flattered, Ben, but that's all it can be. Just words. This is all just a classic *wrong time and wrong place* situation."

"I wasn't planning on meeting anyone else," he said.

"Okay, full truth time, Ben. I started to like you when we met, and I think you knew that. I thought maybe there could be something between us, but then I found out about Tiffany. And I made myself stop. Sometimes it's still difficult, but what's the alternative? We may have been good together, but I can't turn back the clock or wish that somehow, with all our common connections and intertwining paths, we would have met sooner."

"I know."

"I'd still like to be friends."

"Me too."

She stared at him gazing into his cup. She had bottled up her feelings for him, the feelings that were bubbling over at times. Deciding she would be a respectful and responsible friend instead. She knew they both wished for different circumstances. Perhaps in an alternate universe where they would have met first. But the reality was they could never be more than friends.

"But I did miss you," he said in a whisper.

"What?" She asked, wanting to hear the words again.

"I did. I missed you over break."

She sat back with resigned shock. "Ben, um, I, I don't know what to say."

Was he confessing as catharsis or testing the waters?

She felt claustrophobic. No position was comfortable. She leaned forward again, wrapping her long hair around her hand.

They sat in silence until realization dawned on her.

"Wait, is this why you introduced me to David? As a distraction? A deterrent?"

"Not initially, but I hoped it would help me stop."

"Stop what?"

"Stop what I was starting to feel," he said.

Her mouth fell open.

She swallowed, surprised at how dry her throat was given she had downed half her tea. She had tried to ignore what she felt for Ben for months. He wasn't hers, and she had no right to think about him, but she didn't know he felt the same.

"Did it help?" She asked, "Having me with David?"

"No, not at all."

10

February 2003

Knowing they both felt something more than friendship didn't derail their relationship. Maybe it should have, but they couldn't be apart for more than a few days before the need to see each other became overwhelming. Like a thirst that needed to be quenched. They had silently established arbitrary and ineffective boundaries. She never called him but accepted his calls. He never touched her, not even to place a hand on her back as she went ahead of him, but she would gently place a hand on his arm or tussle his hair when she felt something he said was particularly endearing. Nothing helped. She would go home dreaming of him, and he would return to his empty apartment, frustrated.

The added heart and Cupid decor covering the cafe that February didn't help.

"No plans for Valentine's Day?" he asked Camila, picking up the heart candy Bella had placed on his saucer. He grinned reading it and placed it back down.

"Well, usually I'd hang out with Tyler, but now Bobby is in the picture. I think they'll do something romantic together."

"No long-lost boyfriends coming into town?"

She laughed. "How many boyfriends do you think I've had?"

"Well, I only know about the one."

She gestured to the Valentine's candy he had placed on his saucer. "What does it say?"

He picked it up and turned it toward her.

Be mine.

She smiled before picking up her own candy and popping it in her mouth.

"Hey, that's not fair," he said. "What did yours say?"

"That's for me to know and you to find out." She stuck out her tongue with the candy perched on the tip. *Yes.*

He was staring at her mouth, and she retracted her tongue to chew the chalky candy.

"For your information," she said. "I've only ever officially been with two men. Don't look so shocked. Geez, what kind of girl do you think I am?"

"I thought you'd have left a long line of broken hearts."

She smiled. "Mine is the only heart that's ever been broken."

A strange protective urge filled in his chest. "So, you're not in touch with any of them?"

"I mean, I'm friendly with my exes, except Lorenzo, and I'm sure that'll eventually change, but I'm not friends with them. It's a bit weird to see someone naked and then pretend to be *just friends*, don't you think?"

"I don't know," he said, "I guess."

"My first boyfriend was in high school. It was right before graduation, and I loved him as much as a 17-year-old girl can. It was what you would expect—awkward, painful, messy, and quick." She laughed at the memory. "Then there were a couple guys in college I messed around with, but nothing serious until Lorenzo. He was okay at first, but mainly focused on his own needs," she said uncomfortably. "Now I realize I didn't like who I was with him."

Something about the way she described her relationship with Lorenzo made Ben want to smash his fist through a wall, or preferably Lorenzo's face.

"What about you, Dr. Martin?" she said.

It always made him uncomfortable when she called him that.

"Well, I had a high school girlfriend. She was a cheerleader, and I was on the football team, so kinda expected." He nervously ruffled his hair. "I told you about the girlfriend I had my last two years at Yale, but after graduation we broke up. Then I met Tiffany here."

"What happened the first two years at Yale?"

Smiling coyly, he said, "Um, less serious stuff."

"Ha! Were you a manwhore, Ben Martin?" She laughed out loud.

"No," he replied, rubbing both hands down his face.

She grabbed his wrist to expose his face. "You can't hide now!"

"I'm not hiding! I was part of a fraternity, and it was my first time being on my own, so I was, you know..."

"No, I don't *know*, but I'll put you out of your misery. What are you and Tiffany doing for Valentine's Day this year?"

"Nothing. She's working, and we are going to Hawaii in a month, so we're just going to celebrate then." Ever the practical woman, Tiffany had scoffed at the idea of either of them flying across the country for a Hallmark-mandated holiday.

Camila sipped her coffee, looking at him. They would both be alone and two blocks apart on the most romantic day of the year.

*　*　*

The cramping wouldn't let up. It didn't make sense. Bobby and Tyler had both had the soup too. Why were they out romancing it up, and she on the couch in the fetal position? Mamani had advised her to make tea with nabat. The medicinal purposes of rock candy were varied and well-established in their house. Diarrhea? Nabat. Constipation? Nabat. Acid reflux? Nabat.

Unfortunately, this time the effects were not as profound. She still had a painful twisting of what she assumed were her intestines, preventing her from sitting upright.

She had convinced Tyler not to change his plans since it was his first Valentine's Day with Bobby and pulled herself together to shoo him out the door before collapsing and calling her family for advice.

Between fitful naps, she heard a knock on the door.

She groaned from her recumbent state. "Who is it?"

"It's me."

She peeled herself off the couch and shuffled to the door.

She opened the door to see Ben standing on her doorstep.

"Tyler called me since you hadn't picked up your phone, so I came over to check on you."

She turned and fell back down on the couch as he walked in and closed the door behind him. He smelled like soap, a fresh scent that was in contrast to her stale appearance and likely odor.

"You don't look too good," he said. "What happened?"

"I don't know," she moaned, throwing her hoodie over her head and pulling on the drawstrings.

"Is anyone else sick?" he said.

"No, that's what sucks. I made chicken soup, and we all had some, but I was the only one to get sick."

"Who made it?"

"Me."

"Let me look at you," he said. "Can you lay back?"

She rolled over, less than gracefully, in her sweatpants and tank top. He washed his hands and knelt by her side and placed his palm on her forehead.

"Can I touch your stomach?"

"Yeah." She wasn't very worried about igniting any flames of desire given she looked like a wad of used tissue.

He carefully lifted her tank up, exposing her abdomen, and gently lay his hand on her. He felt the warmth of her skin on his palm. Gently, he applied and released pressure across her skin, watching her face.

"Does this hurt?"

"No, but it doesn't feel great."

"Well, I don't think you have appendicitis. Did you eat any raw chicken?"

"Ben, I'm not Julia Child, but I know the basics." Then she smacked her own forehead with her palm.

"What?" he said.

"I used the same knife to cut the chicken and the vegetables."

"Okay."

"Well, I popped a few carrots in my mouth while I was cooking. Fuck!"

He chuckled.

She winced. "It's not funny."

"No, no, not funny at all," he said, trying to stifle his laughter.

"Uh, this sucks."

"Don't worry. It'll pass. I can stay with you until Tyler comes home."

"Thanks, Ben. You're a good friend," she said, moaning further into the fetal position.

Tyler and Bobby returned to find Ben seated on the floor, napping with his head tilted back on the couch Camila was curled on.

"I guess this is one way to celebrate Valentine's Day," Bobby whispered.

Ben woke and sat up, rubbing his eyes, and saw Tyler and Bobby staring at them.

"Oh, hey. When I came over, she didn't look too great, so I stayed until you came home."

"Thanks," Tyler said. "We brought cake home to share with Typhoid Mary over here, but I don't think she'll be eating much. Do you want to join us?"

"Oh, that's okay. I think I'll head home."

Tyler looked at Ben. "Has Tiffany been waiting for you this entire time?"

"No, we couldn't see each other for Valentine's Day this year."

"Okay, that's that," Tyler said. "You are staying for at least a piece of cake. If Tiffany found out I didn't take care of her man, she would literally kick my ass."

Ben smiled, appreciative of the gesture, though Tiffany wasn't possessive like that.

Their relationship was a partnership free of drama and rooted in trust and mutual respect. A grown-up relationship that was now being jeopardized by feelings that he couldn't resolve.

11

Stephanie slipped her sunglasses back down as she walked away from the poolside bar. They had been looking forward to this wedding for months. Ben had come home during the winter break, but they missed him more now that he was going to belong to another woman officially. Also, Maui in the dead of winter was a great escape from the snowplows and icy roads of the East Coast. She walked along the edge of the pool, carefully navigating the slippery floor and small children. She came alongside her younger sister. "Tell me that's not her," handing Amy her umbrella-topped drink.

It was fun to get tipsy with their little sister now that she *looked* like she was legal drinking age. No more elaborate schemes were needed, even though she was not yet twenty.

Amy took her drink, sucking on her straw, and swallowed a huge gulp. "It is her," she said with a sigh.

"Dear God."

The three siblings were close. Closer than most, and as much as Ben tried to protect his sisters physically, they were fiercely protective of his heart. Their mother's trauma had hardened the girls but had the opposite effect on Ben. He was always concerned about their happiness, their safety, more sensitive to their needs than typical brothers. So, when they started to hear Camila's name sprinkled in his stories about life back in LA, they were both curious. But when Amy overheard him call *his* Camila on Christmas morning, locked in their bathroom, using hushed tones, she promptly told Stephanie.

Once Tiffany had arrived, they spent the holiday with their family as planned, and everything seemed copacetic. Until Stephanie saw Ben behind the house on his phone instead of on the trail he had supposedly gone to run on New Year's Day.

Ben had always been steadfast, stoic. They didn't know who this mystery woman was, but he smiled a broader smile, laughed louder, and seemed happier when her name was mentioned. Their reserved, responsible brother had never been so carefree.

Camila and Tyler grabbed their towels and headed towards the lounge chairs, having excused themselves from an overly aggressive game of beach volleyball. They had arrived from Los Angeles the previous night, quickly checked in, and had been planning to start their vacation with a full day of lounging by the pool. Tyler only had a few precious days to curate an enviable tan before the end of the weekend. Camila had just closed her eyes when a shadow fell over her. She squinted upward, shielding her eyes with her hand, and saw Amy and Stephanie smiling down on her.

They introduced themselves, and Camila said, "Hi," and popped up to give them a warm hug, "And this is Tyler," she said, motioning to him as he waved from his chair, sunglasses on, his skin glistening with suntanning oil.

"Charmed, ladies," he called out.

"Grab a seat. I am so happy to finally meet you guys," Camila said.

"And us you," Amy said.

"We've heard so much about you," Stephanie confessed, to which Tyler mumbled not too quietly, "I'm sure you have."

Camila spun around, giving him a scowl. He smiled and resumed his tanning.

"We are so happy you guys made it," Amy said.

His two sisters spent the next hour talking up Camila and confirming what they already knew—Ben's new gorgeous friend was charismatic, funny, and hazardous to their brother's well-planned-out life.

"They are so great," Camila said. She lay next to Tyler and watched the two women greet other friends and family around the pool.

"Darling, you just survived the most sugar-coated interrogation I have ever overheard."

"What? You're nuts. They were just being friendly."

He slid his sunglasses down his nose. "Sure," he said over his frames, "the same way Brutus was Caesar's best bud."

Amy and Stephanie walked back into the lobby. "How is he just friends with her?" Amy asked. "This is a disaster waiting to happen."

"I don't know, maybe he is too scared of Tiffany?" Stephanie half-joked.

"I would be," they both said simultaneously, erupting into a giggling fit. But Stephanie was concerned and would remain so until she could speak to her brother.

* * *

"Is black inappropriate?" Camila called from the closet.

"You're half Persian, aren't you?" Tyler yelled back as he ran his fingers through his hair, praying the extra-strong hold gel would keep everything in place.

She joined him at the mirror, adjusting the flower in her hair.

"Point taken. Still, you don't think I'll offend anyone in this, right?"

She hadn't bothered blow-drying her hair, slicking it back instead, hoping to outsmart the humidity.

Tyler gave her a once-over. "Damn, Camila, you are on fire! I'm pretty sure they named the hourglass after you instead of the other way around!"

"Thanks, honey," she said, leaning over for a kiss.

"Careful! Don't mess up the do. This fucking humidity is a disaster."

"Okay, Paul Mitchell." She said, adjusting the gardenia tucked into her hair.

She stepped back, sat on the edge of the tub, and strapped her heels on.

"Will you be able to walk in those?" Tyler said.

"That's not the point."

"Well, you can't hang off me the whole night. I have to make my rounds."

"Tyler, you can't ditch me! I only know you and Ben."

"And *David*." He sang it.

"I haven't seen him yet. I thought he'd be here already, but maybe not."

"Well, I hope he has his own room because I can't pretend to be asleep in the other bed when you do whatever it is you are going to do with him."

Tiffany had invited them to the rehearsal dinner even though they weren't part of the wedding party. They made their way to the restaurant, and Tyler recognized a few of last year's graduates. Camila was so happy he was by her side. Her heels were not made for walking, and Tyler made a great crutch. But also, together they made a couple. Being single at a wedding was one thing, but being alone *and* single was a different sort of hell.

Tiffany waved at them from across the long table that had been decorated with floating candles in tall hurricanes and cascading bouquets of white orchids. White linens and an array of stemware decorated each place setting. Every aspect was tasteful and chic. Even her knee-length cream-colored shift dress was accented with a flattering, blush-colored belt. It made her look all the more svelte. Her hair was swept back into a tight, pristine bun at the nape of her neck like Camila's, but without the flower.

"You look beautiful, Tiffany," Camila said and gave her a tentative hug.

"Gorgeous," Tyler added.

"Thanks, you two. I'm glad you were able to come. Since you know both of us, sit anywhere you like."

The table had been divided into designated sides—one for the groom's family and the other for the bride. Tyler and Camila grabbed a seat and soon found themselves flanked by Ben's college friends.

Conversation was easy, dinner delicious, and as the guests became more rambunctious, the speeches started.

But when a man stood at the head of the table, distinguished-looking with wire-rimmed glasses and salt-and-pepper hair, Camila understood why Amy looked so different from Ben and Stephanie.

"When Ben came into my life," Dr. Kang started, and for the next few minutes detailed how Ben and his sisters were a blessing in his life and how happy he was that he picked up that extra shift years ago and met their mother.

"What is he talking about?" Camila whispered to Tyler.

"I'm not sure," he whispered back, keeping his eyes on the father of the groom.

"I'm totally confused," she said, glancing over to Ben, who was holding Tiffany's hand and looking up at his father.

"Oh God, look at her," Amy whispered to her sister.

"He must not have told her," Stephanie said, seeing Camila's confused face from across the table. "So much for best friends."

"Maybe she thought I'm just shorter than you two because of a genetic fluke?" Amy said jokingly.

The sisters laughed conspiratorially as their father concluded his speech.

After dessert, Tyler found himself amongst a few of Tiffany's classmates sharing foul stories from their intern year. Camila had strolled toward the restaurant balcony away from the party. She leaned on the railing, watching the waves crash on the rocks below, and heard Ben's familiar laugh from a conversation behind her. She missed him. They had spent no time together since she arrived. She didn't even remember whether they had said hello. It would be ridiculous to expect anything different, but it was still difficult to have him so close but also completely preoccupied with everything and everyone else.

"You didn't want any champagne?" Stephanie asked, coming up beside her.

"Oh, no thank you. I don't drink."

"Another thing you two have in common," she said.

"I guess so," Camila said, turning toward her, "but clearly there is a lot I don't know."

Stephanie smiled at having sensed Camila's confusion at dinner. "You can ask anything, Camila."

"I'm sorry. I don't mean to be rude, but are you and Ben adopted?"

"You're not being rude, and if you're close enough to Ben to be invited to his wedding, then maybe you should have known. Dad is our stepfather. So, we kinda adopted him in a way. Our biological father left when Ben was seven. Well, the truth is we left him, and then he left us."

"Oh, I'm sorry."

"Don't be. Our biological father was an asshole, and I would use more colorful language if I wasn't worried about being overheard. He was horrible. Sometimes our mom would even hide us in her class-room just to give him enough time to pass out on the couch and then sneak us all back home," she said, looking out into the darkness. "It started with drinking," she continued. "That evolved into screaming and hitting. He never hit us, except for once when Ben got in his way."

Camila remembered the faint scar on his lip. "What happened?" she asked cautiously.

"It was towards the end, a month or so before we left. He had come home drunk, yelling and screaming, but this time we had a plan. Me and Ben. We were going to stand in front of our mom since we knew he wouldn't hit us. Because then he'd have to explain to the school if we went in with bruises and cuts. He was an asshole, but a smart asshole. Anyway, he comes home, and we immediately try to get in front of her, but I get scared and hide behind her instead. I was ten at the time. Ben was seven. I mean, you can imagine. He was skin and bones, probably weighed fifty pounds sopping wet. But he gets between them and starts yelling back. I still don't know how he had the courage. I was petrified. That man..." She shuddered.

"You don't have to go on," Camila said, placing a hand on her arm.

"It's okay. He'd get this inhuman look, and that night I wanted to run and hide. But Ben stood there and yelled and screamed. I guess he hit a nerve, and our father hit Ben with a backhand, sending him across the room. He split Ben's lip open. It was a miracle it didn't knock him out."

Camila's hand went to her lip.

"When we went to the ER, Dad treated us. Well, it was Dr. Kang at the time. That's the first time we met him. He didn't buy the story Mom told him about Ben falling. He told her to come to the ER the next time she was afraid. She wouldn't accept his help that night. I think at that point mom knew she had to leave. She had stayed in the marriage because he had never hit us, but after what happened to Ben, she knew we couldn't stay. So, a month later we showed up at the ER, and Dr. Kang was there. The rest is history."

The air between them felt thick with sadness and disbelief. Did Camila even know Ben? What else had he kept from her? "I'm so sorry," she said.

"Nah, it's in the past. Our dad is the best. He adopted us, and then Mom and him had Amy. Ben idolizes him. I mean, like, worships him. He doesn't drink because Dad doesn't drink. He's in med school, and, well, you can imagine why."

Camila swallowed down a gulp of air, and tears welled in her eyes.

"Oh, Camila, it's okay," Stephanie said as she rubbed her arm. "He probably didn't tell you because it still hurts. Men are different. Women talk, and we cry and yell. It's cathartic. But men shove it back down and hope it won't come bursting to the surface one day."

Camila caught a glimpse of Ben in the distance. He was smiling and laughing with his friends, unaware that her heart was breaking for the boy she now knew as a man. A man whose kindness and decency had survived despite the violence of his childhood.

"Oh, it's okay, honey," Stephanie whispered.

Camila backed away, wiping her eyes. "Thanks for telling me," she said with a sniffle.

"Of course. I'm sure Ben didn't want to burden you with the ugly details of our past. He never wants to burden anyone. I'm not sure how much he's processed of what happened to us. But I guess we each have our own way. I became a therapist, and he dove into school. But he did talk about you nonstop when he was home. We know you're important to him."

Stephanie squeezed Camila's arm gently before heading toward her husband and their two young children.

Camila stood there, not able to move. Her heart ached for him. The wind coming in from the waves dried her tears while undoing some of her hair. She caught Tyler's look from across the balcony, and he mouthed, *"Are you okay?"* She mouthed back, *"Yeah."* She motioned to her wrist as if she wore a watch and not a stack of bangles. She wanted to know when they would head up to their room. *"Ten minutes,"* he mouthed. She could clear her head for the next ten minutes before pretending everything was okay.

She started to make her way along the balcony to Tyler, and after nearly two days in the same resort, she finally got a moment with Ben. Alone. He had excused himself from a group of older relatives after locking eyes with her from across the crowd. She flashed him a smile to disguise the sadness that had suddenly weighed her down.

"Hi, you."

"Hey, you," she said, "Are you having fun?"

"Yeah, I can't believe it's finally here. I'm glad you came," Ben said.

"Me too."

The waves continued to crash behind her.

"You look nice," he said quietly.

"Thanks. I didn't know if black was okay, but Tyler said I looked good." She smiled at him.

He bit his lower lip as if he was about to say something that bordered on too friendly. His hand went to the back of his neck. But she didn't press him. In a few hours, this would all be very final. They would be friends with a legal document preventing anything further. No more hoping, no more wishing, no more what-ifs.

"I wish, um, I wish we..." he said, resting his hand on the railing.

"Ben, don't. Don't say it," she said.

She placed her hand on top of his for the briefest of moments as they stood side by side looking out over the ocean. A safe distance separated them, but she heard him exhale a shuddered sigh.

"Exactly," she replied.

* * *

Ben joined his sister in the lobby after the party finally dissolved, and he had said good night to his soon-to-be bride. Stephanie held her youngest in her lap, fast asleep from exhaustion.

"Too much excitement, huh?" Ben said.

"Let me take him," her husband said, taking their son. Ben figured he sensed a private sibling conversation was brewing.

"Let's go down by the pool," Stephanie told Ben.

Ben followed her like so many times before when they had been children. He loved his sister. He trusted her and felt closer to her than even the woman who was waiting to be his wife.

"You really like her, huh?" Stephanie asked as they dangled their feet in the water like when they were young.

"I *am* getting married to her tomorrow," he joked, elbowing her in the ribs gently.

"I don't mean Tiffany," she said.

He looked at her and saw the seriousness in her face.

"Ben, you don't have to do this if you don't want. I'll help you. We can leave right now. Wasn't the entire point of this year to figure out what you want in life?"

They had history, beyond just unconditional sibling devotion. They understood each other silently. They had been there for each other. He knew without a doubt she would help him leave, even right now, if he asked.

"You know I can't do that," he said.

"Can't or won't?"

"Does it matter?"

"Do you love her, Ben?"

He turned to look at her, lips pressed together in a thin line, and gave the most subtle nod. His heart leaped into his throat at the admission. He wanted to disappear.

His sister placed a hand on his back, like she did when he was a child.

"I know you're a good man," she said, "but don't sacrifice your happiness because of bad timing. You can love two people at once. Just make sure you marry the right one tomorrow."

"Stephanie, I can't. I may know what I finally want, but I'm not strong enough to make a choice that will ruin someone's life."

"Ben, but what about your life? Would you have proposed if you had met Camila just one month earlier?"

He honestly couldn't answer, not out loud at least.

"Stephanie, I can't abandon everything now. We're just friends."

She looked at him with a disbelieving glare.

"We can *only* be friends," he said.

"I thought this year was about figuring out who *you* are again," she said. "Maybe *this* Ben would have done things differently, pursued different people and different paths. Just because you are following your heart doesn't mean you're abandoning anyone. Sure, it would hurt for a while, but in the long run, Tiffany wouldn't want to be with someone who's heart always partly belonged to someone else. If you leave now, it doesn't make you like him. You'll never be *him*."

"Tiffany is stable and reliable. She understands the constraints of my career. She's good for me, and we have a well-planned future together."

"Ben, you just described a nice pair of work shoes, not the love of your life."

They were peas in a pod for as long as he could remember, finishing each other's sentences, reading each other's thoughts. Tonight, it seemed like she had just crawled right inside his brain.

"Camila is charming. I'll give you that," Stephanie said. "I don't think she realizes what she looks like either. Most girls that pretty can't be funny or goofy. She's just nice and normal."

He smiled, appreciating how well Stephanie could verbalize his own feelings.

"Why didn't you tell her about all the stuff before Dad?"

"I don't know. Maybe I like that she only knows me for me. I don't want her pity. She just likes me, not wounded me. She's not trying to fix me."

There were a few moments of silence before she said, "Don't be upset, but I told her about all of it. I just fell into it when she asked if we were adopted."

He smiled at her, realizing the predicament she must have been in.

"I don't think I helped you though," Stephanie said. "I think it'll make her like you more."

* * *

Tyler and Camila arrived back in their room to find all six groomsmen and Ben sharing the double next door. Suitcases were splayed open, clothes strewn about in every corner, and a general dishevelment that only a group of unsupervised college friends could conjure. Tyler opened the adjoining door, and the party spilled over into their room. Amy arrived, and the drinking really started. Everyone had changed out of their formal clothes into bedtime clothes, including Camila, who was grateful for having the foresight to bring her longest sleep tank instead of her boy shorts and cropped top. She noticed Ben stealing a quick look, and she dismissed it as pre-wedding jitters. Sometime after midnight, there was an all-out war of pillows, flailing arms, and legs.

"Tyler, you can't hide behind me," Camila yelled as he used her as a human shield.

"Why not? You're all about equality," he said, ducking in time to miss a pillow to the face. She made a dash to the floor on the other side of the far bed. Not a second later, Ben appeared, crouched on the ground beside her.

"What are you doing here?" She said, "You're the enemy!"

"Enemy, huh?" He stood, grabbed her by the waist, and threw her over his shoulder.

"Put me down!" she yelled, laughing, kicking her legs, pounding on his back. "Ben! Put me down!"

Three of the groomsmen cornered Amy, pillows poised and ready for attack. Ben flipped Camila onto the bed before making his way to defend his little sister from a down-feather bombardment. Amy escaped into the bathroom before they followed her, Tyler leading the charge this time, like a bedtime Napoleon.

Ben spun around, eyes landing on Camila as she tried to hide under the sheets. She giggled and kicked as he landed on the bed, throwing the sheets aside. She grabbed the edge of her nightshirt and pulled it down before her backside was exposed. Her hair wildly spread around her. He edged near her with a look like he was going to throw her over his shoulder again or pin her to the bed. She smiled, teasing him, sticking out her tongue. Then, without knowing whether it was calculated or accidental, he made a move to grab her, and his hand slid under her clothes from her thigh up over her backside to her waist and then the curve of her back in one smooth movement. His palm flat on her exposed skin. Hot and intimate. They froze, staring at each other. Suddenly, he recoiled. Her mouth fell open. He was still hovering above her, and she lay motionless. The sound of chaos was coming from the bathroom, but in the room, there was silence. She swallowed as they remained transfixed, the air between them static. It felt like an eternity until he finally peeled himself off the bed and went into the adjoining room without saying a word.

She lay still, shocked. They had never touched like that. Not skin to skin, not underneath clothing. Since the night they had gone dancing, they had made it a point to rarely touch.

Amy escaped the bathroom, followed by a group of pillow-wielding men chasing her at Tyler's command.

"Where is Ben?" Amy said, panting, running around the room.

"Oh, I'll get him," Camila said.

She slowly walked over to the common doorway and stood there watching Ben on the edge of the bed, his head in his hands. Was he that ashamed of touching her?

He glanced up, face flushed, just as she entered. He looked as if he was on the verge of crying, though she knew that wasn't likely. Nothing had happened. But his eyes held an emotion she couldn't identify.

He didn't say anything when she said his name. He just looked up at her. "Ben, nothing happened," she said softly. "It was just an accident."

He sat, immobile. So, she said it again. "It was just an accident. Ben, it was just an accident. It doesn't mean anything."

She hesitated coming closer, not trusting herself or him. There was so much noise and distraction from the adjoining room they could have easily found themselves alone for a few precious minutes.

All she had to do was close the door and lock it. Then she could walk up to him, within arm's reach, and he could slide his hand between her legs to feel her body respond to him. They would have enough time for her to taste his lips. They could whisper the words they hadn't dared acknowledge for the past few months. She could run her hands through his hair and put her mouth onto his.

"Please, Ben," she whispered. "It was just an accident, okay?"

She didn't know if she was asking or telling. She had been diligent in keeping her intentions platonic. Her faithfulness would be paid back in full one day. Sometime in the future but with someone else. She believed it in her heart.

"Ben, I'm going to go," she said, snapping him out of his haze. "It's okay. Nothing happened. We were just kidding around." But what she wanted to say was, *Let's close the door. Let's have this one night.* Before she could test her willpower, she felt someone's hand snake around her. Ben's eyes held disappointment and recognition.

"I've been dreaming for months of touching you again," a familiar voice rasped in her ear. She turned quickly to see David's face inches from hers, and before she could form any words, he pulled her into him, placed a hand firmly on her ass, and kissed her.

"Hey," she said, pushing away as she dragged a finger across her lower lip to wipe the glistening trail of saliva he had left behind. He rested his arms around her, not letting her escape as she smiled up at him, placing her hands on his chest to make space.

"You are still so fucking hot," he said, dropping his face into her neck and kissing her with no regard for their audience of one. She tapped him on the shoulder to get his attention.

"What?"

She cleared her throat and motioned toward Ben with her head.

"Oh, hey man," David said, releasing Camila and walking over to Ben, who embraced him, never taking his eyes off her.

"Hey, Dave," he said softly.

"Dude, I'm sorry it took so long to get here. Some fucking project at work that just couldn't wait."

"It's no problem. I'm glad you're here," Ben said, as David walked back toward Camila.

"Do you have your own room?" He asked into her ear but loud enough to make Ben slightly envious.

"Wow, your discretion astounds me," she said with a chuckle, "But no, I'm staying with Tyler."

"Fuck!" He said, joking. "I need you, a bottle of whatever, and three to four hours, preferably without an audience."

She laughed. "Well, it'll have to wait until after the wedding when this room is available."

Later, she didn't tell Tyler about the near miss. She returned to her room, and around three in the morning, the thoughts of Ben's hands running up and down her body finally dissipated.

* * *

The wedding was beautiful. Camila arrived with Tyler for the ceremony, briefly waving at David as he stood beside Ben, who misconstrued the wave and waved back.

Fucking hell, this was messy. Camila thought to herself as the maid of honor descended the aisle, followed by Tiffany, looking chic and polished as ever in off-white.

The vows were short and thoughtful but not overly romantic. She did notice Ben wiping away a tear as Tiffany walked up to him. He was a good and decent person. She smiled at herself. She thought watching him get married would have dampened her desire for him, but now her longing was replaced with a raw hollowness that was no easier to cope with. Putting him out of her mind would be painful, and maintaining a friendship would be its own special kind of agony.

The large white tent decorated with hanging chandeliers and tasteful flower arrangements of all white spilled over with music and conversation. The night was balmy and warm, the delicate scent of plumeria swirled through the air. Tyler and Camila immediately gravitated toward the dance floor, twisting and gyrating to the music as if they were back at the Abbey. Camila had worn the same red dress as months before when she and Ben had danced together. Her hair was now down, one side tucked with a white hibiscus flower. David hadn't left her side the entire evening, and once she told Tyler of her intentions, he left the two of them alone. David wasn't a particularly great dancer, but his confidence, charm, and good nature made him a wonderful distraction. He was attentive, and Camila had never been happier to be ogled in her life. She needed a diversion, and David's strong arms and chiseled face were perfect for the job.

She closed her eyes and let her mind go numb. She wanted the image of Ben and Tiffany's first dance out of her mind. They looked perfect together. Tall and sleek, and elegant. It didn't matter what Camila felt for Ben. They would have never been a right fit.

"Should we go upstairs?" David asked once the cake had been cut and the newlyweds sent off.

She smiled at him. "Sure," she said.

* * *

The steam fogged up the bathroom mirror. She wiped it with the heel of her hand, looking at herself as she dried her hair. Being with David had been like having sex with an excitable Boy Scout, she imagined, all arms and legs and position changes and an eagerness to please. It was as aerobically demanding as a Tae Bo class she once took. It lacked the selfishness of Lorenzo or what she imagined would be the passion of Ben. Not her proudest moment, but it had felt good to be wanted.

"Hey, sorry man, let me see where it may have dropped," David said, opening the door with only his towel wrapped around his waist.

Ben heard someone in the bathroom, and with an uneasy feeling, he asked, "Do you have a guest in there?" motioning to the closed door.

David smirked, "Fuck yeah," he said quietly.

The room looked like a hurricane of sheets and pillows. David threw the blankets back on the bed along with a wad of red fabric, searching for Ben's wallet. Ben's eyes darted toward the familiar color as the door to the bathroom opened.

"David, do you know where my dress is?" Camila asked, walking into the room, wearing a towel.

She froze. Why was he here? Why wasn't David dressed yet? If it were possible for the room to open up and swallow her and the flimsy towel she had covering her naked body, she would have been elated. But no such luck.

David broke the silence, retrieving Ben's wallet from under a pile of clothes. "Here it is."

Ben didn't break his stare, swallowed hard, and extended his hand to David.

"Thanks," he said, struggling to get out of the room as fast as he could and closing the door behind him.

Ben rode the elevator down to the lobby in silence. He saw his family gathered by the hostess desk waiting to be seated and hoped his nephews would be able to distract him from the mixture of jealousy and guilt simmering inside him. David had just spent a full night with Camila, and all he had were a few stolen moments. But even the memory of those brief moments paralyzed him. She captivated him, and it had felt so good to touch her. Better than good. To feel the warmth of her skin along his palm, to let his fingertips glide along her body. He felt like he was gasping for air. Like he was drowning in a pool of unfulfilled desire and conflict.

Through some miracle, brunch came and went with zero awkward interactions. Camila and Ben stayed as far apart as the restaurant would allow throughout the meal. She shared a cab back to the airport later that evening with Tyler after a prolonged tongue-tying session with David, happy for the affection but ready to return to normal life.

"You've been rather quiet," Tyler said as they buckled themselves in for takeoff.

"Ben walked in on me and David," she said flatly.

He choked on his laughter.

"Do you think we can get those oxygen masks to drop down even if we haven't lost cabin pressure?"

"I know," she said, dropping her face into her hand.

"Cami, he saw you guys together, together?"

"No, I mean David wasn't *in* me at the time exactly but might as well have been. We had post-sex guilt written all over our faces, and we were both just wearing towels."

"Well, you shouldn't feel guilty. You're not married. You can have sex with whoever you choose, consensually, of course, and Ben can't be shocked that you guys got together."

"Yeah, you're right."

"Then why do you feel like shit?"

"I don't know. Maybe because I feel like I cheated in some weird way."

"So, you're supposed to stay celibate, and he can do whatever he likes? That's not fair, and I'm sure he doesn't see it that way."

She stared ahead, watching the last few passengers board the plane.

"Cami, he wouldn't ask that of you, and you shouldn't ask that of yourself."

"I know, but it still feels dirty somehow."

She wished that either she and Ben had never met or they had met before Tiffany. She rested her head on Tyler's shoulder and tried to sleep as the plane took off.

12

For the second week in a row, Camila was greeted in class by the empty chair behind her. She felt a small pang of loneliness. She was happy Ben was with Tiffany. They were probably having a spectacular time swimming and surfing and having sex and snorkeling and having more sex.

She opened her notebook, doodling, zoning out until Señora Escobedo arrived, and the thud of someone sitting behind her startled her. In Ben's chair. She sighed and chewed on the end of her pen, not giving the perpetrator the satisfaction of turning around. She felt a light touch on her right shoulder and a tug on her ponytail. She swung around, ready to unleash her fury on whoever had taken Ben's seat and for pulling on her fucking ponytail, when her eyes locked in on the handsome, albeit more tanned face, she had missed for the past two weeks.

She would have loved to jump into his arms.

"Hey, Camila." He smiled back. She could feel the heat radiating off his skin.

"Coffee, after?" she asked quickly as Señora Escobedo started class.

"Yes," he whispered back, sending a shiver up her spine.

During their break, she called Tyler to let him know he didn't have to pick her up. She had a ride home. She knew he would understand Ben was back.

"How was the honeymoon?" She said, sitting down with their drinks at the cafe. "I can't wait to hear all about it. Of course, censor the steamy stuff." She was trying to make a joke.

He smiled one of those knee-weakening grins as he ran his hand through his hair, hair in need of a trim, hair now with golden flecks. What would it feel like to have that smile hover over her with her legs wrapped around him? She started to feel a rumbling in her pelvis and noticed the golden shade of his recently sun-kissed skin. Fuck.

"First," he said, "did you have fun with Dave at the wedding?"

"Oh yeah, sorry you had to see that." She blushed. "But yeah, it was nice to see him again."

"Did he behave himself?"

"Yeah, he did. Is this you being protective, Ben?" She liked teasing him. "So how was the honeymoon? For real, did you have fun?" She asked, licking her straw. "I've always wanted to go to Bali."

"We went snorkeling and did a lot of lying around. We studied a bit." It was hard for him to remember the details now that he sat before Camila again. Unable to tear his eyes away from her mouth and what it was doing to her straw.

"Wait, wait, wait," she said. "Are you telling me that you took schoolbooks with you on your honeymoon?!"

He looked embarrassed. "Well, I mean, we were there for nearly two weeks straight. There's only so much relaxing a person can do."

She was still staring at him wide-eyed but tried to dampen her shock. "Well, it sounds like heaven," she said, sighing, clutching her hands to her chest and thinking of all the other things besides studying she would have done in Bali.

As they finished their drinks, she toyed with asking the one question that had preoccupied her since Hawaii.

"What?" he said. "You're chewing on your lip. What is it?"

"Oh," she said, smiling, "I was a bit confused when I met your dad, and I, well, I was wondering why you never told me about your father."

"What about him?"

"Ben, you don't have to talk about it if you don't want. Stephanie explained everything."

"I see," he said.

"But why didn't you tell me yourself?"

"It's not you, Camila. I don't like to think about the time before."

She should have kept her mouth shut for his sake, but she asked, "Do you know where your biological dad is?"

He sighed.

"I don't. It wasn't a very happy childhood. My mom did her best, but Steph and I knew what was going on. I still remember the muffled sounds of things being slammed against the wall through the closed door."

"Ben." She reached across the table, squeezing his hand. "You don't have to talk about it."

"You deserve to know. You're my friend, and I've been less than honest now, twice."

She smiled at him. "I'm not going to hold that over your head forever."

"Thanks."

She laughed. "Maybe just a few more years."

He leaned on the table, shoulders slumped. "I think my mom wanted to leave him, but the alternative was also scary. Out there with two small kids and no real job. But the night I got this," he said, pointing at his scar, "that was her line in the sand."

He took a sip of his coffee. "When we finally left and settled down, my mom was able to get divorced. That's when she started dating my stepdad. At first, I didn't want him around. You can imagine I had some trust issues. But he didn't push me. He needed us as much as we needed him."

"How so?"

"Well, his wife and only child had been killed by a drunk driver five years before he met us."

Camila gasped and covered her mouth.

"He didn't talk about them much in the beginning," he said. "But slowly he let us in. He had thrown himself into his work. When he joined our family, it was his chance to rescue us and, in a way, make up for not being able to rescue his own family."

A tear slid down her cheek.

"I didn't mean to upset you," he said.

"You didn't. I'm just so sorry."

"Your family has had its own tragedy," he said.

"Yes, but to lose your child. To never know who he or she will grow up to be. I'm not sure you ever get over that."

"Yeah, I guess it's different to lose the promise of who someone will become and all the memories that would have been created."

"Yeah, I think it's a different kind of suffering," she said. "I mean, when my dad died, I like to think he had the joy of watching me from above. That he could see me have a full life, knowing my mom would make sure it was never lacking. But could you imagine never knowing your child? If the baby you held in your arms were to be taken away in an instant because of a drunk driver. I mean that would break a person, like, irreparably."

*　*　*

There were only a few weeks left with two major assignments looming. They'd watch the movie at Camila's and then carpool to Rosarito with their class a few weeks later.

"Hey, you won't be needing to drive me home for much longer," she said to Ben after class. They were sitting at their usual table in the café.

His heart dropped. "Oh, how come?" He asked, feigning levity.

"Well, I almost have enough for a new car."

"That's great. But do you want to buy a car even though you're planning on moving after graduation?"

"Well, yeah, I can leave it at my mom's place for when I visit."

Bella called to them from the counter. "Hey, you guys, drinks are up," she said.

"I got it." Camila jumped up in her yellow sundress, which skimmed her mid-thigh. Ben had kept the car windows up despite the heat to prevent the flutter of her hem when she first sat in his car.

When she sat back down with their drinks, he told her, "I don't mind driving you if you want to save your money."

"Ben, I owe you like a million favors for driving me around these past few months."

"I don't mind."

"We can still go to coffee after," she said. "Even though we're almost done with class."

He had tried to keep his somber mood at bay. "I know."

She looked concerned. "Are *you* okay?"

He rubbed his eyes with the thumb and forefinger of his left hand. His ring flashing under the lights.

"Yeah. No. I don't know."

"What is going on?" she said, pulling his hand from his face.

He had struggled with telling her the whole truth. What purpose would it serve? The truth. Was his honesty for her or himself?

"I still think about you a lot," he said.

"Ben, we're friends," Camila said, shifting in her seat. "I like you as a friend, but I won't allow myself more."

"I know," he replied faintly.

"It doesn't mean there isn't anything more. If you only knew about the thoughts I have running around in my mind. But I'm able to satisfy myself knowing that at least I have you in my life in some way. Someone to remind me of what type of man I want in my life one day."

"I have a lot to work on, Camila. I wouldn't model anyone after me," Ben said.

"To me you don't, and I have to have faith that this is more than just bad timing. I have to believe we met for a reason, and not so that I can practice self-restraint. If I don't learn something from all of this and just let myself wallow in the emptiness that I feel during those quiet moments when it really sinks in that I'll never have you, then I'm just suffering. There is no point to that."

None of what she said had comforted him. It was a rehashing of what he was struggling with daily.

"Full truth, Ben, is this going to be a problem?" she asked, motioning between them. "Because if being apart from Tiffany makes this harder, then I'll just leave you alone, 'cause this makes me no better than the girl who Lorenzo left me for." It wasn't a fair comparison since Lorenzo was an asshole who would have cheated on her eventually, regardless of how much or little distance was between them, and Ben was a generous and thoughtful man who was struggling.

He rubbed his face. "No, I don't... I don't know," he said, exhaling.

Words were now tumbling out of her mouth, "I would never want to make your life difficult," she said. "And I could never... I mean, you're married... and Ben, I mean, there are only a few classes left. Should we spend some time apart? I can ask Tyler to pick me up after class."

"Camila, it's okay," he said, sighing out his frustration. He looked at her, transfixed. He needed to snap back into reality and roughly ran his hands through his hair. "I don't want to spend time apart. It'll be fine," he said committedly.

"Okay, so, um, that night in Hawaii wasn't an accident then, was it?" she asked.

Everything flashed before him, the softness of her skin, the glint of desire and shock in her eyes. Her full lips. She was sitting in front of him now like torture in human form. All he wanted to do was grab her and pull her beneath him. Take her clothes off and see what he had felt. Lay kisses on the path his hand had taken weeks before.

"Ben?"

"Yeah."

"Was it an accident?"

She needed to know the answer. She had determined it was an accident for them both because, well, because it had to be an accident. It was the night before his wedding, and he had looked so conflicted and on the brink of tears when she found him. She had planned to never mention it again, and his silence on the topic had made her believe that she had placed too much importance on the incident.

"What do you want me to say?" he asked innocently.

"I don't know," she said, rubbing her palm against her forehead. "I want you to tell me the truth."

He didn't answer, playing with the napkin on the table.

"Ben, look at me."

His eyes flashed up, holding her gaze.

"If I would have stayed with you," she said. "If I had locked the door behind me instead of walking away with David that night, what would have happened?"

He looked at her but didn't say anything.

It felt like a lifetime passed. She stood, pushing her chair out. "I think I should go."

He remained seated, looking up at her. "I'm sorry, Camila."

"There's nothing to apologize for. Nothing happened. I'm just going to leave right now before something does."

* * *

Time. Time is what they needed. Time apart. Never had she been more grateful for the stress of her dissertation. Things had been painfully awkward between them, and she needed two weeks away. Away from him and his sweetness, his kindness, his strong arms. The smile that made her lose track of time and the eyes that made her feel like she was known.

She couldn't risk any distraction. Her defense was in two weeks, and she told him she couldn't meet for coffee for two weeks. It was a necessary exaggeration.

"You still need a ride home?" he asked her, smiling.

She was glad for any justified extra time they could spend together. She smiled back. "Yeah, that would be great."

He survived off minuscule fragments of time together for the next few weeks. The fifteen-minute break during class, the short drive home.

They walked in silence, side by side, on the way to his car. It was only a few days until her defense. She was distracted, living in her head. He could sense her anxiety.

"Okay, I just wanted to say good luck," he told her. "I know you'll do great."

"Thanks," she said. Her nerves were visible.

They walked down the stairs toward the parking lot. The campus was nearly empty. He could have easily wrapped his arm around her and coaxed her close, placing his mouth onto hers. No one would see him. He could finally taste her and stop tormenting himself with curiosity. He could slide his palm along her face and rub his thumb across her bottom lip, let her suck on it, and feel her tongue against his skin again.

They were both lost in thought and nearly walked beyond the

parking lot, forcing Ben to steer her sharply to the right and into the lot.

The ride home was as quiet as it had been over the past few weeks. She seemed half present. When he pulled up to her home, she got out and nearly closed the door before saying goodbye.

"Sorry, Ben," she said, snapping out of her stupor. She bent down to see him looking at her. "Thanks for the ride."

"It'll be okay. Don't worry."

"I'll feel better soon. Once I know I passed," she said.

"Yeah, for sure. And please do pass, 'cause I'm going through caffeine withdrawals."

"Okay." She laughed. "If everything goes well, I owe you."

"Deal."

*　*　*

"What are the flowers for?" Camila gasped as Ben entered with a small bouquet of tulips.

"For being finished."

She had called him, the one time she reached out, when she passed her defense.

"Oh, thank you." It took all her willpower to stop herself from throwing her arms around his neck. Instead, she held up a VHS and said, "I got the last copy! I guess *Like Water for Chocolate* is a popular movie in Brentwood."

He laughed. "I'm sure."

"Okay, I got popcorn and soda, and we can order pizza once Tyler gets home."

"Sounds great."

Over the past few weeks, it had become more difficult for Ben to exercise his willpower. With the weather warming, her clothing had become progressively skimpier. Thank God, she was wearing a long white dress today that hid her figure and only exposed her arms and shoulders. But relief was short-lived. The dress was made of the flimsiest of fabrics, and he could see the contour of her legs as she strolled to the kitchen and back.

She rested her hands against the kitchen counter and waited for her pulse to settle. They had both done their part. He was dressed like he was headed to the gym, and she had worn the least flattering dress she owned. It was billowy and could easily be mistaken for maternity wear. Maybe it was? She didn't remember what rack she pulled it off of at Marshalls. But it was light, and she was hot, both because of the weather and his proximity. She placed the vase of flowers on the table and sat on the couch, tucking her leg and dress beneath her as she grabbed the remote.

Two hours later she was even more uncomfortable being alone with him. Camila finally understood how Gertrudis had started the fire without a single match. Willed it from pure lust and desire. Fucking Gertrudis and that damn quail recipe. Fuck! Heat traveled along Camila's skin, and she felt like she had electricity coursing through her veins. She couldn't breathe. Her heart rate hadn't dipped into the normal range since he had arrived. If she didn't do something quickly, she'd implode. He had adjusted himself enough times during the film, apparently equally uneasy. She had to do something.

"Okay, let's watch something less, um, intense," she said.

"Yes, please."

"We answered all the questions for Señora, right?"

He scanned the questionnaire their teacher had assigned with the film. "Yeah, we're good," he said.

Her eyes tracked across all the films they had collected over the years. A collection of rom-coms she and Tyler watched and rewatched as needed. A random gay porn, hidden in a Cindy Crawford workout case (she had learned that lesson the hard way). Her finger landed on a safe, non-sexy movie about surfing, and she slipped the video into the VCR.

"What's that?" he asked.

"*Blue Crush.*"

"I haven't seen that one."

"I'm not really surprised. It's kind of a girl movie," she said, grinning.

"Okay," he replied, not bothering to argue. He needed the distraction. Maybe he could even fall asleep and wake up not attracted to her. Unlikely.

"Do you want anything else?" she asked before pressing play. Only a few more minutes before Tyler would be home, she thought, and relief washed over her.

Somewhere between the first surfing sequence and Kate Bosworth realizing she wasn't football-girlfriend material, they both fell asleep. The room was dark as she squinted her eyes open. The light on the patio created a long shadow on the floor, the TV black, the gentle hum of the VCR the only sound.

Not the only sound.

The soft cadence of breath reached her ears. His arm was draped over her. How did they end up spooning? They had started a movie and sat responsibly on opposite sides of the couch, and it had finished as indicated by the ejected tape, but what time was it? She saw the clock on the microwave door. Still early, not yet midnight. Was Tyler home? Had he found them like this? Together?

She attempted to extricate herself but fell back into him. She didn't want to leave him. But she should, shouldn't she? Yes, she should. He was fast asleep. All of him except...

The incline created when the futon folded into a couch made it impossible to keep even a sliver of space between them. She felt him. All of him up against her. The combination of his basketball shorts and her gauzy dress left little to the imagination. She felt a warm flush spread across her chest, a trembling in her gut. She just wouldn't move. But for how long?

Unfortunately, he pulled her closer to his hardness with the arm belted across her. Her eyes fluttered closed, but she couldn't escape the feeling of him pressed against her. She tried to adjust herself, but all she accomplished was rubbing him against her backside, which made her shudder. Holy fuck.

He was hard, and she was suffocating with lust. And fucking Tyler had flaked on her.

She felt her nipples tighten beneath her dress, but she was already lost. She felt him again and began to writhe rhythmically against him. He was still asleep, and she listened intently to his breath. Carefully pulling her dress up, she slipped her hand toward the front of her panties, and without a consideration for anything or anyone besides her own flaming desire, she slipped her fingers under. She gasped, feeling her engorged body against her fingertips. This wouldn't take long. She licked her lips and bit down hard, trying to settle her breathing and the moan that begged to escape from her mouth. Her chest heaved up and down as her subtle movements exaggerated her need. Suddenly, she heard a deep exhale from behind her. She froze. But he didn't move. She had a few more moments to capitalize on his dreamlike state. But her heart stopped completely when his arm moved swiftly and landed on the exposed skin of her right leg. She was caught. She was literally going to die of embarrassment and prayed to disappear into the couch. But as she was calculating the extent of her mortification, his fingers pressed into her skin.

He had opened his eyes to find her hair spilling over his left arm and her shoulder rising and falling to the pattern of her breath before she had started to move. Each subtle movement propelling him into a state of temporary insanity. He winced as he felt her soft flesh through the flimsy clothing that separated them. When he reached out for her leg, he wasn't certain whether he wanted to dissuade or encourage her. He felt her body stiffen. As he pressed his fingertips into the soft skin of her leg, he had a choice. He had a moment, a sliver of time to change the direction of his life. To ruin one life and start another. To fall into the fragrant, exotic world she had opened to him or to... Fuck it.

He wanted what felt good. Now. Not in the future, right now. And she felt amazing in his arms.

After what felt like an eternity, she felt him pull her body towards him once more. She slowly glided against him, and his fingers pressed deeper into her skin. She let out an audible breath as she heard him whisper her name.

She removed her hand and reached behind, resting it gently on the back of his neck and pulling him down to her. He responded, inhaling her scent, his lips skimming her skin. They moved together slowly as he exhaled her name into her ear. She brought her hand down gently onto his. They interlocked, and with no resistance, she slid their unified hands beneath her dress, resting them on her flat, warm stomach. She released herself from their intertwined fingers, and her hand now resumed the gentle pressure she had been applying between her legs.

"Ben," she moaned. "Oh my God, Ben, I can't stop." She was gyrating with more speed.

"Camila," he whispered, his hand flat on her stomach.

"Ben, I'm close. Please, I can't." She stuttered the words out.

He exhaled. "Camila, fuck." His eyes shot open, and his muscles stiffened. It was as if he woke from a trance. His hand abruptly left her body, gently pushing her off and making space between them.

A stifled cry caught in her throat, and she sat up, running her fingers through her hair.

They escaped to the farthest corners of the futon, like magnets with the same charge.

His respirations were rapid, his heartbeat echoing in his ears. This counted as cheating, right? He was now a cheater. He cheated on Tiffany. No better than his own father. He held his face in his hands, but with his eyes closed, he replayed the scene of her body pressed up against his, his hand trailing up her leg.

"I've never heard you curse before," she said after a few minutes of stunned silence.

"I've never had a reason to before."

"You should probably leave."

"Yeah, I should," he said.

Her arms ached to hold him, and a pulsating sensation still lingered between her legs.

She looked at him, and she hoped he could read what she was asking with her eyes: *Why are you still here if we both agreed that you should leave?*

He looked down at his lap. "I can't exactly get up right now," he said.

She desperately wished she could take his hand and lead him to her bedroom, making use of his predicament. "Oh. Okay, I have to take a shower. Will you just close the door behind you?"

She got up and walked past him to the bathroom. She knew she was playing with fire, but as she pulled down the straps of her dress and let it fall to her waist, she looked over her shoulder. A simple glance, a peek, and an obvious invitation. Then she closed the door.

He rested his head back on the couch. He heard the shower turn on. She was a mere fifteen feet away. Only fifteen feet and a thin plywood door were separating him from her. From her perfectly full lips. From her soft, supple skin. From her perky breasts and curvaceous hips that led to her. . .

This was not helping. He still couldn't stand, and now he was considering heading for the bathroom door instead of the front door. That's all he had to do. Walk to the left instead of the right. Place his hand on the doorknob and open the bathroom door.

He stood and turned.

Ten feet.

He could still turn around and leave.

Five feet.

He heard the shower curtain draw open and again close. She was naked now. Her skin would be moistened and even lathered with some intoxicating body wash. Her dress was in a pile on the floor, whatever lacy bra she wore, matching panties.

One foot.

He placed his hand on the doorknob. All he had to do was turn it. He was already there. His fingers gently gripped the metal, and he began to twist his wrist when he heard a key insert into the front door.

"Hey, Ben," Tyler said as he came in.

He jumped at the sound of the keys being thrown on the table. "Oh, hey Tyler," Ben said as he quickly withdrew his hand and spun around.

"You, okay?" Tyler said, looking from Ben's face to the partial hard-on in his pants.

"Yeah, I am fine," Ben said, embarrassed. "Just leaving. See you later."

*　*　*

"TYLER! Where were you?" Camila yelled a few minutes later as she came out of the shower drying her hair.

"What? I called! There was this nasty ruptured appy that I got to watch, so I stayed late. Why, what happened?"

"Fuck! My phone was on silent. Fuck."

"Oh, shit. What happened, Cami?"

"Well, I nearly rubbed myself raw against him."

"Well, that explains the look on his face, but I'm not sure I understand you correctly. I'm going to sit down, and I need you to say that over again, slowly," Tyler said.

He sat there on the floor, in his dirty scrubs, slack-jawed, eyes wide, as Camila gave him the excruciating details of the past few hours of her life.

"Tyler, say something," she pleaded afterward.

He ran a hand over his fatigued face. He got up and began to slowly pace the room.

"You guys are being reckless. Someone is going to get hurt."

13

Tyler had dropped her off on campus early, and she spent the morning distracted, rereading the same line in the same research article she had lying on her desk for the past month. Two days wasn't enough for the guilt, desire, and confusion to pass. They needed to talk about what happened. She decided to break the promise to herself and call him again. This way she could control the narrative. They could meet before class, clear the air, and everything would go back to normal.

"Hey, can you meet me in the Sculpture Garden before class?" she asked once he picked up.

She had avoided reaching out to him to minimize any temptation, but clearly it hadn't worked. If she saw him in class, that couldn't be helped, but if she actively pursued spending more time with him, she would be complicit. Until now she had only ever called him after her thesis defense.

He was waiting by the fountain when she arrived. The clouds looked heavy and ominous. She was grateful she had thrown a sweater over her short dress, which fluttered in the breeze as she walked up to him.

No hug.

No need for additional physical contact after Saturday night.

"How are you?"

"I'm good, you?" he said.

They walked between the sculptures and headed toward a bench next to a statue affectionately nicknamed *The Freshman Fifteen*. Camila hated the name. To her it was a beautiful woman, basking in the sun, unashamed of her voluptuous curves.

"Ben, I'm just going to come out and say it. I'm sorry about Saturday night. I mean, I'm not sorry it happened, to be honest, but I'm sorry I put you in that position. I know that sounds bad, but what I feel for you is overwhelming, and sometimes it just consumes me."

The silence was deafening. Why was he so quiet? Maybe she had misread his response the previous night. What if she had made something of nothing? No, she distinctly remembered him being a willing participant.

"I mean, I *really* like you as a friend." She was rambling now. "But it's only because I won't allow myself more, not that there isn't more. And I still want to stay your friend, but I can't. I can't seem to control myself, and I'm embarrassed, and at the same time I'm not sorry for what I feel."

He stopped, turning to face her. "It's not just you, Camila. I feel it too."

"What are we going to do?" she asked, exacerbated.

"There's nothing to do," he said.

The wind rustled the branches of the trees. A few students meandered by through the grass.

"I don't want to stop being friends," she said. "Let's just be careful. You leave in less than a month, and after the class trip, we don't have a reason to see each other again." The thought terrified her greatly and relieved her only a little.

They walked side by side, headed toward class as the magic of dusk settled around them.

"Well, tonight will be one less class. That should be helpful," he said, a failed attempt at humor.

"I guess we truly did just meet at the wrong time and place," she said.

"I thought you said everything happens for a reason."

"It does, but sometimes we don't know why. Sometimes we never know."

* * *

After class, they were quieter than usual as they walked to his car that evening.

"Maybe we just try to not be alone together," she wondered out loud.

"Mm-hmm."

"But you can still give me a ride home if you want," she said with caution, "since I hadn't made plans for our new rules of engagement."

"Sure." He smiled, gently nudging her with his elbow.

There's nothing sexy about an elbow, she thought. Still, they touched.

She threw her sweater in the back as the car windows fogged. The music blared from the radio as they each stewed in their own thoughts. She sang along as he drove them through the familiar streets of Westwood, streets they had taken together for months now, when their relationship was purely a friendship and not hampered by the pull of desire.

"Maybe we should stop getting coffee after class," she said, fearful that he would agree.

His jaw tightened at the suggestion. "Baby steps, okay?" he said.

"Okay," she smiled back, relieved that he didn't want to drop her like a bad habit.

The rain picked up as he made a right on San Vicente. Coral Tree was only a block away, but the lights were scattered as the rain became torrential. A car suddenly pulled out in front of them. Camila screamed, and Ben slammed on the brakes, sending their car into a fishtail.

His hand flew out reflexively toward her, acting like a human seat belt as he regained control of the car and quickly pulled over.

"Camila, Camila! Are you okay?"

Her eyes fluttered as she leaned her head back. It was happening again: a dark haziness encircling her visual field.

Inhale. Exhale. Inhale. Exhale.

The rain was so hard she couldn't hear anything but the beating of her heart in her ears.

She heard the faint call of her name.

They hadn't crashed, but she wasn't responding and looked like she had passed out. He undid his seatbelt and hers, grabbed her around the waist, and pulled her onto his lap.

Her head rested against him, and he felt for her pulse. She was still warm, breathing.

"Camila," he whispered, holding her tightly to him with one arm and stroking her hair with his free hand.

She finally looked up at him. "Hey, Camila," he said, smiling.

"What happened?"

"You blacked out after that guy pulled out in front of us."

"Did we get into an accident?"

"Almost, but no, we're okay." He smiled, inadvertently letting his hand rest on her thigh as she sat in his lap. She nestled her head into his neck and closed her eyes.

"I think you had a panic attack," he said.

"Yeah, I get those apparently," she whispered. "I had one after my accident."

He held her, never wanting to leave. He had her in his arms, alone. The rain created the privacy they were trying to avoid but also yearning for. He rested his chin on her head. He swallowed hard and unconsciously started to stroke her leg. His palm lay flat on her skin as he gently moved back and forth. What was once a reassuring gesture now had a completely different meaning. Her dress fell back when he pulled her onto his lap, and his hand easily found its way up her leg. His fingers searching for the edge of her underwear, waiting for an indication of where he should stop.

Higher.

Higher.

Nothing.

She heard him clear his throat as his fingers continued to reach for the thong she was certain he didn't know she was wearing. She smiled to herself. His hand firmly on her now, she pushed herself off his chest, leaving one hand resting on him. They stared at each other. Her eyes moved from his eyes to his mouth and back up. If only he'd move his hand the smallest distance, he would feel what he did to her, she thought. He closed his eyes, leaning his head back, and blew out a long and slow breath. She saw him swallow down whatever he wanted to say.

He looked tormented.

"Are you okay?" she asked.

"Yeah," he said, bringing his face within a few inches of hers.

She bit her lower lip as her hand drifted along his jaw. Her fingers running along the scar now so familiar and over his lips. His hand held her backside and felt like fire on her skin. She ran her thumb over his mouth, and he parted his lips.

"Ben," she said, breathing into his mouth, her lips closer.

This was exactly what they had agreed to avoid a few hours earlier, but being face to face made stepping away much more difficult. The windows were opaque with steam, and the street had emptied out. The world had created a sanctuary for their suppressed need.

She cupped her hand alongside his face, feeling his stubble, and placed a soft kiss along his jaw and moved down his neck, placing kisses like small flutters of butterfly wings. His skin was softer than she imagined. She moved back upward until she faced him again and then gently ran her tongue across his lower lip and felt him stir under her. She pulled him closer, tenderly placed her lips on top of his, and slipped her tongue into his mouth. A moan spilled from both. Their kiss became increasingly more intense. He tasted like mint and honey. She shifted, straddling him. His hands traveled up her back over her dress. He pressed her into him, letting out a groan, and he buried his face into her neck as she tilted her head back. He inhaled deeply, breathing her in, intoxicated by her scent. She could feel his readiness between her legs, and he tangled his fingers in her hair. She pressed herself back into him, starting to shift back and forth slowly. Her mouth was hungry for his, and she sucked hard on his lower lip. His thumb grazed the corner of her mouth, and she turned, giving him a half smile, and took his finger into her mouth, sucking delicately. Rocking faster, she felt a movement deep within her begin to stir.

She guided his hand to her chest, opened the few buttons at the top of her dress, and her breasts pressed against him, cupped in her lace bra. His hand gently traced the curve of her body, and his thumb felt the rigid tip of her nipple, aching for his touch. He lay his palm on her chest, feeling her soft skin and the steady beating of her heart. Before she could slip the straps down over her shoulders, everything stopped, and he froze.

She felt it. The sudden shift in the air, once sizzling, now ice cold. The spell had been broken, and she gasped, bringing both her hands to her mouth.

"Oh my God," she said behind her hands. It had felt so good, so right. But in her haze, she had trampled over the agreement they had just made, and not without his help. She quickly straightened her dress and escaped to the passenger seat, where she should have stayed. Reaching into the back seat, she pulled on her sweater. The less visible skin, the better. He wiped his hand across his face, resting it over his mouth.

"I'm sorry," she said, looking away from him.

"Don't be. It was both of us. I'm sorry too," he said in a hush.

He started the car, and the remainder of the drive to her apartment was in silence. He pulled up along the curb, but before he could get out to open her door, she placed her hand on his arm, "Don't get out."

"Why?"

"Just don't. I think we just need space."

"Yeah, okay."

"I'll see you next week in class."

Back in the apartment, she found Tyler sitting on the floor painting his toenails a deep purple. "What's up, sista?"

"Hey Tyler," she said, sitting on the edge of their couch. She stared ahead of her in a daze. What had just happened? It had been amazing and so wrong, but mutual.

"Camila, what's up? You're being weird," he said. There was an incriminatory edge to his voice, and she sprinted to the bathroom.

"Camila!" Tyler yelled, running after her.

She was kneeling beside the toilet seat, holding onto it and dry heaving. She hadn't eaten much, and all that came up was spit and bile. It coated her mouth with acid and stung the back of her throat. Her eyes started to water as she leaned against the tub. Tyler handed her a towel and sat beside her.

"What's going on?" he said.

"I don't know. I just got a wave of nausea."

"You're not, you know, pregnant, right?"

She wiped her mouth with the towel and looked at him with a small smile. "Tyler, you should get a refund from that fancy med school of yours. You need to have sex to get pregnant, remember."

"Very funny. But seriously, did you give yourself salmonella again?"

She shrugged. "Not that I know of, but maybe I ate something funny at work."

"Okay, why don't you shower, and I'll get you some bubbles to drink with dinner. I think we have some seltzer water hidden in the back of the fridge."

It was the first time she had lied to Tyler. She knew exactly what had prompted her nausea. Guilt mixed with anxiety. Now that she had finally felt his arms around her and his mouth on hers, she felt like she was in a free fall. She couldn't trust herself to control her basic impulses.

The shower helped, and by the time she sat in front of Tyler poised to try his attempt at lasagna, she had more control of her senses. The man was many things—a student, a friend, a dancer extraordinaire—but a chef he was not. The first thing she noticed was that the house didn't smell like Italian food. Before she could object, there was a knock at the door.

"Who is that?" she asked, walking to look through the peephole.

"I don't know," Tyler said from the kitchen.

"Oh, hey Bobby!" She said, opening the door and her arms to him.

"Hola, chica!"

"Hey, honey, what are you doing here, and why do you have pizza with you?" Tyler said emerging from the kitchen in his apron.

"Well, when you told me you were cooking for Camila, I wondered if she had done anything to upset you since we all know your cooking should be used as a form of punishment."

"How rude!" He exclaimed.

"Oh, bless you, you wonderful man," Camila said.

They finished their bottle of wine as Camila ate all the pizza crust Tyler had tossed onto the side of her plate.

"You know, Tyler, this would have been pretty good lasagna had it not had the density of a cheesecake," Camila said.

"Or the taste of cardboard," Bobby said.

"You guys are both assholes!" Tyler laughed, throwing his napkin at Camila across the table.

"Well, this asshole needs a favor. I need to buy a car this weekend, and I was wondering if you guys would come with me. I hate the idea of going to a car dealership on my own."

"Why all of a sudden, may I ask?" Tyler said.

"I need to be independent again. I mean, I can't keep asking people to drive me around."

"But aren't you planning on moving soon?" Bobby said.

"This isn't about her move. This is about Ben. Isn't it?" Tyler said.

She rested her face in her hands and her elbows on the table for support.

"I can't be around him for much longer. We only have like two weeks before he moves away, so I want to be respectful."

"So, you want to spend thousands of dollars to be respectful at the last minute after you've been jerking it off to him for three quarters now?" Tyler said. "Did something happen?" He knew her so well.

"No," she lied again.

14

June 2003

Camila and Ben walked toward the parking lot in silence, heavily laden with angst. They decided against going for coffee. She wanted him, and seemingly he wanted her, but neither wanted to put the other in a more compromising position. But she still craved what little time they shared. It may have been calculated, but despite having successfully purchased a car, she still walked with Ben after class as if she needed a ride.

"I'm parked over here." He gestured to the right down an aisle of cars.

"Oh, I bought a car last weekend. I drove myself in today."

He looked surprised, but his voice couldn't hide his disappointment. "Well, let's see it."

"No, no," she said, placing a hand on his stomach to push him away and immediately regretting it. She felt his muscles beneath her hand, firm and strong. She inhaled and dropped her hand into her pocket before it willed itself to touch him again. She only needed a few more days of self-control. They had to survive a trip to Mexico together, buffered by their classmates, and then life would separate them.

"I'll drive us to Mexico this weekend so you can have the full experience."

"Oh, okay," he said, laughing.

* * *

She arrived at his apartment early Saturday morning. They had survived two more classes, and both made different excuses for avoiding post-class coffee. As a peace offering, she stopped at Coral Tree to pick up two coffees for their drive down to Mexico.

"Ta-da," she said proudly, arms extended wide to emphasize the glory that was her new but used car.

"Wow, look at that," he said as he came closer to the not-so-gently used Jetta that was supposed to take them across the border. He was doubting whether they'd make it back after the class trip given its appearance.

"We'll pick up Señora on our way down. She lives in Long Beach," she said.

"Sounds good," he said, fastening his seatbelt.

She wanted to take this final trip with him but didn't want to risk being unsupervised with him again and volunteered to carpool with their professor for the trip. Even in a moving car, she couldn't trust herself to be alone with him.

It was supposed to be a day excursion, to be fully immersed in the Spanish language and as a final outing for their class of twenty students who had come to enjoy their biweekly gatherings.

She hadn't been to Rosarito, but living in San Diego her entire life, Tijuana was always a quick walk across the border until 9/11, when crossing the border became more of an ordeal.

They started out early on Saturday morning, a week before her graduation and Ben's flight to Boston. Their countdown had begun. If they could keep their hands off one another for seven more days, then this friendship wouldn't have any long-term repercussions.

The conversation was light on the way down, answering Señora's questions about their childhoods and families. It was a welcome change to be near each other without the colossal sexual tension that usually seemed to follow them around.

Ben sat in the backseat. He was quiet for much of the trip, a silent observer watching Camila as she talked. He took in her profile as she smiled, the way she'd wrinkle up her nose right before she laughed out loud, the way she would flip her hair. He watched as she adjusted her grip on the wheel and the bangles slid down her arm or the way she'd lean on her hand and expose her neck, elongated so he could see her pulse rise and fall as she drove. He didn't know when he'd see those features again. He tried to memorize as much of her as he could to take with him.

They arrived in Rosarito in the late morning and met their other classmates at a restaurant for lunch before touring a few galleries. The remainder of the afternoon was filled with shopping before their late afternoon drive home.

"Hey, let's go back to those stores we saw before we meet Señora," she said. "I want to get Tyler a tacky, touristy T-shirt," she said with a smile.

As they headed back to the busy street lined with souvenir shops, Camila's phone rang.

"Who is calling me here?" she said, fumbling in her purse for her phone.

"Hello?"

"Camila?"

"Yes, who is this?" She asked, putting a finger in her ear to aid in hearing over the sound of traffic coming through the speaker.

"It's Señora Escobedo. I'm sorry, I just received a call. My daughter broke her arm at school, and I need to leave immediately. I grabbed a ride with the others. I just didn't want you waiting for me."

"Oh, I hope everything is okay. Drive safely."

She threw her phone in her bag, and a small tickle of anxiety began to gnaw at her. "Señora had to go up with the others. Her daughter had an accident at school."

"Is she okay?"

"I'm not sure. She didn't say."

Camila perused the tables covered with cheaply made T-shirts and tank tops, sure to both offend and delight Tyler with their gaudiness. Ben meandered between the aisles of hot sauce and trinkets, thinking of what would be least useless for Tiffany.

"What did you get?" she said.

"A shot glass."

"For Tiffany?"

He smiled. "Yeah, she can put her jewelry in it or something."

Camila didn't recall Tiffany wearing much jewelry besides her wedding ring. But there was so much Camila didn't know about

Tiffany. Perhaps that was why it was difficult to picture Tiffany with Ben. When he smiled, it was supposed to be for Camila. When she looked at his arms, they belonged around her. When she looked at his lips, parted as he listened to her deep in conversation, they belonged to her. How could the world have gotten it so wrong? She felt with more conviction than ever before that she and Ben were not supposed to part ways. They were supposed to have a life together. She painfully swallowed down the emotion she felt as she walked up to him. "We should head back," Camila said as they exited the store.

They walked in silence. Thin plastic bags of souvenirs in hand, they strolled the length of the beach to her car.

"This is our last day together, you know."

"I do," he replied.

"I'm going to miss you," she said, nudging him toward the tide.

"Me too."

"I'm really happy I met you," she said.

"Not as happy as me," he said.

There was a heavy quiet between them as they walked, the waves crashing, and the sound of children playing in the distance.

Was this how it was supposed to end? he thought. A year to learn about his wants and desires just to turn around and let them slip through his fingers? Maybe discovering what he wanted didn't necessarily mean indulging in that truth. Maybe merely knowing was enough. He didn't have to act on his newfound passion and thereby destroy the hopes and expectations of his wife and their families.

"You know you can come visit," he said, certain she wouldn't.

"Thanks, but I think we both know that's not something we should do. You'll be busy anyway, and I'll hopefully be in some exotic, far-off place by the time you're settled."

She felt bad, dismissing him. He looked hurt, shoving his hands in his pockets and looking ahead as they continued to walk side by side.

She didn't mean to be abrupt.

"Ben, maybe if we had met at a different time or under different circumstances, we could have been more. But I'm happy for the time we did have."

She said it as if she was breaking up with him. As if they knew that despite promises to maintain a long-distance friendship, it would fade. Maybe they would send each other birthday wishes for the first few years or share pictures of their growing families. But over time they would only live in each other's past as faint memories of a time when they each cared about the other more intensely than they could admit.

He didn't reply.

"Maybe in another lifetime our timing will be better," she said, trying to fill the space between them with words and carry the conversation during their last few moments together.

She smiled up at him, hoping to see humor in his face, trying hard to lighten the mood, but all that was looking back at her was a seriousness she didn't expect.

"Just try not to forget me. That would truly break my heart," she said.

"I won't ever forget you, Camila. You've helped me find myself again."

"You were doing fine on your own. I just came along to add a little flavor."

She started the car and pulled out on the main road. The car smelled like the ocean and was covered in sand as they drove. A stillness settled between them as they waited for the light to change. Suddenly the engine stopped running. She reached for the keys and turned them to hear the engine turn over, but every time she let go of the key, the car turned off.

"Pull over," he said. "There's a spot right there." He pointed, reaching over to keep the key turned in place as she pulled the car off the road.

"What the fuck!" She said, slamming her hands against the steering wheel.

"It's okay. I think it's probably the ignition switch. Your car will drive as long as the key is held in place."

"Great," she said, dropping her head onto her hands, clutching the wheel, "I'm cursed when it comes to cars."

"It's not that serious; we'll get it fixed. I think I saw a mechanic on our way in."

The bell over the door jingled as they entered the mechanic shop.

"Hola?" she called over the music blaring from the radio behind the counter.

A middle-aged man covered in car exhaust and a thick layer of grease on his pants appeared, wiping his hands on an equally soiled rag.

"Hola señorita. En qué puedo ayudarla?" he asked while eyeing Ben up and down.

"Hola señor, nuestro coche…" she said.

"I speak English," the man said, leaning on the counter and appreciating her attempt at speaking Spanish.

"Oh, thank you. Um, my car is parked down the street, but when I turn it on, it won't stay on. Can you fix it?"

"Claro que sí, pero," he said. "I'm closing the shop in 10 minutes."

"But sir, we have to go back tonight," Camila said.

"Sí, pero, I'm sorry I can't tonight. My niece is getting married tonight, so I'm closing early. But we can bring your car here, and I'll fix it en la mañana."

"Señor, por favor," she said. "Is there anything we can do to have you fix it tonight?" Not exactly sure what she could offer since all her money had been invested into the same pile of junk she now needed to fix.

"I'm sorry, señorita, pero you and your novio can stay at the hotel down the street tonight, and I'll keep your car here and have it ready by noon mañana."

Camila spun around, frustrated, tears brimming.

"Un momento, por favor," Ben said. The man raised his hands in understanding and disappeared back into his shop.

Ben turned to her, leaning on the counter, "Camila, we don't really have a choice. Listen, we can stay the night. I'll take care of it. Then we can leave in the morning. It's not like we have a lot of other options."

"Fuck," she whispered.

"It's not that bad. We could have gotten stuck outside of town."

She looked up at him. "Do you ever get pissed off?"

He laughed. "Listen, we can't control this. Like someone I know would say, this was destined."

She dropped her head into her hand and leaned into him. He put a soft hand on her back.

"Fine," she mumbled.

With the help of a few extra hands, they managed to get her car into the shop and then walked the short distance to the quaint beachside motel.

They were welcomed by a pleasant woman in her fifties, with bright red lipstick and an embroidered floral dress with a traditional Mexican pattern along the hem. The back door opened directly onto the beach and the sound of the waves crashing in the distance. The TV in the lobby was playing a very intense telenovela on mute that had the complete attention of the older man sitting on a single chair behind the desk, his hands folded carefully over his cane. It was hard to imagine he had ever been young. His skin was so wrinkled, his hair white, and his knuckles knobbly. He was less an employee and more a fixture, it seemed.

"Oh, you must be the couple my brother told me about," the woman said.

"Your brother is the mechanic?" Camila had the sinking feeling that she may have just been tricked into renting a hotel room for the night.

"Sí, señorita, he called over and said your car needs to be fixed but not until tomorrow."

"Sí," Camila said, frustrated even more by the rehashing of the story. "Can we have a double room?"

"Lo siento, we only have one room left." She smiled. "But it has a big bed."

Fuck. Camila stepped away from the counter, exasperated, knowing her self-restraint was being pushed to the limit.

"Señora, we aren't supposed to be here," Ben said, stepping forward to help. "A double room would be a great help."

For the first time, the old man turned his attention away from the TV. With his grey-colored eyes, he slowly fixed his gaze on Ben and adjusted his hands on top of his cane. "We are all exactly where we are supposed to be, hijo."

Ben smiled at the man who stared at him with laser focus.

"Señor, I'm sorry," the woman said. "You can come back to check again in a few hours."

*　*　*

Their room had a small balcony overlooking a courtyard below, but the distant sound of the waves crashing could be heard from the window. A small bed, advertised as a king but at best a full, mocked them from the opposite side of the room.

"Are you hungry?"

"Not really, are you?" she said.

He shook his head. "I'll take the couch tonight," Ben said definitively as he walked over and sat down with a large thud, followed by an unmistakable crack, leaving him sinking a foot off the floor.

She covered her mouth as the laughter escaped.

"Well, so much for that," he said. "Hey, help me out of this thing."

She walked over, extending her hands to help him dislodge from the broken pile of fabric and wood.

"Okay," he said. "I'll go down later to see if another room is available."

She turned on the TV and left it running in the background, the voices helping temper the rising heat in the room. History had proven they should not be left alone, but thankfully, it was hard to feel romantic with dubbed *Tom & Jerry* playing in the background. But as the sun set, the room was blanketed with a warm glow from the window, and guitar strumming filtered in from the courtyard.

Camila considered all the possibilities to escape their four-hundred-square-foot prison of suppressed desire and frayed nerves. Shopping? But they had already done this, and the stores were likely closed. A walk along the beach? Also completed earlier in the day. Dinner? Neither were hungry. Going to a bar? They didn't drink, and the last thing this situation needed was alcohol.

They sat on the edge of the bed, blankly staring at the TV screen. A telenovela had replaced the cartoons. She sat there, an arm's distance from him, upright with one knee tucked into her chest and her foot flexed, ready to bolt. Ben decided at that very moment to lay back on the bed, crossing his arms behind his head but respectfully keeping his feet planted firmly on the floor. She glanced down quickly, her eyes catching the sliver of skin peeking out from beneath his shirt.

It was the final straw. It was a perfect little fragment of unblemished skin covered with soft hair that coalesced in the midline and dove beneath his jeans. She bit down hard on her lower lip and promptly slid down the edge of the bed and sat on the cold, yet welcoming floor. She leaned her head back, listening to the music filter up from below their balcony. The tension that had been held at bay during the morning returned, now hanging thickly in the air between them. It was an awkwardness they hadn't experienced since their car ride home in the rain.

The fan overhead was hypnotizing, and as his eyes followed the blades, he realized his heart was in two places at once. With that reasoning, perhaps only half of him was supposed to be here, so he was only half wrong in wishing he could just roll over and wrap her in his arms. He tried to sleep, but it was useless. To say he was conflicted was a vast understatement.

"Hey, I think I'm going to go see if another room is free now," he said.

"Okay, I'll come grab some bottles of water."

Thankful for the distraction, they both left the room.

A short while later, they both returned. Only one successful in their mission.

"So, I bought four bottles of water, two to drink and two to swish and spit with."

He looked at her with utter confusion.

She shrugged. "Well, we don't have toothbrushes, so it's the best we got," she said, putting the bottles down on the small coffee table.

"Well, one of us got lucky then," he said, plopping down on the bed, immediately regretting his choice of words.

She resumed her seat on the floor, extending her legs before her, tapping her feet together, shaking off the sand. It was dark outside now, and the music had become livelier. Ironically, the wedding delaying the replacement of her ignition switch was being held at the hotel. She peered out over the balcony to watch the hotel receptionist and her mechanic dance with the rest of the wedding party. The old man was now sitting on the periphery of the courtyard, still resting his hands on top of his cane. He looked up and saw Camila watching him and placed a hand over his heart, locking eyes with her. She smiled and waved at him subtly.

"What's going on out there?" Ben said.

She laughed. "Well, it seems like the entire town is downstairs, so even if we had found another mechanic, most likely he would be at the wedding too."

There was a sudden knock on their door, and she gasped, startled that anyone would know their room was occupied.

Ben gave her a look that expressed everything she was feeling. He walked over to the door and opened it as she backed away cautiously.

"Hola, señor," said a bright young girl, who looked like a carbon copy of the receptionist, but smaller. "My mother told me to bring you this," she said, holding two plates of wedding cake.

"Oh! Gracias." Camila said, pushing Ben aside to take the plates.

"De nada," the young girl said, giggled, and then turned quickly, heading down the stairs.

"This is fantastic!" Camila said, positioning herself on the bed with one plate in front of her and the other waiting for Ben.

"Do I get one?" he asked, with a smirk.

"Yes, here," she mumbled, mouth already full of the first bite. It was a delicious white cake with hints of pineapple. The only thing it was missing was a cup of coffee.

He sat across from her, holding the plate in his hand.

"Oh, this is good," he said after his first bite. "As long as it doesn't have the same effect as the cake in that movie."

Camila dismissed the reference to the movie that had led to their first awkwardly intimate encounter.

"If it did, I'd already be crying," she said, shoving another bite into her mouth.

With a cake this delicious, it wasn't difficult for both to lick their plates clean. On their way to a spectacular sugar high, Ben lay half asleep, watching TV from the bed. She stretched out on the bed and propped herself up, leaning on her elbow, and absentmindedly followed the ending of the telenovela.

He turned his head toward her, watching the images of the screen in her eyes. As her hair fell around her, he moved to tuck it behind her ears.

"Thanks," she said softly.

"You're welcome."

It was difficult to focus on the TV. No further deterrent of cake or the overly dramatic telenovela, they were forced to face the stillness in the room as the credits ran on mute.

"You know it was your hair I first noticed." He ran his fingers through her waves as they fell on the bed.

"Really?" She felt the heat start to climb up her legs. They had done well so far. The energy in the room had been tolerable, and the sounds of the wedding a welcome distraction.

"And what do you notice now?" She knew she was playing with fire.

"Everything else."

"That's nice."

"It's the truth."

She placed her palm on his chest as he placed his hand over it. He brought it to his lips for a small kiss.

"We have shit timing, don't we?" She said with a small smile, pulling her hand back and placing it securely on the bed between them.

"The worst."

She dropped her head down on the bed, intending to close her eyes for a moment, but she must have fallen asleep because when she woke, Ben was missing, and the shower was running. She sat up listening for the party below. It had quieted down, but there was still the faint sound of a guitar. She sat and stretched her legs before walking to the balcony and leaning over the railing as the bathroom door opened.

The shower was supposed to help him clear his head. He leaned his arm against the cool tiles and let the water hit his face, hoping to wash away all the angst. He always assumed he knew what he was doing, where he was going, and what he wanted. But he was exhausted. Exhausted after a lifetime of always doing what was right and not what was right for *him*. And she was everything he never knew he wanted. He was confused and beyond conflicted. He had dedicated his life to being good, caring, and selfless, someone who didn't sacrifice the happiness of others for his own. He wasn't sure if he believed in destiny the way she did. He did believe that there was more than one possible partner for each person. That an honest, solid, and long-lasting union could be made with more than one person for a lifetime, meaning he wasn't necessarily destined for Tiffany. But they had met, and they had agreed on the fundamentals of life and their plans for a family and future career goals.

Of course, this was all before Camila. Camila, who believed with devotion that in this life two people are destined for one another, and though a tolerable life could be had with another partner, there was just one person we were fated to be with. And sometimes that person slipped through our fingers, and other times we pushed them away, but it was written in the heavens and could not be denied.

"Camila?"

"Yeah."

She turned to see him standing in nothing but a small towel, hair soaking from the shower, water dripping down his solid chest and defined arms, his skin dewy. She swallowed hard and diverted her eyes.

He sat on the bed, a move that exposed one muscular thigh beneath the worn towel.

She tried to avert her attention away from him. She could feel a flush spreading along her chest and neck and hoped it was not visible.

"I think I'll shower too." She needed to cool off, literally. To put a wall between them.

She closed the door behind her and leaned against it, eyes closed and head tilted back, and prayed. Prayed to be strong, prayed not to tempt herself or him, prayed to keep herself from flirting, which felt like the most natural thing to do, prayed to stay away from him and survive the night. The room filled with steam, and she wiped the mirror clean, staring at herself.

Camila, you do not mess around with married men. Camila, you do not mess around with married men. Camila, you do not mess around with married men.

Maybe if she said it enough times, it would manifest into reality.

The soap lathered into a thick white foam that smelled like summer, and she lingered under scalding water hoping he would be fully clothed when she emerged. She towel-dried her hair and pulled on the shirt she had bought for Tyler, thankful it hit well below her waist and was like a potato sack, highlighting none of her attributes.

She stepped out of the bathroom resolved to resist the colossal urge that was propelling her to throw herself at him. That was until she saw him still seated on the edge of the bed wrapped in only a towel. So much for her prayers.

The room was illuminated solely by the moonlight coming through the window. Her hair, damp and hanging loosely around her shoulders, did little to put out the fire beneath her skin. Even the water droplets soaking into her shirt barely cooled her down.

"Are you okay?" She said, noting his troubled expression. "What's wrong?"

"Listen, you know you are the closest person to me. I never thought I'd care about someone the way. . ." He stopped himself, rubbing a hand through his hair. "I guess what I'm trying to say is that I care about you in a way that scares me, but I can't give you what you deserve."

She lied. "Ben, I don't expect anything from you. We're friends." Why did this feel like a breakup speech again? They were *just* friends.

"I know, but you deserve more. You deserve a relationship and a commitment. Not me staring at you whenever I have a chance. I want to give you more, but my hands are tied."

She stood still. Trying to process what he was saying. "I don't think I understand." They were each moving away in a matter of a week. Away from each other, away from the incessant pull.

"Listen, we've both felt it from the start," he said. "I'm happy to admit it now. It wasn't just you all those months ago. I felt it too."

She stood there mute. Redeemed from his confession but more confused than ever.

"Ben, that's okay. We've talked about this before."

"But we're stuck here now."

Where was he going with all this, she thought. "Yeah, so?"

"I can give you what I have now, and what I have is tonight, and that's all."

Her mouth was dry, trying to grasp what he was offering.

"No more hesitation or making excuses to touch you. I feel like I'm stealing parts of you when I do that. Like you have no choice but to let me because we can't do anything more. But for one night I want you, all of you, and I want to be with you without holding back what we both want."

She blinked her eyes slowly as if she were in a dream. "All of me?" How could she be with him? He was married. She had been there when the vows were spoken for God's sake.

"What about Tiffany?"

"It's my marriage, not yours."

"I appreciate that, but how could I ever look at her again? It's bad enough I'm in lo..." She squeezed her eyes shut to truncate her accidental declaration.

He smiled at her as she looked at him wide-eyed.

"It's out of our control. I've never wanted something I knew I shouldn't have this badly," he said.

She walked across the room toward the balcony. She needed air. The courtyard had emptied, but the faint smell of food still wafted up to her. With her eyes closed, she tried to clear the turmoil that had settled over her, never imagining that she would have to choose between what her heart wanted and what her head knew was right. But all the karmic retribution seemed insignificant now. She would be willing to burn the entire world down for one night with him.

She turned to him. "One night and we'll never speak again. Ever?"

"If that's what you want."

"One night at the price of our friendship. Forever?" she asked. "Because you know this," she said, motioning between them. "This will never get easier. We will never be *just* friends. There is just too much here."

"I can't give you more than just tonight, you know that, so I'm leaving it up to you. I want this, but I'll agree with whatever you decide.

And I'll never ask you for more," he said.

She walked over, sitting on the bed a few feet away. Struggling with the contest between wrong and right, desire and denial, her head and her heart.

"I know you like me, Ben, but you love her, and those two things can't exist at the same time and place, so if this happens, when we return home tomorrow, that'll be it."

"I think it's a bit stronger than just *liking* you, but yeah, if that's what you want."

"It's not about what I want. It's about what's possible. We won't ever see or speak to each other again. We can't."

He turned his head, looking at her, pain and hope tethered together. Agreeing to indulge in the desire he had fought against for months was coming at the greatest price. Would he be able to live a lifetime without her? Losing the woman, he felt, in some ways, was destined for him. What kind of life could they have built together? He couldn't dwell on those possibilities. They were futile.

"Okay," he nodded.

"Ben, are you sure? All we have to do is make it until morning. I can sleep on the floor," she offered, knowing with each passing minute, it had become nearly impossible to keep her hands off him. She felt giddy but also queasy at the thought of being able to have him to herself for one night.

He smiled. "I think we both know I'd take the floor," he said, "but Camila, I've never felt this. I can't even think when I'm around you, and when I'm not, all I think about is you. I'm paralyzed."

"Well, it's good that we're both moving away then, isn't it?"

She moved to stand before him. He tilted his head back and looked up at her.

He could see the struggle masking her features, the same struggle he held in his heart.

"Camila, it's okay. We're not crossing a line that hasn't been crossed before."

"But we are. This is the ultimate betrayal," she said in a whisper.

"Camila," he said, rubbing his face. "The betrayal started months ago, when I started to crave being near you. Every time we said good-bye, there was an emptiness inside me, and when I'd see you, I could feel you replace the void. It wasn't physical yet, but I was already emotionally wrecked. I've never felt this."

He reached for her hand. "Stay with me tonight, Camila." He hadn't asked before. He had made the offer and asked her to make the ultimate decision, but now he was asking.

She stood between his legs. She nudged closer to him, their legs touching, the hem of her T-shirt grazing her thigh. She was scared. If this last bit of self-defense was compromised, she wouldn't be able to turn back. He moved his hand slowly off his lap and let his fingers hover over her skin. She could feel the electricity between them when she looked down at him. She felt the readiness between her legs before her mind had decided her body should prepare. Her nipples were hard against the coarse cotton of her shirt. Every cell in her brain was screaming *no*, while every fiber in her being was begging for her to fall into him.

He looked up at her, "Please, say no if you have to, but do it now."

She rested her hand along his face and gave him a barely perceptible nod.

"Camila, I need you to say it."

And then, after what felt like an eternity, she softly said, "Yes."

The fingers that had fluttered over her skin now wrapped themselves around her thigh, gently pressing into her. Lightning spread across her skin.

His hand traveled along her leg up underneath her shirt. He tried to slow himself, but months of physical and emotional deprivation had made him ravenous. Yet, he tried not to rush, to savor every moment he had finally been allowed to take. He felt the curve of her hip and the thin band of her thong before stopping beneath her breast. The same path he had taken months before.

Her breath was rapid, her chest rising and falling. She wrapped her hand around his wrist and, with a slight tug, invited him to go further and let her head fall back. He brushed his thumb across her breast, and she licked her lips at the sound of his exhale. His hands running along her body, resting on her waist, pulling her toward him, his head on her stomach, not moving but feeling her body rise and fall.

She tilted his face upward. Their eyes darted back and forth, silently acknowledging the gravity of their decision, as she leaned toward him and tenderly placed her mouth on his. A warmth flowed through her, the anticipation of physicality, the elation of touch she had only dreamt of filled her as he kissed her back. His lips soft and full against hers. Their mouths opened to each other in a soft tangle of tongues, making her moan. She pulled back as he leaned in for more.

"Touch me, Ben."

One of his hands traveled along the front of her abdomen, stopping to lay flat on her skin. He slid his palm down before stopping between her thighs. His fingers moving along the inside of her leg, pausing at the top. He felt the moisture through the fabric, and running a finger along her front, her legs started to quiver. He removed his hand and felt her exhale.

"Can I take this off?" he said, gently tugging on her shirt.

"Mm-hmm," she hummed. He took the edge and in one swift motion pulled it over her head. He leaned in and kissed the skin below her navel, then ran his tongue up between her breasts. He turned his head slightly, placing one delicate kiss along the underside of each breast.

Her nipples were firm at the thought of him, his mouth so close. He moved along the half-moon curve of her breasts with small kisses, making her insane with desire. His lips wrapped around her, and she felt his tongue play with her. She let out an involuntary groan. She couldn't have imagined how purposeful he would be with his movements, how restrained, given she had only envisioned attacking him and ripping off his clothes in a much less thoughtful way for the past few months.

"Do you want to lie down?" he said.

She nodded, her lower lip sucked into her mouth. He lay back as she straddled him, and he pulled her into him, running his hands down her side and bringing their bodies together. She could feel him through his towel against her leg. He kissed her as she pushed her tongue into his mouth and tasted him more earnestly. Her body pressed against his as he slid his hand down her back and along the curve of her backside. He reached between her legs, now wet and glistening.

"Can I take these off?" he asked, curling his fingers around the edge of her thong as she placed soft kisses along his neck, her hot breath making him come alive.

"Yes."

She moved, lying on the bed next to him, her hands along his face, pulling him into her as she kissed him, and he pulled the fabric down her legs. He took a moment to stare at her.

"You're beautiful."

She smiled at him. "Can I take this?" she asked, tucking her fingers into the towel still around his waist. The last remnant of modesty separating them.

"Yeah."

As it fell away, she saw all of him for the first time. The parts that she had felt but were always hidden from her. She reached out and gently touched him, propping herself up on her elbows. He lay back, one arm behind his head and the other resting by his side, his fingers digging into the bed. He exhaled for a moment as he enjoyed her hands on him.

"Camila, please."

"Should I stop?" she asked cautiously, letting go and backing up quickly.

"No, no, I just need us to go slower," he said.

He grabbed her around the waist and pulled her down beneath him. She ran her fingers through his hair, gently tugging at his mouth with her own. His hands traveled down along her skin as he focused his mouth on her breasts. She closed her eyes as he moved down her body, touching her, finding her.

"Just tell me to stop if you need to."

"I don't think that'll happen," she said, breathing out slowly, head tilted back.

She opened to him as he carefully placed his fingers alongside her. He continued to move down her torso, placing soft kisses on her skin, and then ran his tongue between her, making her gasp and arch back suddenly.

"Was that okay?" he asked.

She relaxed again, letting her body fall back on the bed. "Yes."

"Are you sure? We don't have to."

"Please, Ben. I want you to," she panted, sensing his hesitation.

She gripped the sheets beneath them as he pushed his finger inside with one gentle move and used his tongue against her as she let out a moan. She brought his face up to her and kissed him deeply as his fingers continued to move methodically. His thumb rubbed her simultaneously, making her ache deep inside as she pushed their mouths together, her tongue thrusting into his. She felt a rush build up deep inside. She pulled back with a whimper as he began to move more rapidly.

"Ben... Ben, I'm going... Ben, I'm so close."

Suddenly, she threw her leg over him, pushing him back on the bed, and climbed on top. She positioned herself so she felt him beneath her. She began to slowly rock back and forth, feeling him firmly, sliding along her bare skin but not letting him inside. When she felt his hands on her thighs moving up to her backside, she knew she wouldn't last much longer.

He looked up at her while his hands rested on her hot skin. Her silhouette in the dark room was illuminated only by the moonlight. He could see her contours, the soft curve of her hips and breasts. The fullness of her lips and the glimmer in her eyes. Her dark hair cascaded around her when she tilted forward.

"Ben," she groaned into his ear.

"Camila, fuck, Camila, I can't..."

Relief washed over her knowing she didn't have to hold back and nudged herself back and forth more rapidly as he dug his fingers into her hips. She leaned forward, bracing her hands on his chest, her hair a curtain hiding them from the outside world.

"Oh, God, Ben," she whispered softly and then let out a small cry as she trembled. She felt him writhe beneath her, spilling out. He pulled her onto him and wrapped his arms around her. She rested her head on his chest and listened to the pounding of his heart as his hands traveled along her skin.

A few minutes later the sound of his breath was distinctively of sleep.

* * *

The sky was pitch black when she opened her eyes again. His arm draped over her waist, but this time she nestled back into him without hesitation. Only when she was certain he was awake did she speak.

"Ben?"

"Yeah," he answered back in a whisper.

"You know I love you, right? You don't have to say anything back," she said, facing the window, her body rising and falling with the cadence of her breath. "I just want you to know that this is not something I planned. I'd want a life with you if..."

He turned her toward him, kissing her softly, "I know. We have a lot of 'ifs' between us." He considered all the options that had occupied his mind for a way to make this work. To somehow create a scenario where they could be together without ruining the future for all three of them. Because truthfully, there were three people involved. He wanted to blend into Camila, become one, and never let her out of his arms. He knew the raw intensity of his emotions for her was unrivaled. What he thought he felt in the past with others was a mere fraction of the force he felt now. A diluted version of the passion that was running through him. He wanted each minute to last a day.

They faced each other, softly kissing as his hands gently moved up and down her back. She ran her hand along his arm, across his shoulder, and behind his neck. Sensing his readiness, she whispered, "Ben, do you have a condom?"

Up until now, it hadn't been necessary. They had been careful. They hadn't risked everything yet. They hadn't experienced each other fully.

He pulled back, realization and disappointment marring his face.

"I, I don't, I mean we don't use..."

Of course, why would he carry condoms? He was married.

"I'm not on the pill either."

He dropped his head and puffed out a frustrated sigh. She placed a hand on the side of his face, forcing him to look at her.

"But you can pull out," she said. "I don't mind. I was tested after David, and everything was okay. I haven't been with anyone since."

"Are you sure? You're okay without one?"

"As long as you are. I've never not used one, so this is a first for me."

He pulled her to him, pressing his mouth onto hers, and wrapped his arm around her thigh and dragged it over him. She felt his weight press into her as she lay back, wrapping both legs around his waist. They intertwined their fingers against the bed.

"Are you sure?"

"Yeah, just pull out before, you know..."

He smiled down at her. "Yeah, I know."

She gave him a nervous laugh and then arched up to kiss him. He kissed back, tightening his grip on her hands with his own, dragging them above her head. She was ready for him, and he slowly pushed himself in. She let out a stifled gasp, freed her hands, and wrapped her arms around his shoulders, pulling him into her. He moved slowly back and forth, her legs holding him tightly as she closed her eyes. His movements quickened, and she dug her nails into his skin, and he groaned. She loved the weight of him, the feel of his skin moving against hers, his muscles tightening beneath her touch.

"Ben, be careful," she whispered.

"I know," he panted.

She ran her hands down his back, firmly placing them on him as he moved deeper inside.

"I've wanted this for so long," she breathed out.

"Me too. I've dreamt of you."

She pulled him down to her for a long, deep kiss and swallowed back the tears that gathered quickly at his words. He braced himself up on his palms. A few more quick movements, and he suddenly pulled out, releasing himself on the bed, and collapsed, exhausted from the near impossible exercise in self-control. She watched his chest rise and fall quickly, his arms tense under the burden of his weight and effort.

"I'm sorry it was so quick," he said.

"It's okay. It's better to be careful."

He lay behind her, holding her close as he slowed his breathing. He had wanted to hold her for so long and now, didn't want to let go. He had no regret. He would have been incapable of living a life having never known what she felt like. He lost himself inside her. His body and mind aloft, experiencing both a freedom and purity of emotion that was transportive.

* * *

The sun peeked through the window. The sound of the city coming alive. She had fallen asleep in his arms. She felt him trace the curve of her hip and drag the thin sheet that had been covering her back. He pressed himself firmly against her, and she held his hand against her stomach.

"Buenos días," she said coyly.

"Good morning, Camila," he said in a deep, groggy voice.

He kissed the back of her neck and down her shoulders. They started to move together, and she wrapped her hand around his neck, pulling him down to her as he slipped his hand between her legs. A shiver ran up her spine as she felt him within her. They moved slowly in unison, her mind fogging over as she felt his strong body beside hers.

Before she could remind him, he whispered, "Don't worry. I'm being careful." A few minutes later, she felt him shudder behind her, and his body went limp as they both fell asleep again.

"I'm going to shower," she said when she woke a few hours later. The sun was now high and bright outside, but the light that shone across their floor brought with it an inexplicable grief. They had to go home, unable to avoid the inevitability of their future.

He rested his arms beneath his head, and she smiled as his eyes followed her across the room. Pausing at the bathroom door, she turned and asked, "Want to join me?"

The shower washed away the tears that fell uncontrollably down her face as they made love one last time. She ran her hands down his chest and along his stomach as he tensed beneath her touch. The water trailed down the muscles that flexed as he moved. She held onto him as he pressed her against the cold tiles, kissing her with an urgency that exposed his sorrow. His arms wrapped around her tightly, and she sobbed into his chest. It was no use trying to hide the heartache that had arrived as night had faded into morning.

* * *

They pulled up to his apartment five hours after checking out of the hotel and receiving sideways glances from the front desk girl, four hours after they paid the mechanic, who gave them a knowing smirk, and three hours after they were given suspicious glares from the border patrol as they crossed back over the invisible line that pushed them into reality. Their hands had been locked together, even after she had dozed off, savoring the last few moments of touch available.

He drove, glancing over to her, her eyes closed, and wondered. Maybe they could just stay friends. Send each other Christmas cards and catch up with a call once or twice a year. He and Tiffany would start a family, and surely Camila would meet someone and settle down, even if it were in another country. But then he realized this fantasizing was a juvenile attempt at making all the jagged pieces of his life fit neatly. If she was available to him, by phone or email or even pen and paper, he wouldn't be able to give himself completely to the new life that awaited him. Camila made him feel like the world was in technicolor. Sadly, he knew, with certainty, he would have loved her if the temporality of their fucked-up situation had been different.

She woke up somewhere near LAX. He didn't notice her staring out the window, watching the planes hovering over East LA, waiting their turn to land. She always wondered where those planes departed from. Was it someone's first time in the U.S.? Was someone coming home after a long time away? As long as she could remember, she had been aching to cross continents, to see every corner of the world. But now, seated in her car beside a man she had known for no more than a few months, she felt most at home. She wished they were going home together, to a domestic life she never knew she wanted. She could move with him, and they could buy a home and have children. These thoughts bounced around her mind as they sped along the freeway. The mundane life that she now longed for was unrecognizable to the old Camila. The Camila who hadn't met Ben. Adventurous, thrill-seeking, globe-trotting—those were the words used to describe her. Domestic, stable, and common were not in Camila's DNA. But now, she wanted nothing more than to live a simple life with Ben. He had crept into her heart through friendship and now resided deep inside, surrounded by love.

They stepped out of the car, he to leave and she to get behind the wheel as quickly as possible and head home to sob in the privacy of her own room. He slowly made his way around the car as she stood on the sidewalk waiting for the painful severing of ties.

"Here you go," he said, placing the keys in her hand and letting their hands linger together. He gave her a smile that did a poor job of hiding his true feelings. She preoccupied herself with shuffling her feet and desperately avoiding eye contact. She was succeeding too, until he placed his hand beneath her chin, bringing her face up to his.

"Hey," he said softly.

"Hey," she said, before looking away, swallowing painfully. The tears started to flow uncontrollably.

"Camila, we can stay in touch. Maybe we shouldn't have agreed to such an ultimatum."

"No. No," she said, backing away and wiping her face with her hands. "No, we agreed, and it's for the best. I can't keep feeling like this, and if you're still available to me, I'll never move on." She took a step toward him and tugged at his shirt, mustering a small smile. "I'll miss you, Ben Martin. I hope life is always good to you."

"Camila," he said, pulling her into his arms.

She shook her head against his chest as his hand came up along her face, and he kissed her. They lingered for a moment before she finally pulled away.

PART 2

March 2014

15

"I'm almost done, just checking out," she said hurriedly into the phone as she dove into her bag looking for her wallet.

"Camila," Tyler said calmly.

She froze. After nearly twenty years of friendship, she could decipher an entire conversation with a small inflection of his voice.

"What? What's happened?" She asked, grabbing her bag of sour cherry jam and pickles from the cashier and rushing out of Jordan Market.

"Nothing. Well, something, but just stay calm."

"I hear you driving. Why are you driving? Weren't you guys supposed to wait at home for me?"

"So, I may have been showing Cole how to use the table saw and…"

"Holy fuck, Tyler! Is he okay? Does he still have all his fingers?" A cold sweat immediately appeared along her brow.

"Camila! Calm the fuck down!"

She was panting, feeling the beginning of one of her long-lost panic attacks making an ugly resurgence.

"Mom, I'm fine!" She heard Cole yell through the phone.

Oh, thank God.

"Camila, we are going to UCLA just to make sure he doesn't need stitches. Just meet us there."

She yelled into the phone. "Aren't you a doctor?"

"I'm an anesthesiologist! I don't deal with kids or their hands! Just meet us there."

She didn't know how she got there. She crossed every single intersection with a symphony of honking cars and upheld middle fingers. She slammed her car door shut and bolted for the entrance to the ER. She was scared, furious, and sweating as she burst through the doors, with everyone staring as she made her way through the waiting room.

"I'm sorry. My son, I'm the mother of…"

"Ma'am, take a deep breath," the kind clerk behind the glass partition said. Used to hysterical mothers, the woman chewed her gum as Camila composed herself.

Inhale. Exhale. Inhale. Exhale.

"Now, who are you trying to find, ma'am?"

"My son is here."

"What is his name?"

"Cole. Cole Malik. He's 10 years old."

The clerk pulled down the glasses perched on top of her head. Camila could see the pages of the computer reflected in her lens as she scrolled through the census.

"Okay, there he is. Bed twelve. If you just make a left and then go down the hall, his room is on the right."

"Thank you so much!"

"It's okay, honey. Just try to breathe."

"Thank you," Camila replied more calmly, straightening her back and smoothing down the front of her dress.

She walked briskly down the hall, her eyes frantically searching for the number twelve. The space looked different. Years earlier, Tyler had brought her here after her car accident. The accident that sent everything into motion. She had been so lost then. Convinced she would never find love, and now the person she loved most in the world was a few feet away.

She made it to the glass door and stood for a moment trying to regroup so she didn't transfer her anxious energy directly onto Cole.

It didn't work well.

"What the fuck happened, Tyler?" She said when she slid open the glass door and threw back the curtains. "I left him with you for like twenty minutes."

"Mom, I'm fine," Cole said, his hand wrapped in a blood-soaked towel, his face looking one shade left of chalk white.

She gave a half-gasp. "Oh honey," she said, sitting next to him and pulling his head into her chest.

"He's fine, Camila. We were just doing some renovating around the house." Tyler smiled at Cole.

"It was so cool, Mom. Uncle Tyler had me cut all this wood for the sauna he is building out back and..."

"What the fuck, Tyler?! *Renovating?* You mean *Bobby* was renovating. The only renovation you know your way around is in the new shoe department at Barney's!"

"Well, I am both flattered and offended! We were just being men!"

She looked at him speechless.

"Camila! Chill!"

"Chill my ass! Look at all that blood," she said, standing again and looking at her son's hand.

Lucky for Tyler, they were interrupted by the clerk. "Ms. Malik, I'm sorry to interrupt, but we need you to fill out some insurance forms for Cole."

Camila glared at Tyler. "No problem. I'll be back," she said, kissing Cole's head before leaving.

The resident who had initially triaged Cole's hand returned a few moments later with his supervising physician.

"Mr. Bradley, this is my attending physician, Dr. Martin."

"Hiya, Cole," the doctor said. He looked at Tyler. "Mr. Bradley?"

Silence. Deafening silence and disbelief.

"Ben?"

"Tyler?"

They exchanged looks before it fully set in. Tyler hadn't even thought about Ben in more than, well, more than ten years.

"Wow, how are you?" Tyler said. "Are you back in LA?"

"Yeah, we moved back for my fellowship at CHLA. What are you doing here?"

"We had a little woodworking accident. I'm actually an anesthesiologist at Cedars," Tyler said.

"That's great. It's so good to see you." He looked over at Cole. "Hi, buddy. I'm Dr. Martin. That looks like a pretty big cut."

"Hi," Cole said shyly.

He looked at Tyler. "Is this your son?" he asked, inspecting Cole's hand as the resident leaned closer for a better look.

"No, my godson. His mother... well, here's his mother," he said as Camila pulled back the curtain to enter the room.

Camila froze. She knew that voice. She knew the tenor and the depth. She knew what that mouth had once done to her. Her eyes shot up to meet Tyler's. He fixed her with his gaze and gave her the slightest, barely perceptible nod when he saw the fear and recognition in her face.

She moved slowly. Ben turned, and her eyes landed on his chest, the green scrubs underneath the white coat. She slowly moved from the chest to his mouth, the familiar scar near the upper lip. She exhaled a long, slow breath and met the soft brown eyes that had changed the course of her life more than ten years before.

Time had slowed, and the edges of the room became blurred. She saw Ben, and she saw Cole with his hand cut open on top of a blood-soaked towel. Her ears heard the words in a mangled and distorted way. She shook her head and glanced down to where the resident was pointing only to see blood pumping from the palm of Cole's hand. And then everything turned black.

* * *

There was a faint beeping as she opened her eyes in the dim room. It looked like the room she had just been in with Cole. But there was no Cole. No Tyler. *Oh my God.*

She turned to the source of the beeping and found she wasn't alone. He was sitting there. Arms crossed at his chest, his head forward. Asleep. She watched as his chest rose and fell. The same chest she had laid her head on all those years ago when they had their one night. The one night that changed everything. She didn't want to wake him, but shifting on the gurney was not as graceful as she had hoped.

He pushed himself upright in the chair, rubbing the sleep from his eyes. His hair was short but messy, and he had earned some wrinkles over the years they had been apart.

"Camila," he said.

Hearing him say her name warmed her. It felt familiar but also a painful reminder of time lost. She rubbed the back of her neck. "How long have you been sitting here?"

"You fainted."

"Oh," she said, bringing her hand to her head and feeling the tender knot that had formed.

"Don't try to sit just yet," he said.

"Where is my son?"

"Tyler took him home after we stitched up his hand. He's going to be fine."

"Thank you."

She hugged her legs to her chest. She placed her head on her knees, looking at him.

"I didn't know you had a son," he said, bending to rest his elbows on the edge of the bed.

That was a nonsensical statement given the vastness of what he didn't know about her now.

"Well, it's been a few years."

They had never had so many moments of silence between them. She wondered if she looked the same to him. He was the same, and yet different. Her eyes fell on his wedding band. Reliably still there.

"How is Tiffany?"

"She's fine. Just home."

"Do you live here? In LA?"

"Yeah, we live in Pasadena."

She had so many questions, but her head was pounding, and her hand went to rub the pain away instinctively.

"Do you have pain?" He asked as if she were any other patient needing an evaluation.

"Yes, a little."

"Let's get you something," he said, brushing her arm as he reached for the call light. Her skin tingled where they had barely touched.

A nurse quickly appeared. "Dr. Martin, how can I help you?"

"Can you get 1,000 milligrams of Tylenol out of the Pyxis for Ms. Malik? I'm putting in the order right now."

"Absolutely," she said, turning quickly and pulling the curtain closed again.

He finished typing and logged out of the computer. Turning back toward her, he said, "You changed your hair?"

"I cut it after Cole started walking. It was too hard to chase after him and deal with this chaos," she said, motioning at her now sleek black hair. She was trying to lighten the mood.

"You didn't take his father's name?" he said.

"I'm not with his father. We were never together, not really," she said, looking down at her feet under the sheet.

"Oh," he said, visibly thinking.

"You don't have to stay with me. I know you're working." She wanted to start over, but she didn't know how to salvage their reintroduction to avoid the uncomfortable place they now inhabited.

"I'm done with my shift," he said.

"You should go home then. To Tiffany." As if it wasn't clear.

They had an agreement. An understanding. She didn't have the capacity to navigate this unexpected reunion.

He ran his hand through his hair and then rubbed the nape of his neck in that painfully familiar way he had years ago.

"What?" she said.

"What, what?"

"You only ever did that when you wanted to say something but weren't sure if you should."

"I guess some things never change."

He smiled faintly. They hadn't smiled at each other once. The wind was knocked out of him. He had wondered about her daily for years. Always hesitating before opening his internet search window or attempting to find mutual friends on Facebook, just to make sure she was okay. The day she left, the last day he had held her, had broken him. He had taken the time to prioritize his life when they had met, a full year to determine what he valued. And he found her, but hadn't been able to tear himself away from the life he had already started and let her slip away. In a certain way, he had lost a part of himself that day and had been resolved to move through life with a hollow space in his heart. Now she was here, in the same room, and he had no idea what to say or do.

"I think I have to go," he said, standing. "It was nice seeing you, Camila."

"You too," she said with a half-smile as he got up and left the room.

A heavy weight fell in her stomach, and she turned to her side and curled her knees in. That was all? That was all they could say after ten years?

Why did she feel like she had seen a ghost?

An emptiness filled her chest, an ache that sent bile up to her mouth. She turned in bed and closed her eyes, trying to fend off the nausea that had set in. He was so cold. So numb. Maybe he had been happy without her in his life. Maybe she was just a reminder of all his mistakes.

He stood in the middle of the hallway rubbing his temple with one hand.

"Dr. Martin, are you okay?" the nurse asked, heading for Camila's room, carrying two white pills in a small paper cup.

"Yes, thank you."

"You've been working so much lately," she said with an undeniable maternal concern.

"I'm fine. If her headache resolves, please discharge her home with precautions."

"Yes, doctor."

He made his way to the doctor's lounge, where he had left his backpack. He needed to leave. He yearned to sit in the dependable LA traffic and forget that his life had just cracked open, letting his past ooze into the present.

An hour later, charting finished, and a bit more settled after his fourth decaf coffee of the shift, he made his way through the parking lot. But not before his eyes landed on Camila hunched over with her hands braced on her knees. She was leaning against her car, bent over with her head hanging. Worried that she may have a concussion, he approached her against his better judgment.

"Hey, are you okay?" he asked, startling her upright.

Her head pounded from the sudden movement. She quickly wiped her face with the back of her hand. Tyler had texted to say Cole was fine, that she should take her time getting checked out, figuratively and literally. But she had taken the opportunity to sob incessantly instead.

"I'm sorry. It's just. I just. I need to go home."

"Camila," he said softly, like no time had passed. Like they hadn't spent a lifetime apart.

"This is just too much. I missed you so," she blurted, the tears falling freely.

"I called you, emailed you," he said urgently. "You never replied. I even asked David if he had heard from you. He said you never called him back. You just left."

She dropped her head in her hands, and her entire body was shaking from heartache. He wrapped his arms around her, pulling her into him. He started to stroke her back, and as her crying slowed, she steadied her breath. His hand gently caressing her. She leaned her face into him, feeling his chest beneath her, inhaling his familiar scent. Finally, she pried herself off him, her face blotchy and moist.

"I'm sorry."

"Don't apologize," he said. "Didn't you always say things happen for a reason?" He looked at her with a kindness she didn't know she had missed.

"I should go," she said, reaching for the handle of the car, and he held the door open for her as she got in and fastened her seatbelt. The engine purred, and she looked up one last time through her open window.

"Camila, wait, we should talk."

"We shouldn't. We had an agreement."

"Camila, please."

"I have to go."

"Wait!" He yelled after her as she pulled out of the parking lot.

* * *

"You what?!" Tyler yelled at her through the phone.

"I just left."

"Are you crazy?"

"Tyler, what was I supposed to do? *'Hi Ben, remember me? We fucked once while you were married, and I got pregnant, and by the way, the hand you stitched up belongs to your son.'*"

"Okay, well, maybe not in those exact words, but haven't you said that Cole keeps asking to meet his father? Maybe this is the universe telling you the time is now."

"What is with you two and throwing my own karmic philosophy in my face?"

"All I'm saying is that you should talk to him. Tell him he has a son. If not for him, do it for Cole. It's not fair, Camila. He shouldn't have to be raised without his father because of a promise based on lust years ago."

She was silent on the other line.

"Camila?"

"Yeah, I'm just thinking. I'll be home in a few."

She pulled off Bowling Green into the driveway but had been lost in thought. It wasn't until she heard the door slam behind her and jumped at the sound of her name that she realized Ben had followed her home.

She spun around. "What are you doing here?"

"I followed you. Do you live here?"

The front door opened behind her before she could answer. Out walked a handsome, tall, dark-haired man who looked vaguely familiar. He stepped toward Camila. It never occurred to Ben that she would be married. But why not? She had a son he didn't know about. He knew nothing about her anymore.

"Oh, sorry," Ben said, stopping abruptly, realizing that his impulsive gesture may not have been well thought out.

"Ben," she said, grabbing his wrist and quickly letting go as he faced her.

"I'm sorry," he said. "I didn't mean to. Do you live here?"

"No, this is Tyler's new home. We're visiting."

"You and your son?"

"Yeah."

"And that guy?" he asked, a ball of bitter jealousy in his mouth.

"That's Bobby. Tyler's husband."

Relief washed over him.

"You, okay?" Bobby called out after her.

"Yeah, thanks," she waved at him.

Ben paced a few steps back and forth along the driveway, tussling his hair.

"Don't you need to go home?" she asked.

"I need to see you again. We need to talk."

"We don't."

"How long are you staying?"

"Through the weekend. But Ben, really, we should just pretend today didn't happen."

"Meet me tomorrow night. Please."

"Ben, I don't think this is a good idea. Let's just let things be."

"No," he said more forcefully than he intended.

Camila was shocked. He had never taken that tone with her before.

"Can I have your number?"

She hesitated.

"Just so I can text you, so we can talk," he said. The world had given him another chance, an opportunity to welcome her into his life again.

"It's the same number as before," she said, looking down at the pavement.

His heart fell. He had called her. He had texted her. He had convinced himself she had changed her number. But really, she had just cut him out of her life.

She had received his calls all those years ago and listened to his messages. But she deleted them. All of them. Except one. One she kept to listen to.

Hi Camila, I miss you. I know we agreed on something, but maybe we were wrong. Call me. I love you.

She played the message daily at first, then weekly, and then over the years listened to it on her birthday as a gift to her previous self. Tyler had told her to join Facebook, that their paths would electronically cross, but she dismissed him, saying, "Facebook is not natural. People come and go in your life for a reason, not because of a computer algorithm."

"Cami, there are very intelligent software engineers who can now alter fate to your liking."

"It's been so many years. I can't."

"Can't or won't?"

"I can't, Tyler," and for the first time, she was outwardly honest. "I'm afraid he doesn't remember me or, worse, he doesn't care anymore. And maybe I've spent all this time thinking of him, and he's moved on. I don't think my heart could take it. Maybe it didn't mean as much to him."

Tyler was thoughtful for a few moments before replying cautiously, "But you'll never know until you reach out."

16

A few months after their trip to Mexico and their final goodbyes, Camila had a run-in with some bad sushi. Or so she thought.

Camila and Tyler were still living together, and she was working extra shifts at CPK to save up for her move.

"Are you done in there?" Tyler called from the kitchen. "There can't be anything left."

"Yeah, I think so," she said, wiping her mouth on the back of her hand as she exited the bathroom.

"That sounded horrible," he said as he threw out all the leftover sushi he found in the fridge.

She walked into the kitchen. "How come you didn't get sick?"

"Stomach of steel!" he said, slapping his abdomen.

"Okay, I'm going to go to bed. I have the early shift tomorrow."

She had been distracting herself relatively well since Ben left. She picked up more shifts and signed on to be a TA for the summer quarter for some extra cash. They had successfully ignored each other, cutting off all communication as planned. At least for the first few weeks.

Her life was moving forward, and he was across the country with his wife. Camila longed for him mostly at night, but exhaustion had left little time to dwell on his absence. As usual, she climbed into bed and fell asleep as soon as her head hit the pillow.

The next morning, she barely made it through the door at work, bolting straight to the employee restroom. Everything she had eaten came hurling back up. The lack of food toward the end resulted in painful retching.

"Camila, you okay?" her shift manager asked, knocking on the door.

She emerged wiping her mouth with a paper towel. "Yeah, I just had some bad sushi last night."

The woman gave her an inquisitive look. "Are you having diarrhea too?"

"No, thankfully."

"Camila, you sure it was bad sushi? Last time I was sprinting for the toilet like that, I was pregnant with my second."

"Well, to be pregnant you have to be having sex," Camila said.

After she finished her shift, there was no more dry heaving, but a low level of nausea had persisted since morning. On her way home she stopped to pick up some Gatorade and Pepto Bismol from the store. She walked down the aisle toward checkout and saw the shelf of pregnancy tests. She couldn't be pregnant. She had sex once in March and once in June. Her period between March and June was normal. After June she had some spotting, but now, she didn't recall an actual normal period. She made it home and found Tyler on the couch studying for his board examination.

"Hey, how was work? You feelin' any better?"

She shrugged. "Well, I only threw up once since morning."

"No free pizza today?" They had been sustained by the free pizza Camila would earn per shift for the past two years.

"Oh, sorry, Tyler. I had to go to the store and totally forgot. I've been so absentminded lately."

With the bathroom door locked, she pulled out the pregnancy test tucked in the back of her pants. She read the instructions and proceeded to pee as directed onto the stick.

She undressed, turned the shower on, and stepped in, leaving the test on the counter. As the aroma of her shampoo filled the room, she started to breathe easier but was caught off guard by the scent of tomatoes. Strange, she didn't recall that fragrance coming from the bottle in the past. She dismissed it, and as she pulled the shower curtain back, the steam from the shower engulfed the small room. She stepped out drying her hair and glimpsed at the pregnancy test. The bright pink cross staring back at her from the counter was unmistakable. It was as if she had been slapped.

It couldn't be right. She must have left the kit on the counter longer than directed. Clearly, the test was faulty if left to process for too long.

She took out the second test, the backup test. The *just-in-case* test and proceeded to pee on the stick and left it on the counter as she brushed her hair and applied toner to her petrified face. This time she set a timer.

"Cami! Are you okay?" Tyler yelled hearing her scream. "Did you fall?" He busted through the door. "Why are you sitting on the toilet naked? Are you okay? Did you black out again?"

"Tyler," she said, sobbing. "Look." She nudged the two tests toward him with a shaking hand. Both tests with bright pink crosses.

His eyes went wide. "Cami, let's get you off the toilet and into some clothes, and then I'm going to ask you what the hell is going on."

After he helped her into her clothes, he started with the most fundamental question, "Cami, who's the father?"

She couldn't look at him. She had never not used a condom. She had never been pregnant. She had never been with a married man. She had openly ridiculed her friends who would pursue "attached" men, as she called them.

She sniffled. "I had sex once in March with David at the wedding and once in June."

"Well, it's not David's based on that timeline alone. Who did you have sex with in June? You weren't dating anyone."

She dropped her head in her hands and wept. Tyler rubbed her back gently, pulling her into him and dropping back on the couch.

"It's okay if you don't remember his name. One-night stands happen sometimes." He was trying to reassure her.

"Tyler, I know his name," she said between gasps. "Oh my God, what have I done? My life is over," she cried, dropping her head into her hands, again.

"Cami, we can get through this. Your life isn't over. Whoever he is, I'm sure he'll want to help once he knows. And if not, I'm here."

She bolted upright in her seat. "I can never tell him!"

"Okay, Cami, you're freakin' me out. Who is he?"

"Oh Tyler, you'll never forgive me."

"First of all, I will always be by your side, and unless you slept with Bobby, I'm pretty sure I'll get over it." He smiled.

She didn't crack a smile. She looked at him as the tears rolled down her face.

"My God, Cami, who is he? You're really scaring me. Is he a criminal? Or worse, a celebrity?"

She hid behind her hands. "It's Ben's," she murmured.

"Wait, what? I can't hear you."

"It's Ben's!" she yelled, flopping herself back on the couch.

"Cami, what the fuck are you talking about? He's married."

The sound of her sobbing filled their apartment.

"Wait. Were you guys having an affair?"

"No, no," she yelled. "It was just one night. One time! It happened when my car broke down in Mexico. We were together once, and we agreed that we would never see each other again." She was hyperventilating.

He looked stunned. "Is that why he wasn't invited to your graduation but showed up anyway?"

She nodded.

"I'm sorry because I know this obviously doesn't matter now, but didn't you use protection?"

She dropped her head into her hands again. "We didn't have anything since it wasn't planned. He pulled out, but I guess..."

"Oh, Cami."

She cried into his arms, and he held her, lost for words.

* * *

"I can't believe it took so long to get an appointment," Tyler said as they sat in the waiting room.

"I know, but I'm so happy you could come with me."

"When are we going to tell your family?"

"Once I find out everything is okay."

They walked into the exam room together, and Camila quickly put on the gown.

"I never know if the opening is in the back or front," she said, as she struggled to tie the strings behind her neck.

"Don't worry. He'll be seeing everything soon enough," Tyler said.

The visit was short but long enough for the doctor to mistake Tyler as the father, advise Camila on her options for genetic testing, and show them the first images of her son. She clasped the ultrasound pictures in her hand as they drove home.

Her heart was full. "Look at that cute profile, Tyler!"

She had never been happier. All her plans would have to change. She wouldn't be traveling. She wouldn't work for the CDC in Mexico City. But she had a part of Ben with her now and always would.

"When are you going to tell him?"

"Tyler, are you fucking kidding me?"

"No! Are *you* fucking kidding me?"

"Never, I'm never telling him," Camila said.

"Cami, stop it," he said. "It's his child."

"Tyler, he's married, remember? We were at the wedding."

"Convenient that you remember that now!"

"Tyler! That's fucked up!"

He motioned to his head. "I'm sorry, there is just a lot swirling around in here."

"I get it. It's okay. But Ben and I had an understanding. We were never going to see or talk to each other. Ever again. And don't you dare say a thing. I forbid it."

"Ok, listen, I may have a big ass mouth, but even I understand that this news is not mine to share."

They drove without speaking down La Cienega, passing familiar restaurants and shops that would now be impossible to frequent with a newborn.

Tyler was the first to break the silence. "So how was it?"

"What?"

"You know. Being with him. Was it worth it?"

She went silent again. The images of their one night together flashed before her. Finally, she said, "Absolutely. It was better than... I've never felt anything like it. I don't think I ever will. I love him, Tyler. And he loved me."

The light turned red, and they sat there, staring out the windshield.

As if reading her mind, Tyler turned to her, squeezed her hand, and said, "You loved him enough to let him go."

"Exactly."

17

March 2014

She pressed her lips together, blotting them on a tissue before throwing it in the trash, and glanced at her mirrored image, her figure accentuated by her knee-length black dress. Simple makeup, a simple dress. This was *not* a date. He was married. This was to clear the air, to answer questions yet to be asked.

She leaned on the doorway, slipping on her heels.

Tyler nudged Cole, who was glued to the TV. "Doesn't your mommy look pretty?"

She blew out her nerves. "So, what do you think?"

Tyler whistled. "You look hot!"

"I don't want to look hot!"

Tyler motioned to her breasts. "Well, then maybe tuck those bad boys in more."

"I can't shove them in any further. If it's inappropriate, just tell me. I'll go change."

Cole looked up from the TV. "Don't change, Mommy, you look pretty."

"Thanks, baby," she said, leaning down and kissing the top of his head.

"Where are you going anyway?" Tyler asked, getting up to walk her to the door.

"Some place in West Hollywood. I have the name in my phone." She fumbled in her purse for her phone. "Here it is. Susina. He wanted to go to Bouchon, but I said no."

"Why? That place is great. So romantic..."

She gave him a look.

"Right," Tyler said, "Okay, well, you're not taking your car looking like that."

"And what is wrong with my car?" She asked, hands on her hips.

"Nothing, nothing. You're saving the planet. Yeah!" he said and threw his fists up in the air in a mock cheer. "But you look BMW-good, so please take my car, not yours."

"Take his car, Mom! It's so fast." Cole yelled.

"Okay, okay," she said.

"Have a good time," Tyler said. "Don't worry. He may be angry when you tell him, but he loved you once. That doesn't just evaporate."

"Tell who what?" Cole asked, half paying attention.

Camila glared at Tyler.

As she headed out the doorway, she whispered to Tyler, "I don't know if I can tell him."

"Cami, you can, and you will."

"He's a stranger to me now," she said. "What we had is gone. I don't know him anymore."

"Do it for Cole. You have been given another chance. Take it. Now go out there and handle your business."

"Oh, Tyler."

"*Oh, Tyler*, nothing. Remember the two most useless human emotions are guilt for what's been done and worry for what might be done. Go to him. Talk."

"Why couldn't *you* just marry me?" She whispered as she hugged him.

"Ewww, you're a girl," he said, winking at her.

* * *

Her text had caught him off guard. It had taken her more than a week to reply. He assumed that they had fallen into the same pattern from nearly a decade ago. He contacting her, and she leaving him unanswered. But only now did he realize she had purposely avoided him. That her number and email never changed.

He was in the middle of rounds when the familiar ding sounded, but with an entire hospital to cover, it wasn't rare to hear a few chimes in the middle of his day. Nurses confirming orders, pharmacy rechecking a dosage, families wanting updates. He acknowledged the subtle nod from his attending and stepped out of the huddle that had gathered outside a patient's room to discuss the events of the preceding night. When he looked at his text and saw her name, he nearly dropped the phone.

He had sent the text more than a week ago, and when she didn't respond, he had resolved to ignore what he felt. If she couldn't reply, then he wasn't going to beg. She must have thought what they shared wasn't even worth a conversation. Maybe he was too sensitive. Maybe she easily discarded the memories of their one night together, but images of her had haunted his dreams.

He read her text.

Camila: Hi, I'm sorry it took me so long to reply. I didn't know what to do. I'll be up next weekend if you're free for coffee.

Ben: Hi. Sure. I'm free Saturday night.

Camila: Ok, I'll meet you.

Ben: Fine. I'll send you details later. Have to get back to work.

Camila: K

* * *

She waited at the light on Third and La Cienega, and her mind meandered back to a decade ago. Why her mind insisted on taking her down memory lane at the most inopportune times, she didn't know. Graduation had been joyful, an accomplishment shared with her mother, grandmother, and Tyler—the three people who had loved and supported her through the years. But she remembered the vacancy in her heart, a palpable absence. The source of passion that had sustained her for that past year. A man who had come into her life, unexpected and unpredictable. A love that had filled her and torn her to shreds. A dichotomy of agony and joy. She kept smiling the day of her graduation, mustering as much happiness outwardly as she could, but it was shallow. It had been six days since their return from Mexico, and the ache hadn't ceased. With each passing day, she knew the window to abandon her agreement with Ben was narrowing.

She recalled the quad thinning out as graduates filed away towards their cars and restaurant reservations and celebrations. She had looked up at the sky, exhaling a shaky sigh. It was all so vivid. She remembered it as if it happened yesterday. Her grandmother's smile telling her, *Camila, I know you miss him. Camila, you'll be okay. Camila, he's not yours.*

Now, her chest felt like it was caving in from heartache even at the memory. It was too much. She shook her head and pressed down on the accelerator, turning onto 3rd.

The scene flashed before her again. The hallways and paths they had taken together, learning about each other. She had thought severing all ties and erasing him from her life would have made the separation quicker, cleaner. She had removed his information from her phone the day after they returned from Mexico. Refused to answer his calls. She didn't answer when he had banged on her door a few days later, begging to see her again.

She had ignored Tyler when he had suggested perhaps they could see each other one last time.

"I can't, Tyler. Never."

"Cami, just say goodbye."

"We already did."

She had been so naive. Why did she think something as tangible as distance could separate what had bound them together?

Her family saw through her mask during graduation. Mamani worried Camila would miss out on love. Elena worried she would be crushed by it.

"Mija," Elena had whispered as they were leaving. "I think someone is here to see you."

Camila scanned the crowd of families and professors and found him, half-hiding behind the pillars by the courtyard.

"Go talk to him, Camila," Tyler had said softly. "We'll be here for you when you're done."

She had wiped her face with the sleeves of her graduation robe and pinched her cheeks for some color.

"You look beautiful, honey," Elena had told her, as Mamani gave her a gentle nudge.

As soon as she had approached him, she asked what he was doing there.

"I had to see you again," he told her, pulling her behind a column.

"We had a plan," she said. "You shouldn't be here."

"I don't care about our plan. You didn't answer my calls. I even came to your house. I had to see you again. We can figure out a way to make this work. This can't be the end."

She remembered choking on her tears as she said his name. "It has to be," she told him, placing her hand along his face. He had kissed her palm, pushed her gently against the bricks, kissing her mouth deeply, hands roaming across her body as if he was searching for something to hold on to, to bind them together. She had gently pushed him away.

She remembered the hollowness that grew in her core that day. She remembered how he looked down at her, his eyes heavy with desperation. How he had opened his mouth to speak but quickly tightened his lips.

"Here, take this," she had said, taking off her necklace, the one she always wore. The one she wore when he had first seen her. She had pressed it into his hand. "That way I'll know you'll be safe."

"I can't. You always wear this one."

"And now you'll always have a part of me with you."

"I don't have anything to give you," he had said.

"You've given me enough." She smiled through tears.

"I love you," he told her.

And then, between gasps of air and sobs, she said, "I love you too."

She was only a few blocks away and needed to put an end to the mental slideshow threatening her mascara before it was too late. She glanced in the rearview mirror.

Fuck, she looked like a slobbering mess. She patted away the dark circles of makeup beneath her eyes thanks to her prolonged memory reel. Predictably, parking was an issue, but two blocks away she tucked Tyler's convertible into a tight spot. She welcomed the cool night air as she walked and attempted to harness the calmness it offered.

He was outside waiting, and she smiled as she walked up to him.

They didn't hug, just a cordial greeting with a vastness between them that could not be traversed.

"You've come a long way from your little Jetta," he said, motioning to Tyler's BMW keychain.

She held the keys tightly in her hand, an old habit from her college days when she'd hold the keys between her fingers as a makeshift weapon when walking to her car at night.

"Oh, yeah, it's Tyler's. He said my car didn't match my outfit." She laughed, realizing the absurdity of the comment, and dropped the keys into her bag.

He looked painfully handsome, his crisp white shirt open at the neck. She had missed seeing that notch at the base of his neck, the softness of it, the perfect depth to hold a kiss.

"You look great," he told her.

"Thank you," she said, looking down at her hands.

He opened the door to the café. "Shall we?"

He had wanted to take her somewhere nice, a place they could never have imagined going to when they were younger, when they were happy just sharing a cookie. She walked ahead of him, her delicate shoulders funneling down to her narrow waist, with that familiar yet subtle sway of her hips. Despite her more sleek and polished appearance, she still stole glances from customers.

How he had missed her. She had made him question so much when they met all those years ago. He had been searching for his purpose, his passion, and she had swiftly landed in his life with color and conviction and nearly turned his world upside down. But he had safely steered himself back to the world that he knew, safe and reliable, and she had let him go. He didn't know what he hoped for now and tried to quiet any expectations. He was surprised that even after all this time, what he had felt for her was easily reignited, like a smoldering ember of a fire not fully extinguished.

As soon as she sat down across from him, she asked, "Where's Tiffany tonight?" No need to pretend there wasn't a third person involved.

"She's with her parents. Her father isn't doing well."

"Oh, I'm sorry to hear that. Is that why you moved back?"

"Partly, yes. I'm finishing up my fellowship at CHLA."

"Then why were you at the ER at UCLA?"

"I'm picking up extra shifts to save up."

Her delicate fingers broke off a piece of scone to dip into her cappuccino. "For a house?" she asked.

"No, um, actually we are trying to start a family, and it's not really working out all that well."

They had jumped straight in, hadn't they? She felt like a jerk but had assumed that life had proceeded smoothly for them while she had been elbow-deep in nipple cream and diaper blowouts. They were the perfect couple. Two doctors, two salaries, two tall, intelligent people with presumably perfectly working anatomy.

Her eyes met his. The shyness evaporating around them.

"I'm sorry, Ben."

He blew out a sigh and dropped back into his chair.

"What?" she said.

"I've missed hearing you say my name."

She looked away briefly and dismissed the comment. "How long have you been trying?"

"Two years," he said. "Right now, we are in the evaluation phase. I get tested, and she gets tested to figure out who is the problem." He took a sip of his tea. "Maybe it's both of us, but it's all cash. Insurance covers nothing. And that's why I ordered this," he said, motioning to his cup. "No alcohol, no caffeine, no nothing. We have to watch everything, I'm told."

It wasn't him. Her proof was at home sitting on Tyler's couch, likely devouring more ice cream than he was allowed.

"Do you know how much I missed you?" he said. "How many times I tried to remember why we stopped being friends and how stupid that was?"

"Ben, we couldn't."

"We were miles apart. Nothing would have happened."

"It would have. You and me," she said with a small hesitation. "You and me, we can't just be friends. It wasn't possible back then, and

I'm not sure it is now. Honestly, I'm not sure if I would have met you today if not for Tyler and my grandmother."

"Well, I guess I'll have to thank them," he said flatly.

"Listen, a part of me wanted to come here and didn't need convincing, but there is another part that isn't sure what the point of this is."

"Why can't this just be two friends catching up?" He sounded irritated.

"Ben, we aren't just friends."

That all came out too fast. They needed a warmup topic, a shared memory or experience they could rely on to bring them back together emotionally. A way they could recapture a fragment of the chemistry they used to share. There was a hesitation to their conversation. For two people who had been so close, they were now strangers. Perhaps she was right. Too much time had passed.

He wanted to know everything but had no idea how to restart the dialogue. Every bit of her was now a mystery. He decided to stick to a safe subject. "How's Cole's hand?"

"You remembered his name."

He smiled. "Of course. He's your son."

She smiled back. The first genuine smile of the evening.

"His name?" he said, without asking the obvious.

When he mentioned their son's name, her stomach dropped. She wasn't ready for this conversation and had to be certain it didn't veer off course.

"Ben," she said abruptly, "I'm going to ask something of you," not answering his question.

"Okay."

"I want full truths tonight. Please. I don't know why we were thrown back together, but if we only have tonight, let's be completely honest."

Immediately, she regretted her choice of words. They had *just one night*. She wondered if he was also transported back to the small room in Rosarito. The bed where he had held her.

"Fine," he said, a shift in his voice, more direct and less cautious. "If we're going to do this, then I get to start."

"All right." *Shit! Why had she agreed?* She wasn't used to the demanding tone of his voice.

"Are you married?" He thought it best to ask since she wasn't wearing a wedding ring but had a son. She told him no.

He looked straight into her eyes. "Did you name Cole after me?"

She was nervously folding the edge of her napkin, "Yes."

"Did his father know?"

"Not until recently," she said, now tearing the napkin into small pieces and shifting in her seat.

"Did you love him? His father?" he asked, his lips tightening. He had been calculating when she could have conceived Cole after memorizing his birth date from his hospital chart. It must have been with someone right after he left for Boston.

She piled the tattered napkin fragments into her empty cup and sighed back into her chair. "Yes, with everything I had."

"Why aren't you with him?"

She crossed and uncrossed her legs beneath the table, taking care not to rub against him. "He left."

"Camila? There is more to that answer. You were the one who said we have to be honest."

"He wasn't mine. He left, but I loved him. I loved him more than…"

He saw her trying to hide a cry behind a cough, her hand held up to cover her quivering chin. She smoothed her hair. It was as if she was resetting herself. She lifted a cup of water to her lips, and he noticed the familiar charm dangling from her wrist. A similar evil eye to the one she had given him when they said goodbye. He reached out and ran his finger over it. "I still have mine. I always keep it with me."

She watched him take out his wallet and dig inside for her old necklace, the one she had worn daily when she had fallen in love with him.

"Has your life been lonely without him, Camila?"

"My life is full of love, Ben. I'm happy, but if you're asking if I have a boyfriend, then the answer is no. Cole is my priority, and I have other responsibilities."

"I didn't mean to pry," he said.

She smiled at him as if offering a truce. "It's okay. I would want to know the same about you if I didn't already know you were with Tiffany." She had often wondered about his life. With his wife. Did they do boring married things like grocery shopping, planting flowers, and making love on lazy Sunday mornings? Things that she now envied when she imagined doing them with Ben.

"Are you happy?" she said.

He smiled.

"I love my work, but I'm tired from working overnight so much. It's everything I wanted professionally, but right now things with Tiffany are a bit rough. It's not her fault, but she blames herself for all the infertility stuff. It's hard when she's always been good at everything. I wish I could do more to help her, but I know she wants space. So, I work. There is so much unspoken pressure from everyone around us, and in a way, she's closed herself off. But mainly between the two of us, I worry she resents me."

"I'm sure she doesn't feel that way," she said, based on no fact whatsoever.

"Yeah, I'd like to think you're right, but when I'm home it feels like there is a huge cloud hanging over everything. I'm hoping if the testing gives us an answer to the infertility, then it'll help expedite the process. She has a vision of what her life is supposed to be, and being a mother is a part of that."

"I'm so sorry."

It was now or never. Tell him and put him out of his misery, she told herself. *Inhale, exhale, inhale, exhale.* She brushed away a tear.

"Don't cry, Camila. It'll all work out."

"It's not you," she said, looking directly at him.

He froze and cleared his throat. "What?"

She knew she had to somehow let him know that Cole was his son. That he had been able to father a child and that he could stop wondering.

"I mean, aren't most fertility issues related to the woman?"

"Well, yeah, more things can go wrong for the female, but I'm still getting checked out."

You are a coward, Camila thought to herself, and he was a fool.

"So, you didn't move to Mexico?" he asked.

"No, that dream went out the door once I found out I was pregnant.

But another door opened, and I was lucky to get a job in San Diego, so I moved in with my mom and Mamani." She laughed, rolling her eyes. "I know, glamorous, right?"

"So, you've been in San Diego the entire time?"

"Yeah."

All the time he had been in LA, she was just a short drive away. When he thought she was in Mexico, she had been in San Diego. When he had tried to contact her and blamed the faulty third-world cell service, she had been ignoring him. He felt the betrayal boil to the surface.

"You look angry with me," she said.

"I looked for you everywhere. Even when it didn't make sense, every time I saw someone who reminded me of you or who laughed like you did. My heart jumped. But it was never you, and you never reached out. You broke my heart," he said softly.

"Ben, you were married," she said. "What did you want me to do?"

He didn't have an answer. He could have also changed the course of his life for Camila, and he hadn't. At the time he wasn't strong enough, or confident enough in his own ability or dedication to a life yet unexplored, to abandon Tiffany and the path everyone around him expected him to pursue.

"Listen, what we did was wrong, and I'm sorry for it every day," she said. "I blame us for being young and careless, and I blame my shitty car that left us stranded together when we should have never been left alone."

"You're sorry for being with me?" he said.

"Ben, come on, you know what I mean."

"You really regret it? Because I don't. I don't regret a moment of being with you. Ever."

"Ben, I meant, Ben, please, look at me."

But he couldn't. He had confessed everything, how she had occupied his mind and his life for years after they separated, and now to find out it meant nothing to her. That breaking his marriage vows when they were still so new meant nothing to her. His anger morphed into shame and embarrassment. He had replayed their night together countless times. Hoped for years that she was thinking of him too. But now he realized that whatever hope he clung to was one-sided. That, despite the passion she once had, her belief in fate and destiny, he alone had kept the memory of them alive. He finished his tea and prepared to leave.

"Thanks for meeting me," he said, standing. He was hurt and felt stupid, a sentiment he was unfamiliar with. "Maybe you were right. This wasn't the best idea."

"Ben," she said tenderly, reaching for his hand, but he pulled away.

She remained seated, unable to move. He had walked away from her. Again. She was numb. Her heart felt cavernous, a shell of the organ it was intended to be. She took out her phone and sent a text to Tyler telling him she was headed home.

Tyler: already?!
Camila: yeah
Tyler: that bad?
Camila: yeah
Tyler: did you tell him
Camila: no

She turned off her ringer and threw her phone in her purse. She didn't have it in her to be reprimanded right now. Straightening her dress, she tidied up their table, an old habit from years of waitressing, and walked out the door.

The street was dark and empty. A cold chilled her from inside and out. She rubbed her arms and walked quickly to her car. Once sequestered safely inside, she rested her head on the steering wheel, her sadness catching painfully in her throat.

It could have gone worse. This wasn't the best outcome but not the worst. There was too much distance between them, and now she knew. She could put an end to all the wondering, all the time spent considering the "what ifs" and willing him to think of her at the same moment and with the same intensity. Closing her eyes, she urged herself to start the engine. She needed to get home.

Home.

Where she was loved and safe from the hope of having Ben in her life again.

A sudden knock on her passenger window startled her.

"Camila," he said, her name muffled through the glass.

It took her a moment to decipher which button controlled the window.

"Camila, I'm sorry. Can we talk?"

With a nervous hesitation, she unlocked the door. "Get in. It's cold."

The car was warm, and steam started to gather along the edges of the windows.

She kept her hands firmly on the steering wheel though the engine was off.

"Full truth, Camila."

She smiled at the memory of the term they used to use to indicate seriousness.

He turned toward her as she slowly unbuckled her seatbelt to face him.

"Ben, we had an agreement. We had an understanding," she said.

"Camila, we weren't business partners. We were friends. . . lovers," he whispered. "I want the full truth."

He deserved an explanation, but she was terrified.

"Ben, I told you years ago that I wasn't going to be someone's wife and had no intention of being someone's mistress. And that's what I would have been, right? You'd be living your life in Boston with Tiffany and giving me scraps of your time because that was all you had. I deserved more than that. *We* deserved more than that." She took a breath in, defeated. "And we can't restart now. There are too many other factors."

"What other factors? So, you have a son. That doesn't matter."

If he only knew, she thought.

"Ben, we can't be just friends. It will always be more between us. We are tethered together in a way that I can't explain. That's why the agreement was what it was."

He blew out a frustrated sigh.

"Camila, we were kids. You can't hold us to a conversation we had in our twenties."

"You are married!" She didn't intend to yell.

"I was married then too!" he yelled back. He ran his hand over his face.

"This wasn't a good idea," she said softly.

"According to the old Camila, this was all destined," he said much more calmly.

"A lot has happened to the *old Camila*."

"Why did you disappear on me?"

She rested her head on the steering wheel, exhausted. "Ben. Please."

"Camila, just tell me. It won't change anything that's passed. I just need to know. For closure."

How little he knew. "It will change everything."

"Camila," he said softly, placing a hand along her face.

She looked up at him. Those same eyes that had smiled at her, laughed with her, and loved her. How she had loved him. And still loved him. How could she tell him that Cole was his son now that they had finally been reunited? When they were dancing around the broken pieces of their fragile relationship. Would he ever forgive her for this? She wasn't sure if she would lose him with her confession, but she was certain Cole would gain a father, and that was more than enough.

"He's yours," she said in a hushed voice, almost mouthing the words. Terrified.

Well, that's one way of doing it, she thought.

His mouth fell open. His hand dropped.

She couldn't look at him.

He rubbed his hands up and down his face and fell back into his seat.

It was so quiet, it was as if a black hole was swallowing her, the calm strangling her. She yearned for him to say something, anything.

"Ben?"

"Just give me a second," he mumbled.

She felt her eyes brimming, and then the panic set in. The same cold feeling she had experienced last week when she saw Cole's bloodied hand.

Ben didn't say a word, and she interpreted his silence as anger, disappointment, frustration. Anything but happiness.

"Ben, this was a mistake. I'm sorry, I um, I shouldn't have told you this way. I need to leave. You can't even look at me, so let's not try to. . . to make something of nothing," she said in a panicked and pressured way. She opened the car door to escape, and the air slapped her face. Where was she going? She needed to get back in her car and drive away but started walking away instead. She could feel the cold sweat running down her back.

"Camila! Camila, stop!" He called after her.

She froze. She didn't know where she was going, by herself, at night, with her car sitting right there. All she knew was that she wanted to leave, to get as far away as possible.

"Camila, I just needed a moment," he said, reaching for her wrist and spinning her around. "That's all. Please. Get in the car so we can talk."

She slowly returned to the car with him, partly because there was nowhere else to go, partly because she remained hopeful.

After an agonizing few minutes, Ben said, "When I saw him the other day, a part of me recognized something, but I thought it was nostalgia. That it was you I was seeing in him."

"Are you angry?"

"Honestly, I don't know how I feel."

Her heart was slowing into a reasonable two-digit rate for the first time that evening. She leaned against the door, creating as much space as possible between them.

"Why didn't you tell me?" he said.

"Ben, your life would have been destroyed."

"We were adults. We could have made it work. We would have survived."

"We were kids. Everything was so black or white. Wrong or right. Good or bad. I couldn't be a good girl who did a bad thing. I could only be fully good or fully bad," she sighed, "and I had done something very bad. But the world, well, it's mostly gray, and my mistake was to fall in love with a taken man. We had one night, and I knew I came along after promises had been made to Tiffany and plans had been set into motion, but it didn't make a difference to me in here," she said, pointing at her heart. "So, when I found out about Cole, I was happy to have a part of you with me and let you live your life."

He knew she was right. The contradictions of youth were what had prevented him from putting a stop or at least postponing his own marriage. Exploring what a life would have been with Camila instead, but his younger self could not have fathomed changing course once a decision had been made. He understood exactly what the confines of black or white, wrong or right, can do to a person.

"Camila, I never stopped loving you. I just put it on pause. I would have helped."

"How would you have done that, Ben? Really, I appreciate you saying so, but how could you have helped without ruining everything for yourself and for Tiffany?"

Ben couldn't answer. He knew it would have destroyed his marriage, but his heart would have been full in a different way. A fullness he had missed for ten years.

"I've loved you from the first moment you held me in your arms," she said. "That night at the restaurant, and then every moment after. I never stopped, but I didn't expect anything from you, and I only had room for you in my heart, but then Cole was born. And now he's my world."

"Who knows he's mine?" he asked.

"Tyler and my family."

"Oh my God," he whispered. "They must hate me." He dropped his head into his hands, wondering if the women who had welcomed him into their home now cursed him. He had unknowingly been turned into an absentee father.

"No, Ben," she said, reaching out for his hand instinctively but pulling back. "All they asked me was whether we were in love. And I told them we had been. I never had again what we shared that night. Not before. Not since."

He closed his eyes and hung his head as he braced himself against the dashboard.

"Ben, I couldn't imagine love being possible again. But I told them the truth, that you didn't know about the baby. They kept telling me to call you, to let you know, to let you have the choice to be a part of it. Tyler was furious with me and stopped talking to me for a few weeks, but I just couldn't. Your life with Tiffany had just started. You had all these plans. I wasn't going to ruin that."

"Camila, what about *your* life? You did everything on your own. I wasn't even there to hold your hand."

Her heart fluttered hearing his words. She smiled at him with a tilt of her head as he looked toward her.

"Oh Ben, how I loved you. I ached for you. For years," she said, placing her hand on his arm.

"I've never loved like I loved you," he whispered.

If the circumstances of his world had been different, he would have taken her into his arms right then. Held her and told her all the ways she permeated his life. The way the scent of orange blossoms reminded him of her. That anytime he heard "Mi Tierra", at a store, in a restaurant, in a movie, he thought of her swaying hips the night he held her for the first time. How, in the midst of punishing night shifts when exhaustion swept over him like a wave, he would close his eyes and the memory of her would sustain him until morning. That for years he would seek her out in crowds. If he saw wild, long, wavy hair or if he heard carefree laughter, he searched for her. His longing had made him lonely in his own home. What he felt couldn't be shared, not with David or his sisters, and definitely not with Tiffany. He and Tiffany had built a dependable life together. They were puzzle pieces that fit together safely and securely. Any move on his part would impact not only him but Tiffany and both their families. It was all woven together too tightly. Even still, he couldn't pull away from Camila.

"I want to know him, Camila."

"Ben, I don't..."

"I want us to get to know each other again, too."

"Ben, you're married."

"I can have friends who are women. I do have a bit of self-control, Camila."

He knew he sounded irritated, and she reminded him about their lack of self-control the last time they were alone.

"We have no business being friends again," she said. "Don't make me be the bad guy. You know it's true."

He knew from the urge to pull her into him at that very moment that she was right.

"What did you tell him about me?" he said. "Did he think I left him?"

"No. I would never let him think that. I told him his father helps sick children and needs to travel all over the world."

Another partial truth.

"How did you know what I did for work?"

"Tyler had said you were a surgeon, and when I was embarrassed to ask more, I would Google you. I'm very proud of you."

Unexpectedly, he felt a tightness in his throat and pushed down the feelings that were rising to the surface.

"Please let me see my son, Camila," he said. "You had no choice growing up without a father, but he does."

18

Toward the ninth month of Camila's pregnancy, the insomnia had taken over. When she was still a reasonable size and had felt the baby's first kicks, it was a daily reminder of the baby, yes. But also, of him. It was Ben's baby. A part of him was growing inside her and let her hold onto a piece of what they had. Tyler had said she still had time to tell him.

Swollen feet, acid reflux, and constipation made the days drag, but still the weeks quickly passed, and now they were days away from the fated Match Day when residencies made non-negotiable offers to their top choices, and Ben would be gone forever. She wondered why this day held such importance for her. There had been no communication with Ben for months now. No voicemails, no emails.

At night, when she waddled around her room rubbing her lower back or trying to sleep upright on the sofa, she would wonder. What would it have been like had he asked her out before he had ever met Tiffany? And not to the Coral Tree, but on actual dates to actual restaurants. Would he have had the same restraint? Would she have been as alluring to him if nothing were holding him back? Would they have memorialized their first anniversary with gifts or a weekend away like normal couples? She leaned back, stroking her protuberant abdomen, and fantasized about the excitement of what would have been their first kiss. Not a stolen, guilty kiss. One that didn't require an apology. Maybe after a few weeks they would spend the night together, and she would have felt the tingle of anticipation instead of the dread of the inevitable separation. Maybe slow, patient love would have built between them instead of the urgent, desperate love that pushed her into his arms one night. She dozed off with memories of him, of them, of what might have been.

* * *

It was the first week back at her family's home. She had inhabited her old room with its twin bed, the same bean bag, and posters decorating the walls, now sun-faded. The reality of her loneliness weighed on her as her due date approached. She needed to be close to family.

The pain had started suddenly, waking her from sleep. She went to the bathroom thinking it was gas or her perpetually overactive bladder. Over the past two months, she would congratulate herself if she could avoid a restroom for two hours. She washed her hands before she doubled over in pain. It was as if a hot skewer was being shoved into her back and through her stomach. She cried out, grasping onto the counter in excruciating pain, and heard the familiar shuffle of feet.

Mamani appeared in the doorway, wrapped in her shawl. "Azziz, are you okay?"

With fear in her eyes, Camila replied, "Mamani, I can't."

Before she could explain, there was a faint pop and a sudden gush of fluid splattering on the floor. They looked at each other, one with terror, the other with excitement.

Thankfully, the streets were empty as they drove toward the hospital. Camila's pain became exaggerated to the point of incomprehension. She held on to the seat in front of her and closed her eyes in agony. By the time they were in the hospital room, it was all she could do not to scream with every contraction.

She counted the tiles on the ceiling between her bed and door. One, two, three...seven. And then repeated it. With this focal point, she calmed herself as the nurses started her IV and strapped the belts to her abdomen that would tighten and release with increasing frequency.

The mind-numbing pain sent regret surging through her veins. Why had she cut him out of her life so completely?

"I can't do this!" She cried out a few hours later. "I need him! I can't do this by myself!"

The doctors and nurses had carefully avoided asking about the missing FOB. She had seen the acronym in her paperwork once and asked her nurse about it. She had answered with indifference.

"It means father of the baby."

Between peaks of pain, she wondered what the staff thought of her. Unmarried. Or unloved. Alone. They were all so cautious. Dancing around with their aseptic terminology. Did they think it was a one-night stand? An act of carelessness?

Why shouldn't they? It had been, hadn't it?

"We are here for you, Mija. You are not alone," Elena said in a calm, tender voice.

"Azziz, focus on the love you had for him," Mamani said. "The love you shared together. The pain you have now is the price of the love you had then. You can't savor the sweet if you haven't tasted the bitter." She stroked Camila's face and swept her hair back.

Camila cried out Ben's name as Cole started to crown.

Her mother too had cried out the name of her one great love twenty-seven years before, but unlike Camila, Elena's love was by her side. Holding onto her hand with all he had and whispering a prayer in her ear, in a language she didn't understand but knew was meant for her.

Sweat beaded on Camila's face and arms. Sweat from fear, from heat, from anguish. As each wave washed over her, she felt it in her core, in a place separate from the outside, pushing from within, a tsunami of agonizing pain. She had kindly been offered an epidural on multiple occasions but declined repeatedly. She couldn't tell them the truth. That she wanted to feel the inverse but equally intense physical pain to atone for what she had done. For what they had done, all the pain they had been willing to cause. For betraying Tiffany, for ignoring all that was right. And for loving Ben when she should have walked away. For tempting a good man who loved her when he knew he shouldn't. She wanted to feel it all, and when it felt like she may just break in two, she finally heard the cry of her son.

And the storm stopped. She was surrounded by love. By strength. And then tears of relief, exhaustion, and joy.

His small body rested on top of her bare chest as she exhaled.

"Look at him, mija. He is beautiful," Elena said through her own tears.

Camila looked down and was greeted by the same soft brown eyes that she had met a year before. The same eyes that had stolen her heart once were again looking up at her in the face of her son.

* * *

To say it was difficult would have been a gross understatement. Besides the fatigue and general sense of confusion that accompanies living with a newborn, Cole's features were a constant reminder of the man she had lost. Her family tried to help. Even Tyler had come around, putting aside their differences about what Ben's involvement should have been. But despite the physical help, Camila fell hard and deep into a depression that could not be considered merely the baby blues. Her grandmother cooked foods that were supposed to improve her mood and enhance her breast milk. Nothing worked.

"Mamani, I can't eat any more ghormeh sabzi," she said. Begging to try supplements instead to pump her body full of fenugreek.

Her mother brewed homemade teas purported to decrease the intensity of postpartum depression. They watched her drink and eat, cautiously optimistic that the light would return to her eyes knowing the only cure was approximately three thousand miles away. Her obstetrician offered her a short course of an antidepressant after she refused to go to group therapy with other mothers in similar situations.

Similar situations? How absurd. There was no one in her position. And sharing her story with a group of married women would likely invite scorn and judgment, definitely not what she was after.

She tried to convince her family she was improving. That the teas and stews and powders were helping. Her only solace was the privacy of the bathroom, where she sequestered herself, knowing she would be granted a few minutes of solitude. With the water running, she would cry to her heart's content, but it was never enough. There were always more tears, more regrets, more ridiculous scenarios to conjure where they could have been together. But the weight of the world would never ease from her shoulders. She knew she could never reach out to him now. She could not and would not.

Eventually, the newborn weeks blended into the monotonous infant months, and then she earned the joy, though nonstop chaos of a toddler. Cole filled her life with more love than she could have imagined. This small little boy had infused their home with more energy and excitement than anything since, well, since she herself had been a child. He was boisterous and bold, like his mother, but thoughtful and kind like his father. A man who was never discussed.

As Cole grew, Camila fell into the comfort of a predictable pattern of parenting and work. She didn't have time for social endeavors, especially since Tyler had started his residency. "Uncle" Tyler had grown fond of little Cole, and Camila credited his masculine presence for delaying Cole's questions about his father. The rare times Mamani and Elena convinced her to leave Cole for the evening and go out like other young twenty-somethings, she was riddled with guilt. In those times, Tyler would drive down and drag her out on his one weekend off in eight.

"Listen, I'm sleep deprived and horny, and so are you!" he said. "So, you're coming downtown with me, and we're going to dance, and you are going to have a good time whether you like it or not."

He was right. After a reasonable amount of hesitation, she would start to apply her makeup and pick an outfit, and the excitement of years before would slowly creep back.

The moment she walked through the heavy, red curtains of the club, the sound of bass would reverberate through her body, and she'd forget. Forget that she was a mother, forget that most of her clothes had food stains from her child, forget that she was alone and hadn't had sex in over three years, and forget that she missed Ben every day. There wasn't a night that she didn't wish he was in bed beside her. But before she could find herself crying in the middle of the dance floor, Tyler would gently nudge her in the direction of the nearest handsome man to distract her. She let the music ripple through her as a stranger's hands roamed her curves and ran through her hair, and she would lose herself for a while, reminded of who she used to be.

Tyler was her only link to Ben, though she was unaware. He had stayed in touch with Tiffany once intern year started. Despite her seriousness, Tiffany was an excellent mentor and now friend, who guided him to excel with tips and tricks that could only be gained through experience. A few times, he had heard Ben in the background asking who she was talking to, and after her reply, Tyler heard him leaving the room. Toward the end of intern year, Tyler had called to let Tiffany know about a teaching award he had received. But as he was preparing to leave a message, Ben answered.

"Oh, hi Ben, It's Tyler. Is Tiffany there?"

"Oh, hey. Um, yeah, she's just getting out of the shower. Hang on a minute."

Tyler heard a rustling in the background.

"She said if you can hang on a minute, she'll be right out," Ben said.

"Yeah, that's fine." They made small talk, Tyler asking Ben about his intern year.

"It's what's expected for surgery, I guess," Ben said. "You?"

"Same, but Tiffany helped a lot."

Tyler was certain there was no room large enough to house the elephant they were trying to avoid.

Finally, Ben asked in a whisper. "How is she?"

Tyler felt he was asking so much more. He must have wondered about Camila in the years since their last conversation. Where she was living, if she had a boyfriend, if she thought of him.

"She's fine," was all Tyler said. He wasn't sure why he lied, though. "Well, she's not fine, but she's okay." He knew what Camila would want him to say, but he also heard Ben's genuine concern through the phone. He would be as honest as possible without betraying Camila.

"Is there something wrong?" Ben asked.

"You should reach out," Tyler said and immediately regretted his words. He had crossed the line.

Ben let out a sigh. "I stopped trying. She never replied."

"I didn't know that."

"Yeah, not once. If you see her, tell her I...just let her know...oh, here's Tiffany. Nice catching up," Ben said.

Tyler vowed never to call their landline again.

19

April 2014

Ben had finished his rounds early and was on his way to meet with Camila. And for the first time, his son.

His weekly calls to her had been cathartic through the dark and murky fog of doctor's appointments and the long hours of fellowship. Ben loved his wife, but over these last months, their relationship seemed more a blur of timed intercourse, ovulation sticks, and basal body temperature. He didn't remember the last time they had spontaneous, unscheduled sex. It had been a calculated move on his part, not being completely transparent with Tiffany about his weekly calls to Camila. He had mentioned running into her a few days after the ER visit, and Tiffany seemed less than interested, so why belabor the point with the details of their conversations?

He had been in the kitchen making a sandwich when he said, "Guess who I ran into today?"

"Who?" Tiffany said, scrolling through the most recent fertility article from ASRM. The benefit of having friends in medicine was access to an abundance of research. Experts a phone call away. The negative was what most of the data pointed to—sometimes things just don't work.

"Camila," Ben said and waited for her response.

"How can this be?" Tiffany said. "Fifty percent of infertility has no cause? What the fuck? That's bullshit."

Had she not heard him? He felt no need to repeat himself; maybe that was confession enough.

She looked up at him. "Sorry, who did you see again?"

"Camila."

"Camila?" She removed her glasses. "Oh, Tyler's old roommate. She was fun. What's she up to? It's been like, what, ten years?"

"Yup, ten years."

"Wasn't she going to travel the world and cure malaria or something?" She walked into the kitchen and took a bite of the turkey sandwich he had made for himself.

"Yeah, well, she has a kid now and lives in San Diego."

"Who's the husband?"

"None that she mentioned," he said.

"Geez. Wait, where did you run into her?"

"Oh, the ER. Her kid cut his hand."

She braced herself on the counter, shoulders slumped. "I guess it's just us who are fertility-challenged, huh?"

He went to her, wrapping her in his arms. "We'll be fine too."

She shrugged, dislodging herself from his embrace. This had become their pattern. Moments of her self-doubt, Ben trying to console her, and Tiffany rejecting his gesture.

He turned her around, forcing her to look at him. "It'll all be fine. It'll happen if it's destined." He kissed her forehead before pulling her into another embrace.

"It's not destiny," she said. "It's science. Once they can give us a treatment plan, we can get started. Just line up the hoops, and I'll start jumping. I've come this far. This is not where my success ends."

Tiffany approached her fertility like her career, with Type A ferocity and a cold-hearted determination. But for Ben, his energy was divided into equal portions for the son he hadn't met and the children he was yet to father.

Camila had finally agreed to speaking on the phone after their initial outing. He had nearly convinced her to bring Cole, but she was still playing mental ping-pong between the pros and cons.

"Listen, I want to be a part of his life," Ben told her. "But I would never force you if you felt it was bad for him, if you thought it would set him back or create issues."

"He's strong. But I'm worried, sure. And I'm worried about myself too."

"What do you mean?"

"I don't know what I'll feel if I start seeing you again regularly."

He heard the hesitation in her voice.

"Honestly, Ben, I don't know. It's my fault that he hasn't had a father, and now what if, what if meeting you somehow makes him resent me? I'm stuck. I'm terrified."

"You can't blame yourself for everything," he said on what had now become a routine biweekly call.

"But I was the irresponsible one. I'm the one who said we could keep going."

"But I agreed."

"Yes, but I should have known better."

"Camila, stop. I'm to blame too. We both are. We can't keep going in circles. There's no point."

Most of their calls digressed into a tug of war over who was most at fault.

"But *my* car broke down, I was the one who agreed to the arrangement, and I was the one NOT on birth control," she said.

He finally blurted it out. "I never asked for a second room."

"What?"

"In Mexico, I never asked for a separate room."

She remembered the night vividly, the wedding and guests, the hotel with only one available room. "But there weren't any. They told us so when we checked in. That was the whole problem, remember?"

"Yeah, but when I went down again to ask, I found out there was another room. But I didn't want it anymore. I wanted to be with you."

"Wait, what?"

He had never said the words aloud, but he recalled clearly that day at the hotel, the small smile on the old man's face when Ben had politely declined the second set of keys.

He adjusted himself on the small mattress in the hospital's call room, the springs creaking under his weight.

"Camila, I wanted to stay with you. Deep down, I guess I was hoping something would happen. I was looking for any excuse to spend the night with you. I knew we would never see each other again, and I was desperate. I was consumed. You were all I could think of, and I was young and scared."

He had beaten her at her own game with the ultimate partial truth.

Tears filled her eyes when she thought back to that night, all those years ago. Some details had faded with time, but certain images would resurface when she remembered the gentle tug of his mouth on hers or his weight pressing her into the bed.

"Are you still there?"

"Yeah," she murmured.

"Are you angry?"

She thought for a few minutes. "No, actually, I'm kind of relieved. All this time I thought I had tricked you somehow. That you were coerced into being with me."

"Camila, I didn't need convincing."

She let out a sigh. As if a huge weight had lifted.

"I don't think either of us could have stopped it," he said. "There was such a momentum by that point. If not in Mexico, it would have happened back home."

"Yeah, I guess you are right."

She heard his beeper go off.

"Shit!" he said.

"It's okay. I know you're on call," she said.

"Just hang on a minute."

She heard shuffling as he put down his own phone and answered his page.

"Dr. Martin here... Pain? He had PRN meds ordered... Okay, I'll put in a one-time IV dose. Yup... Sure."

"Sorry," he apologized, picking up his phone again.

She could hear him furiously typing. "What's going on?" she asked.

"Oh, some 17-year-old kid who could bench press me can't swallow pills."

She laughed. "Ben, he's a kid. Shouldn't you, of all people, be more compassionate?"

"I know, I know, Camila. But it's one a.m., and I'm barely caught up and just had cold pizza for dinner, or an early breakfast depending on your perspective."

"Well, I'll let you go so you can get your work finished."

"No, no, I love talking to you. I mean, I really look forward to catching up with you and hearing about Cole."

She had resisted the urge to ask about Tiffany beyond that first night over coffee. She assumed he was the same truthful and devoted man she had met years before, minus one major transgression. She still felt the need to ask, given what she and that truthful and devoted man had done together.

"So, does Tiffany know we talk?"

He let out a long sigh. "She doesn't know we talk as much as we do, but I did tell her we ran into each other."

Camila was only somewhat relieved.

"Would you meet me again?" he said. "Just for coffee?"

"I don't know Ben. It'll never be just coffee for me, if I'm being honest. I can't risk feeling more for you again."

"I know I'm irresistible, especially now, twenty hours since my last shower, but I promise I'll behave myself."

She laughed out loud. "As appealing as that sounds, I'm not worried about pouncing on you. But I don't know if it's a good idea. Tiffany doesn't even know we talk."

"I don't think she'd care, to be honest. She is totally consumed with getting pregnant."

"Aren't you?" Camila asked.

"I was, but now, I kinda want my wife back. She was always serious, and I loved that about her, but now she's like a full-blown robot. Every little thing is viewed through the lens of fertility. If anyone she knows gets pregnant, she's affected. If her labs aren't perfectly within normal range, she reads every article she can get her hands on trying to understand exactly why. She's only thirty-eight, and she's already looked into egg donors. We don't even have sex unless it's during an optimal fertility window." He blew out his breath. "I'm just exhausted. My conversations with you are the only fun I have right now."

"I'm sorry, Ben."

"I'm not sure if I would have… I'm just not sure I would have made the same choices if I knew where I'd be right now."

She didn't reply, just let the words hang between them.

Ben sighed. "It's okay. You were always my escape. That was part of the reason it was so hard to lose you. I felt like I had lost everything joyful in my life in one person."

"I'm so sorry. I just couldn't be near you. I was shattered. I loved you."

They had focused their conversations on Cole and their current lives, but the past loomed overhead like a shadow, regardless of whether the words were spoken.

"I never stopped," he said.

"Ben, how can you say that? You're married."

"I was married then, too," he said, more softly this time.

She felt a twinge of shame. "Yes, but we know better now. Anyway, I look different now and have had a baby, so things aren't quite as taut or together, so to speak," she said with a deprecating giggle.

"You're still beautiful. And you had *my* baby. You're remarkable."

"Ben..." Her voice cracked.

"Camila, we've always had bad timing. I can't leave my wife, and I know you're not asking me to, but never forget I loved you. From the start, before careers, before marriage, before Cole, before it all."

She brought her hand over her mouth to stifle a cry.

"Don't cry," he said.

"I've thought about you for so long," she said. "I dreamt of you. I felt your hands on me like it was yesterday and wondered if you even remembered me. Especially after you stopped trying to reach me. I thought you hated me, and I was embarrassed, thinking you had forgotten me while I thought of you all the time and wished you were still in my life. Sometimes if I'd go a day or two without you occupying my mind, I'd congratulate myself. How sad is that? But I missed your friendship the most. I missed your laugh, the way you would look at me. I was so stupid. I wasted all that time when I could have told you earlier."

He could hear her crying through the phone.

"Camila, I thought about you too. I wondered how you were and who you were with and if they made you happy. I wondered why I had been such a coward."

"You weren't a coward."

"I was. I should have stopped it the moment I knew what I felt for you was so strong, so real."

"But we tried, and it didn't work."

"I don't mean between us. I mean I shouldn't have gotten married."

"Oh God."

He heard her try to suppress a small sob.

"Ben, why didn't we just meet earlier? Why didn't we stay friends?"

"Because there's a reason for everything, even if we never know why," he said. He heard her breathing calm. "You taught me that, remember?"

"Yes," she said.

"Just please don't leave my life again."

20

May 2014

"Mom, what does he look like?" Cole asked, balancing on the edge of his seat.

Camila smiled down at her son. "He looks like you."

She had tried to subdue the butterflies in her stomach. Cole had been ecstatic when she told him they were meeting his father. But then he withdrew, no doubt scared to meet the man he had wondered about for years. She had given him the choice knowing the little boy who drew imagined versions of his father would jump at the chance.

With his backpack at his feet, he was quiet as she drove them past the beaches and Camp Pendleton to the small cafe she had suggested to Ben.

"Why there?" Ben had asked her.

"Well, it's halfway, and also no one knows us there. It's private but out in the open."

It was also the safest place to meet. A place that held no memories. She had to be honest with herself. Weeks of easy, hour-long conversations had bridged the distance that initially separated them. It was a revised version of their dates at Coral Tree, only this time they had a son.

Mamani and Elena were hopeful Cole would finally have a relationship with his father but apprehensive to welcome Ben back into Camila's life. They hadn't seen another man enter her life since Ben. Cole, their small family, and her career had filled her life but left a vacancy in her heart. Mamani knew Camila needed love. Not the love of a child or a mother, but of a man and one who she had loved and continued to love.

"Camila, there are these places on the internet where you can find a man now," Mamani said with enthusiasm, having heard about online dating from one of her friends at the Persian Senior Center.

Camila laughed, "Mamani, I'm shocked you would consider a computer a proper matchmaker."

"In my day, we had matchmakers," Mamani said. "Now, Mr. Internet has made it much easier and without all the nonsense of suitors and tea ceremonies."

She smiled at her grandmother. "Thank you, Mamani, but I think I'll take my chances with fate."

Cole pushed the straw in his chocolate milk and arranged his toy cars on the table. The pictures he had drawn for his father were still tucked inside his backpack. Camila wondered if he worried the man he was about to meet wouldn't live up to his expectations and be deserving of such a gift.

She heard the jingle of the cafe door opening and stood, smoothing her dress and smiling at Ben. She gently tapped her son on his shoulder, "Cole, honey, he's here."

Cole glanced behind him and saw Ben approaching their table.

"Hi, Camila," Ben said, as she placed a kiss on his cheek.

She pulled her son into her. "This is Cole," she said.

"Hi, Cole, I'm Ben."

Cole looked up at him, and Camila felt a joy in her heart that she hadn't expected.

"You're my dad?" Cole asked.

"Yes, I am."

* * *

It was effortless. As if the genetics were strong enough to compensate for years of separation. There was some trepidation initially from Cole, but Ben was certain that trust would build between them in time. He devoted what little free time he had between the requirements of his fellowship and his wife, and unbeknownst to her, to Cole. Initially, they met for lunch or walked around campus passing around a football Ben had brought for him. Camila would tag along, usually in the background, reading or busying herself with work, but allowing them to build a relationship free from her supervision. But these meetings eventually became broader in scope and didn't focus solely on Ben and Cole, but Camila too.

Cole ran ahead to play catch with a dog, and Ben and Camila strolled behind together. To the outside observer, they looked like any ordinary couple. But they were careful, cautious to a fault. Never touching. Communicating by phone had been safe. Now they were playing with fire.

"He talks about you all the time," she told him. "His class had to do a report on the 'Most Important Person in My Life,' and he picked you."

He didn't recognize the feeling of parental pride that formed in his chest. "He did?"

They had been seeing each other monthly for the past 6 months. He had come close to telling Stephanie about Cole but hesitated. He wasn't sure how to divulge his secret—that he had a son—information he had purposely withheld from his sister and, more importantly, his wife. He had become more distracted trying to balance his two worlds, and it affected his performance at work and home. He would forget to take out the trash cans or to pick up dinner on his way home. Tiffany dismissed the change in his behavior, attributing it to chronic sleep deprivation and stress. But the seasoned nurses at work who had spent hours with him over the past few years were quicker to pinpoint the cause of his absentmindedness.

"Dr. Martin, I'm sorry, but did you want to remove the Foley on bed three or not? There was no order."

"Oh, I'm sorry, Lauren," he said, shaking his head. It occurred to him this was the third time he was being asked to clarify an order he had promised to place an hour before.

"It's okay, Dr. Martin, but if you don't mind me saying, you've been a bit, well, not yourself."

"Don't sugarcoat it, Lauren," the charge nurse said. "Dr. Martin, there's only one thing that distracts a man," she said from her desk. "Lady problems."

He smiled. These women knew his idiosyncrasies better than his own family. He rubbed his eyes and leaned back in his chair, swiveling toward the small group of nurses.

"I'm just tired, Janice, thanks for asking," he said.

"Mmhmm. When Dr. Patterson started getting 'tired,' he was fooling around with Kim from the fourth floor."

"Don't mind her," another nurse said, handing him a much-appreciated cup of hospital-grade coffee. "We know you are as good as they come."

But was he? He had been seeing his lover from a past life, though not romantically, while his wife was at work or taking care of her ailing father. He knew he was acting like an asshole, but he couldn't stop. Even if he could, there was Cole. He had never expected to love someone so fast and so deeply. Even with Camila, it had been gradual, and he had fought against it. But with each passing month, he and Cole were growing closer. And to complicate things further, so were he and Camila.

They had met in Manhattan Beach. The briny wind sweeping her hair. Cole skipping along a few feet ahead of them.

"How is work?" Camila asked him.

"Tiring, but I'm near the end."

A gradual panic crept up her spine. Would he have to leave again? If they were going to be separated again, it would be even more painful now that Cole was involved. "Will you move when you're done?"

"God, I don't know. I can't even figure out what I'm doing tomorrow. Tiffany will want to stay close to her parents, especially if we have kids. But we're not having much success in that department."

"Still no luck?" Camila said.

"Well, we don't see much of each other, but I still have to go through the humiliating act of submitting a specimen for analysis."

"I wish I could help. I mean, not with that, but you know," she said, turning beet red.

He smiled, "Yeah, well, you can't help with that."

"Doesn't it count that we have Cole?"

She had never referred to them as *we*. Though she had been careful, her feelings for him had begun to swell. Seeing him interact with Cole made it all more intense.

"Yes, it proves I can do it, but they still check."

They walked ahead, the sun setting behind the clouds. She hugged herself as the wind picked up.

"Are you cold?" he said, opening his jacket. He pulled her into him, and she felt the heat coming off his body and the strength of his arm, and she nearly burst into tears, not realizing how starved she had been for his touch. She relaxed into his side, and Cole ran up to them and nestled his head into his mother. There they stood. The three of them. And for a moment Camila was whole.

21

Plans were underway for Cole's birthday. Camila had called Ben at their son's request. "He would love for you to come."

"Really?" Ben said. "He asked for me?"

"Yeah, we asked him what he wanted for his birthday, and he said a chocolate cake and you to come to his party."

"Where is it?"

"It's at our house next weekend," she said. "Are you working?"

"I'll get it covered if I am."

He drove down after Tiffany fell asleep. She had worked the past three nights, was exhausted, and still planned on seeing her parents later that day. He felt conflicted leaving on the one night they could have spent time together, but his feelings of isolation from his wife helped ease the guilt. They were living a life in parallel. She never asked what occupied Ben's free time, not that there was much of it, and for months hers had been full of family obligations. She was grateful something was keeping him busy.

As he walked up to Camila's front door, he heard the shouts of at least a dozen 11-year-old boys. No one heard him knock, and he entered the small house, and the scent of cinnamon, cumin, and saffron transported him back to Camila's birthday years before. He stopped, closing his eyes, and inhaled.

"Hola, Ben," a vaguely familiar voice said.

He opened his eyes to see Elena standing before him.

"Hello, Ms. Malik."

"I'm so glad you are here," she said, wrapping her arms around him.

He noticed the tears in her eyes.

"We've missed you," she said.

"I'm happy to be back," he said, nervous about what they thought of him all these years after Camila had discovered she was pregnant and alone.

Cole ran up to him. "Hi, Dad, I mean Ben." He grabbed the gift Ben held in his hand. "Is this for me?"

"Yup, happy birthday." Ben tussled Cole's hair and noted how it stood on end like his own.

"Thanks! Mom is out back."

"Okay, I'll be right there."

Elena took his hand. "There is someone else who would like to see you," she said, leading him into the backyard where a much smaller version of Camila's grandmother sat beneath the gazebo. He walked outside and saw Tyler and Bobby across the yard acknowledge him with a synchronized head nod.

"Azzizam," Mamani said in a fragile voice, standing and opening her arms to him.

"Hello," he said, gently wrapping his arms around her now slightly hunched back. He didn't remember her looking so frail. But whatever time had taken from her physically, she still held the same shimmer of strength in her eyes.

"Sit," Mamani said.

A few minutes later Elena appeared with a tray of tea. He remembered the perfume of cardamom and roses that infused the tea he brought to his lips.

"We told her to call you," Mamani said, immediately diving into the details of the past decade. "We told her you had a right to know, that you were his father, and her son needed a man in his life," she said. "She never told us exactly what happened between you two, but we knew. From the first time we saw you, we knew there was something powerful between you. Something that couldn't be controlled."

She stared ahead, watching her great-grandson play happily amongst his friends.

"Her eyes were dim without you. Cole joon brought the light back, but she's only partly full in here." She motioned to her chest with her slightly crooked finger. "I know you have a wife. So, I only ask this. Be careful with the three hearts you hold. If you push too hard, they will all crumble."

Before he could reply, Camila came up to them, and he rose to greet her. She looked beautiful in a black dress. Her red lips were vivid and lush in contrast to her dark hair swept back.

"Hi, I didn't know you were here already," she said, hugging him into her and slipping her hand into his.

"Mamani, do you remember Ben?" Camila said.

"Yes, azzizam, he looks the same. Still a good boy."

"I'm going to get him some food."

"Yes, good, make sure he eats my dolmehs," Mamani said.

Camila gave his hand a quick squeeze and pulled him toward the table of food. "I'm sorry, I didn't know you were here. They had already sequestered you, huh?"

"I don't mind," he said. "I always liked your family."

She smiled at him. "So, what can I get you?"

He looked out across the backyard, the bunches of balloons bordering the fence. Tables with colorful tablecloths overflowing with pizza and dessert. The boys had started a game of soccer that devolved into a high-speed game of tag. "Are these all his friends?" Ben said.

"Yeah, from school and soccer."

They sat at a quiet table, and he looked at his overflowing plate of food. "I'm supposed to eat all of this?"

Laughing, she said, "Yes, and if you don't, they'll think you hated it."

"Thanks for inviting me."

"Don't thank me. It was Cole's idea," she said. She crossed her legs and dragged her hand down her shin. She watched him follow her movements and reached out to run her fingers through his hair.

He watched his son playing with his friends. "I've missed so much."

"It's not your fault, and you're here now," she said.

"Hey, Ben," Cole said, running up to them. "I mean Dad. Come play with us."

"Sure," Ben said, getting up.

* * *

The last of the cake was put away, and Cole had been put to bed by his father for the first time in his life.

Ben had sat at the end of his bed reading to him until he had fallen asleep.

Camila appeared in the doorway. "Hey, I think he's out," she whispered.

He sat there, memorizing details of his son's face, comparing them to the baby pictures Camila had shown him. He stood quietly. "I was worried I'd wake him if I got up too soon."

"Once he's asleep, he sleeps like a rock," she said.

She took his hand in hers as they made their way down to the kitchen. There was an unfamiliar melancholic song playing through the back door. Bobby and Tyler tidied the remnants of the party in the yard, and the hum of their conversation was soothing. The light was dim, and they were alone for the first time.

Silently, he pulled her into him, and they swayed with the music. She rocked, pressing against him. He felt her hips move beneath his hand. Her head resting against his chest. He knew this intimacy was bordering on inappropriate. It was a matter of time before one of them would end it. But for now, he tightened his grip.

"Camila, did you..." Elena said, descending the stairs.

They sprang apart. Camila straightened her dress, and he moved a few feet away.

"What, Mom?"

"Your grandmother wanted me to make sure you packed cake for Ben," she said.

"Oh, thank you, but I can't, Ms. Malik," Ben told her, and Camila understood it was because of Tiffany.

"It was very nice seeing you, Mijo."

"Where is Mamani?" Camila asked.

"Oh, honey, she went to bed an hour ago. She wanted me to say goodbye to Ben for her. She can't stay up as late anymore."

"Please thank her for me," Ben said.

"I will. Please come visit us again. You are always welcome here," Elena said, placing a kiss on both of his cheeks.

"I'll walk you out," Camila said, taking his hand.

The sky was speckled with stars against a canvas of indigo. There was the smell of someone's fireplace burning, and the sound of music carried from the backyard as they strolled down the walkway.

When they reached his car, he told her, "I'm getting to that uncomfortable place again. Where I worry, I can't stop myself."

"I know. I feel it too," she said.

She leaned into him, and his arms engulfed her, trapping her into him. He felt solid. Strong. Everything she missed and wanted in her life.

"What's wrong with us?" she said.

"I don't know."

She tucked her hair behind her ear. "For a moment in there, it felt like we were a family."

"I wish I could take you with me."

She smiled at him. "And where would we go, Ben?"

"I don't care. I just want you. I can't explain it, but you make me feel like myself, like I'm whole."

She placed her palms on his chest, and he held her. She lifted onto her toes and nestled her face into his neck, breathing him in, letting her lips hover over his skin. She wrapped her arms around his neck, and he leaned his forehead against hers, tightening his grip at her waist. They pulled away, their faces a few inches apart.

"I want more," he said.

"We can't," Camila said.

"I know, but it doesn't make it feel any less right," he said. "Can I see you again?"

"Anytime. I'm yours."

22

April 2015

Tiffany was exhausted and already late for dinner with her parents. She opened the front door of their apartment and glanced down at the mat and saw an envelope addressed to Ben. She recognized the lab's logo. Finally, the long-awaited semen analysis. It had taken him much longer to give them a sample. She wanted him to avoid any unnecessary stress that might impact his results, and she told him it couldn't be at the end of the day, or after one of their timed sessions, or after an overnight shift, but two months had passed.

She tore open the envelope and pulled out the results. She confirmed his name, date of birth, and the test date. Her eyes scanned the numbers and reference ranges, and a cold shiver ran up her spine.

A feeling of free falling.

An error, that's what it was.

But she didn't make mistakes, and neither did he.

* * *

Since Cole's birthday party, Ben's level of distraction had become nearly insurmountable. The only place he had any clarity was in the operating room. Tiffany's father's health had improved, but her visits were no less frequent, and now that Ben's semen analysis had been submitted, he was anticipating the start of the arduous process of IVF. He wasn't sure how bringing another child into his life would help lessen the complications he was already struggling with, but they had been trying for so long. Tiffany didn't deserve any of this—his betrayal, the lies, or the infertility. She was a good wife and partner. An excellent physician. He loved her and was terrified of telling her the truth, but more of hurting her. He knew what she would say—that each day he hadn't told her counted as another lie. Every day for the past ten years was one betrayal on top of another, and their marriage was built on a foundation of deception.

She would be right to leave him. He couldn't stomach the thought of destroying the life she had worked so hard to build, but he was sunk so deep now that he didn't even know if he could crawl back.

His mind was full of these thoughts as he navigated from one day to the next. Work was his only reprieve. He started staying longer at the hospital, finishing his charting, and rounding for a third time on patients he had already seen. If he came home on the brink of collapse, there was the chance of falling asleep instantaneously and avoiding another conversation sidestepping the truth. He and Camila had been talking daily since the party, each call more tender than the last. Each conversation teetering closer to the line separating friends and lovers. They had briefly discussed meeting. Just the two of them. Both knowing it would be catastrophic.

A few weeks later he walked through his front door after work, exhausted but content, expecting to find an empty apartment. There was a single light on in the hallway. Tiffany was on the couch watching reruns. She hated TV.

"Hey, Tiff, why are you alone and sitting in the dark?"

She didn't answer, taking a sip of the wine she had poured herself and staring straight ahead. She had been abstaining per the recommendation of their doctor since their first consultation.

"Tiffany? Are you alright? Is it your dad?"

She leaned over, without making eye contact, and drummed her finger on the papers spread on the coffee table.

"Care to explain this?"

"Explain what?"

Now he was concerned. He threw his keys on the kitchen counter and walked over to the table and the results of his semen analysis from the lab. He picked up the papers and scanned them.

"What's wrong? The results are normal."

She didn't look at him. "First page, top right."

His eyes traveled across the papers.

There. Two little words. In black and white: *Proven paternity.*

Next to them, in black and white: *Yes.*

Fuck.

How could he have been so careless, so stupid? He had called the office to update them on his history. He forgot it would be printed on his medical records, and he had granted Tiffany access to his information. In his determination to be factually accurate, he had divulged everything.

She glanced up at him, not moving from the couch.

"Tiffany, I'm so sorry. I can explain."

"So, it's correct?"

He could barely form the word, but quietly said, "Yes." He made a gesture to sit next to her, and she said through gritted teeth, "Don't."

"Just let me explain," he said.

"Start from the beginning and don't fucking lie."

* * *

Camila had tried to subdue her eagerness. Their friendship had quickly resumed its cadence with an unexpected level of depth that surprised them both. Perhaps this time it would work. But that was the problem with hope. It was based on nothing but emotion, devoid of reason, fact, or evidence.

The bell jingled as she walked in. The walls of their old cafe were a different shade of yellow, and the aisles had been rearranged, but the familiar scent of coffee flooded her mind with memories.

It didn't take long for her to spot him seated at the same corner table that had been theirs years before. She smiled. This is what my life is supposed to be, she thought, walking toward him.

We're supposed to be together. We'll make it work. Somehow.

As she came closer, she saw in his eyes a mixture of conflict and regret.

He stood as if an afterthought when she pulled out her own chair.

"Hi," she said.

"Hi," he said, placing his arm around her shoulders for the briefest of moments.

She saw the two cups of coffee on the table. "You ordered already?"

"Yeah. Sorry, your coffee is probably cold by now. Latte with almond milk, right?"

She sat across from him, a knot forming in her gut. "Yes, thank you."

When they had agreed to see each other, alone, without Cole or her family or Tyler, she assumed it meant her feelings were reciprocated. That he felt the same pull. That this time it would work. But now she only felt a frigid energy emanating from across the table.

"I can't stay," he said abruptly.

She searched his eyes. "Okay. Can I ask why?"

"Tiffany found out."

"Wait, I thought you had told her that we're talking again?"

"Not that. But I only said I ran into you."

"Just that you ran into me?" she asked.

"Yes, she didn't seem to care, so I never elaborated."

Camila dropped her hands into her lap.

"She found out about Cole," he said. "I was going to tell her eventually, but she found out before I had the chance." He rubbed his neck with a ferocity that did little to hide his frustration. "I'm sorry, Camila, I can't stay."

A subtle ringing had started in her ears. "Does Tiffany know you're here now?"

"Yeah. She said I should come and explain."

She felt the end hurling toward her, knowing whatever she did, she couldn't stop it. She shifted uncomfortably in her seat, bracing for the impact. "I see," she said, clearing her throat. "Does she hate me?"

"No. I think it has very little to do with you. For her, it's more about my betrayal—the secrets, the lies. And then there's the infertility. It's everything."

Camila was silent. Minutes passed. She heard cups clinking against saucers, the soft drone of conversation around them.

"Camila, say something. Please."

"What's there to say, Ben? I knew we were being emotionally reck- less. But I didn't listen to my gut. I knew I could get hurt again, but being with you is always worth the risk."

"Camila, I never meant to hurt you. Then or now."

"I know, but that's the problem with hope, Ben. It doesn't care what is possible. It just springs up like a weed."

"I'm sorry, Camila, I am."

"Don't be sorry. We both felt where this was headed, and we didn't do a thing to stop it. That is our fault, not just yours. She's your wife. That's the relationship you need to focus on. Not me." If she could stay strong, then she could end this with a finality that was lacking ten years before.

"I'm stuck. I'm sorry. I feel like we are reliving the past. I don't want to hurt anyone, and I feel any direction I choose will cause someone pain," he said and reached for her hand. She pulled back after the slightest brush of their fingertips.

She fell silent again. She knew he would rather do anything than hurt her, but he was wedged between two impenetrable options. Leave his wife for a long-lost love and a son he barely knew or stay the course with the woman he had wed in front of friends and family and God ten years ago.

Camila wasn't angry, but a cold, heavy sadness had settled in her chest, replacing hope.

"Well, it's very poetic," she said.

"What is?" He looked at her, his eyes bloodshot.

"That we come here, where it all started, to say goodbye forever to the possibility of us."

"And Cole?"

"I'd never keep him from you. But we can arrange for the two of you to see each other without me. It's not fair to me or to Tiffany, but Cole doesn't need to be punished for our mistakes."

"It wasn't a mistake, Camila. I know this sounds selfish or impossible. I love you, but I'm married to her. I'm part of a life she and I have built. There are too many people involved now. To say I'm torn is..." His voice trailed off.

She knew he was trying to get through whatever this conversation was—confession or breakup—without falling apart. He took a deep breath and rubbed his eyes.

"Ben, I don't want to make this harder for you. I'm not angry. I'm devastated, but I love you and don't want to make this more difficult. I don't know why we met when we did or why we were thrown back together again. But if it was all to bring Cole into the world, then that's enough for me."

They sat across from each other, like so many times before, but now a lifetime had passed. Vows had been spoken, love had been exchanged, a child had been born, and now the death of a future together for the sake of all those things before.

She continued to try and explain what they both already knew. "I can't be around you for just the sake of friendship because, well, there has always been more than that between us. If I'm going to be truthful, we just..."

He dropped his head. "I understand."

She gathered the courage to reach out and gently place her hand on his, giving him a small squeeze.

"Want to walk me out?" She said, standing and grabbing her shawl. She felt the scaffolding of her heart beginning to fall.

He pushed up from the table and, as always, gestured for her to walk ahead.

They stepped out into the night, and she pulled her shawl around her arms, hoping it hid the shivering that had little to do with the weather.

"I'm sorry, Camila."

She smiled. "Don't be." Despite her efforts, her eyes brimmed with tears.

"I love you," he said.

"I know. I love you too."

She balanced on her toes and placed a feather-light kiss on his cheek before stepping down the few steps to the sidewalk and turning, "Bye, Ben."

"Goodbye, Camila."

She glanced down the street and made her way quickly across to the parking lot. The same path he had watched her traverse countless times all those years before. She knew no other love would replace him. She would never feel again what she felt for him, something pure and honest and natural. Other men would enter her life, but no one would occupy her heart again like he did. No one could.

She reached her car and turned. He was standing where she had left him. Hands in his pockets, his shoulders slumped. Their eyes met, and she raised her hand to wave, like she had done so many times before. When their lives were simple, and the pull between them hadn't yet become complicated and insurmountable. He raised his hand in return before she disappeared into her car.

Acknowledgements

First, to those of you who see yourselves or recognize familiar events in the pages of this book thank you for being a part of my life. Please know that the time I shared with you inspired the characters and stories on these pages. It is all intended to be complementary and not judgmental. I'm so grateful to have had the ups and downs that brought me to this point in life.

I have so many people to thank.

To everyone, who offered to read my project or put me in touch with their contacts (Melissa Manzarian and Megan Johnson) or enthusiastically supported me with their periodic inquiries of 'How's the book going', I can't thank you enough for encouraging me to venture into a world I do not naturally belong.

Thank you to the authors/agents who took time out of their lives to share their experiences with the challenging and mysterious publishing world: Mary Pauline Lowry, Michael Oates, Aubrey Hartman, Sam Polk, and Valerie Noble.

To everyone who said no, passed on my project, or didn't even answer: thank you. You helped bring me to exactly where I am now. If I was ever deterred by rejection I would not be who I am today.

To my friends who were kind enough to be my guinea pigs, AKA my readers. Thank you so much for the gift of your precious time:

Manuela Vazquez	Charity Brewer	Lisa Solomon
Beth Hamilton	Ceci Perez	Cambria Kang
Sepi Samzadeh	Jenny Jaque	Jasmin Omrani
Eline Wilson	Stephanie Kusiak	Tiffany Wong
Akta Patel	Kari Bray	Ingrid Hernandez
Paula Richter	Deb Gaal	Johanna Dubyak
Alexa Richter	Hilary Tordai	Gina Chang

A special thank you to Sepi, Beth, and Deb who read the manuscript when it was raw dough and lacking salt but still were kind enough to give me their thoughts.

To Barbara De Santis, thank you for your editing expertise and suggestion for the ending.

To Courtney Cowgill, thank you for looking at the book with your kind, thorough, and thoughtful eye. Especially for your suggestions and help to put into words what I kept tucked away in my mind about Ben.

To Monique, for your creative expertise and beautiful cover design.

To Andi Domjan, thank you for making the photo session not only painless but fun!

To Kari Bray, who is the matchmaker of all matchmakers, thank you for vouching for me.

To Trinity, I am so grateful for your friendship and expert guidance through this process and for encouraging me to come out of my social media shell. Thanks for being my friend despite my clear lack of promoting/marketing intelligence.

It must have been a true test of patience to work with me as I poo-pooed getting my picture taken and asked you riveting questions like "What is a reel and how do I make one?"

To Alison, for being my partner in crime for decades and always pushing me to be a kick-ass lady by example.

To Gina, for supporting me and being with me through all the different iterations of my personality and for being instrumental in my musical taste.

Ladies, your friendship has been a gift.

To the 'Cousin Crew', thank you for the laughs, dorehs and your unconditional support.

To Noori, who has been my 'sister' since birth. Thank you for all the laughs.

To my lovely in-laws, thank you for years of support and raising me like I was your own.

To my brothers, thanks for trying to hide your surprise when I told you about this project.

To my parents, thank you for leaving everything and everyone you knew to give me a better chance. And I'm sorry Mommy that I wouldn't let you read this book. I hope you aren't too shocked if/when you finally do.

To my kids, who were always supportive of this project and cursed the countless 'passes' I received on my submissions. I hope you can look back on this book when you are older (much older) and think your mom was kind of cool for trying to do something different than her day job and learn to never let anyone put you in a box. Also, thank you for teaching me how to use Spotify.

And to Gabe. Thank you for ignoring me that day back in 2004 when I thought I was too cute to be ignored. I'm so glad I didn't graduate on time so we could end up in the same orientation group. And I'm so happy you skipped lunch that day so I had to offer you some of my animal crackers. You know there is a little bit of Camila in me so I can't say what I really feel here for everyone to read (evil eye and all). You are everything Camila hoped for and everything Ben wished he could be.

SHAHED GHANIMATI

PARTIAL TRUTHS

SHAHED GHANIMATI, is the child of Iranian immigrants and raised in California. She received her doctorate from The Chicago Medical School and trained as a resident and fellow at Los Angeles County/ USC. As a mother, wife, and physician, she's a believer that life and love can be complicated, and happy endings are never guaranteed. Shahed lives with her family in Orange County, where she is always in search of her next pastry shop and bookstore (and if you find one within the other, please send her a message).